The Let Go

Also by Jerry Gabriel
Drowned Boy

The Let Go

STORIES

Jerry Gabriel

Queen's Ferry Press
8622 Naomi Street
Plano, TX 75024
www.queensferrypress.com

These stories originally appeared in the following publications:
"The Visitors," *Alaska Quarterly Review*, winter 2014
"Panic," *Atticus Review*, spring 2013
"The Defense," *The Missouri Review*, spring 2013
"Long Story, No Map," *Big Fiction*, spring 2012
"Dishonor," *The Missouri Review*, fall 2011
"Above the Factory," *Five Chapters*, August 2011
"We're in Danger, All of Us," *Epoch*, 60:2, May 2011

Published 2015 by Queen's Ferry Press

Cover design by Brian Mihok

First edition May 2015

ISBN 978-1-938466-25-0

Printed in the United States of America

Praise for *Drowned Boy*

2008 Mary McCarthy Prize in Short Fiction

"These [stories] are rust-belt blues, then, a vision of and lament for a past time and a swiftly changing place. They're not showy—the language is plain, the tragedy muted, the comedy low-key and wry—but they stick in the mind. Ray Carver would recognize these characters and situations, as would poet Philip Levine. I like to think that they would share my appreciation for this fine first book, built slowly and carefully over some years, and worth the wait."

—Andrea Barrett, from the foreword

"In Gabriel's first volume of fiction, the bare and austere landscape is reflected in the tightly written, almost stripped, prose."

—Ann H. Fisher, *Library Journal*

"Eight linked stories, set among boys and men in southern Ohio, have the masculine virtues of honest craft and plain, carefully chosen language. The author, who grew up in rural Ohio, put years into writing that sticks with the reader much longer than showier fiction."

—Karen R. Long, *The Cleveland Plain Dealer*

"In prose as spare and enchanting as the town's landscape, Gabriel paints a beautiful and sobering portrait of Middle Americans trapped in a world of snow, ice, and inevitability."

—Jonathan Fullmer, *Booklist*

"The prose is spare, but hardly minimalistic. . . . if there are slower moments in the earlier stories, they do echo beautifully, not unlike our own memories."

—James Tate Hill, *Bookslut*

"Gabriel connects all of these stories through location, anchoring them to the lone highway or the river that run through Moraine, Ohio. . . . It's a nuanced and complicated examination of the way grief is contagious, sparking dark emotions in people who initially are barely affected."

—Jonathan Messinger, *TimeOut Chicago*

"With the publication of *Drowned Boy*, his first book of fiction, Jerry Gabriel has produced a devastating vision of the post-industrial experience in the American Midwest. Set in Moraine, Ohio, this powerful collection of stories is reminiscent in both its symmetry and spirit of Sherwood Anderson's classic, *Winesburg, Ohio*."

—Jesse Freedman, *Rain Taxi Review of Books*

"Committed to the experience of youth in a land 'dark from the rain,' *Drowned Boy* proceeds with unyielding candor, slowly revealing the poverty of post-industrial Ohio. By the end of this book, I was defenseless against Gabriel's haunting, penetrating prose and prepared to advocate on behalf of his wounded, often desperate characters."

—*The Literary Review*

"Set in the hardscrabble borderlands where Appalachia meets the Midwest, Jerry Gabriel's *Drowned Boy* reveals a world of brutality, beauty, and danger in the forgotten landscape of small-town basketball tournaments and family reunions. Selected by Andrea Barrett for the Mary McCarthy Prize in Short Fiction, these stories probe the fraught cusp of adulthood, the frustrations of escape and difference, and the emotional territory of disappointment."

—Sam Katz, *One Story*

"Sublime and stark, the stories in *Drowned Boy* showcase Jerry Gabriel's lean diction, crisp characterization, and exquisite storytelling. Readers eager to experience the very best in contemporary short stories need go no further than this perfect collection."

—Tim Davis, *ForeWord Reviews*

"Ultimately, the novella demonstrates Gabriel's ease with writing a longer story. "Drowned Boy" might make some readers wish that Gabriel had written a novel. However, the collection as a whole refuses tidy conclusions and long-term relationships; it reveals people in isolation with only brief moments of startling connection."

—Rachel Bara, *Prairie Schooner*

"In her forward to the book, author Andrea Barrett says that Jerry's fictional world calls to mind poet Philip Levine and short story writer Raymond Carver. Both write about people from this milieu, and Jerry further resembles Carver in the understated way that he captures the small twists and turns of everyday life. Tragedy and comedy mingle quietly and we must pay close attention lest they pass beneath our notice."

—Robin Bates, *Better Living Through Beowulf*

Praise for *The Let Go*

"The characters in Jerry Gabriel's *The Let Go* are the most memorable I've read in a very long time. They're war vets and immigrants, ex-cons and small town middle-schoolers, whose lives intertwine in ways both inevitable and unlikely. As they trap mink, repair roofs, harbor fugitives, and try to figure how the hell to run a factory in the basement, they stand in that place—familiar to all of us—where life shifts imperceptibly and something has to give. They cling hard to integrity and do what they have to do."

—Ana Maria Spagna, author of *Test Ride on the Sunnyland Bus*

"Like Alice Munro's stories, these wonderful stories by Jerry Gabriel often have the scope of novels. They take a particular interest in characters who are just barely hanging on and who fear 'The Let Go': the day when they will be laid off. The stories have great urgency and momentum and carry you headlong through to the end. *The Let Go* is one of the best books of short fiction that I've read in the last few years."

—Charles Baxter, author of *There's Something I Want You to Do*

"*The Let Go* is a knife-twister, sharp, sad, sneakily funny. Jerry Gabriel writes with bracing authenticity and insight, but what's most impressive is how he's able to chart and deepen the pathos of these unmoored lives without ever marinating in it or succumbing to easy revelations. A terrific collection."

—Kevin Moffett, author of *The Silent History*

"An enormous heart pulses through every page, every line of *The Let Go*, a collection of stories somehow diverse enough to include poachers, roofers, scientists, dropouts, basketball stars, war vets, office workers, and accidental factory owners, all of them full of longing for something they can"t quite name. With his careful attention to their rich interior lives, it's obvious Jerry Gabriel loves every one of his characters for exactly who they are, and you will too. *The Let Go* is a work of great literature."

—Matt Burgess, author of *Uncle Janice*

"Jerry Gabriel's wry, fierce stories are about Ohio in the same way Breece Pancake's stories are about West Virginia, which is to say they tenderly, vividly evoke a singular merciless landscape while also being deeply engaged with the larger world and the politics and history of the United States. In *The Let Go*, Gabriel elegantly distills the disorders of our perilous times into marvelously strange fiction that is sometimes surreal, often wickedly funny, and profoundly moving. These stories bring us the news that stays news."

—Maud Casey, author of *The Man Who Walked Away*

For Eva, Clara, and Henry

Contents

The Visitors

THE MECHANISM WAS SIMPLE: a phone call to a laundromat payphone in Rush, all the way up in Wyatt County, nearly forty miles north of Shallsville—Hansen Cleaners and Laundry, an anonymous place on the square. There, no one knew them. The call only ever came at eight in the morning on a Saturday. Camille—pronounced in the French style after her Breton grandmother—and her father would make the drive most Saturdays, occasionally with her little brother Robbie in tow, though generally not. With a couple of dryers running, it was hard to hear much of anything. These were perfect conditions. Her father had examined every payphone within a hundred miles of Shallsville, she knew, because she had been with him for much of the search. She knew, too, that in his head he had a list of backups strewn across the state: one in Mapleton, one in Collier, even one in Columbus, where she knew he didn't like to go for fear of getting lost.

At Hansen's, they did the week's laundry stationed adjacent to the bathroom corridor, at the table closest to the black GT&E payphone on the wall. Camille often did her homework sitting beside her father. When she was older and would recall the strange days of their safe house, she would sometimes think about the unspoken tenderness that passed between them as she puzzled over French conjugations or the Missouri Compromise and her father read a newspaper or, more often, scribbled strange designs on a small tablet he carried of the contraptions that he might one day build.

A few hours or a day or maybe even a week after a call, someone would show up at the house outside Shallsville looking tired, stinking of sweat and sometimes alcohol, their hair tangled, their clothing rumpled. On a few occasions it was more than one, but usually just a lone driver in a decade-old car, a nondescript dark sedan or station wagon whose plates could have been from just about anywhere. Camille, though, remembered the colors of the common ones—Illinois and Texas, white; California and New York, blue.

Her mother, a thin woman with a closet full of frayed floral-print dresses, smoked her way through the visits. She was just twenty-nine in 1972—young to have a thirteen-year-old—but she looked a decade older from a lifelong bout with insomnia, a two-pack-a-day Pall Mall habit, and her strained marriage to Luc Mills.

It was obvious to Camille from the start of it, in the summer of 1970, that the visitors had to do with her father and that her mother was enduring the arrangement, though no one had taken her aside and explained. On occasion, Camille would hear her parents bicker about the visitors, usually just before an arrival or after a departure. They bickered about other things, too, but there was a special intensity to these arguments.

Their house stood a couple miles outside Shallsville, discrete and sheltered by a long forested lane. It butted up to County Road 28 on the west, and Bryant National Forest on the north and east; there were neighbors a few hundred yards distant on the fourth side, the Smolts—a compound of trailers and squat cinderblock structures that housed a large extended family of ne'er-do-wells, nominally mechanics and autobody guys, but Camille's father had confided to her, by way of telling her to steer clear, that they were chopping up stolen vehicles and probably dealing drugs. Real drugs, he'd said, for the sake of some kind of clarity, which she eventually came to understand meant heroin. It obviously didn't mean the pot that the visitors sometimes smoked out in the woods.

The Smolts kept to themselves. A few times she and her dad had come across one of the Smolt men in the forest, all three of them holding the shotguns with which they were hunting deer or out-of-season pheasant. The man and her father would exchange nods and that was about all.

There wasn't a steady stream of visitors, but for nearly two years it was rare that a season passed without at least one's arrival. They never stayed long, usually a day or two, and then they were off again, on toward one coast or the other, maybe Chicago.

When they didn't lodge in a large storage closet across from the bathroom, they were put up in a converted shed out along the property line; it was never clear to Camille if this was their choice. The shed had a potbelly stove and a Quikrete floor and tarpaper walls reinforced with straw stuffing.

On occasion the same faces reappeared, months later. A woman who went by Sam stayed with them three times during the period. She was memorable because she spent most of her waking hours pecking on an ancient black typewriter, at work on what she told Camille was a treatise about the failure of capitalism. She carried a large cardboard suitcase full of books on the topic—the only real luggage Camille could discern—which she read in that storage closet, the picture of which was fixed in Camille's mind: Sam laconically turning those tattered pages as smoke from her Lucky Strikes curled into the ceiling fan above her. Sam was unique in her willingness to talk about herself, and Camille's conversations with her were some of the first sparks of knowledge of who these people were and what their family was involved in. Sam told her that she had attended a revolutionary conference in Cuba in 1969; even as a young teenager, Camille knew that Americans couldn't go to Cuba anymore.

Most of the visitors had a studied look of nonchalance and downward mobility. They wore clothes that suggested labor—lumberjack, longshoreman, seamstress—though there were things that belied the subterfuge: smooth hands, obviously, but also the language that slipped out unwittingly—"insatiable," "taciturn," "ascertain"; even their gait didn't always seem quite the part, though these distinctions were not ones Camille made then.

They laughed easily, though, and were surprisingly good with kids—telling jokes and asking about school and on a few occasions even reading bedtime stories to Robbie. Camille was always especially struck by the beauty of most of the women—their faces symmetrical, their skin unblemished, their necks long like Jackie Kennedy's—even though they attempted to conceal it with bad haircuts and ill-fitting pants.

Above all else, the visitors wanted to talk about Vietnam. It came up the way Camille knew sports scores came up in other houses—battles, White House maneuvers, responses from Hanoi, demonstrations around the country and world. Her knowledge of Tet and My Lai easily outstripped her knowledge of photosynthesis, which she was supposed to be learning in third period Life Sciences the last winter of the visitors.

Years later she pieced all of this back together the way you might a dream after waking with just a shard in your mind. She knew that there was something strange about all of it, even if she hadn't been able to make it make sense. She didn't need anyone to tell her that other kids had no such visitors in their homes. There were many things that she did not get from her father in the end, but she did get his common sense and his practically infallible intuition about people. She also got his complex moral compass, which was for her, as it was for him, at once asset and liability.

—

A young man who went by Hunter stayed with them in the winter of 1972. He was somehow memorable, or at least noteworthy, even before all that happened, in part because he seemed to lack many of the others' qualities and social graces. He was arrogant and lazy, extravagantly lounging around the shed, sleeping, drinking when he could convince her father to purchase some Ten High bourbon for him. There was a bigger tell, though: he wouldn't leave. The average stay was two days; after two months, he still had not left. This was not deep cover, but a way station, and two months was far too long for the sake of safety.

Also, Hunter had very few questions. The visitors were, to the person, information gatherers. They wondered, even though they usually didn't leave the premises, about the location of things in Shallsville—banks, municipal buildings, schools, fire and police stations. They wanted to know what events had been going on locally; they wanted to read the newspaper. They wondered if the postman or the electric company man came to the door, if neighbors or friends were likely to drop by, if they—the Mills'—knew, personally, any member of law enforcement. Most of this information they got from Camille's father, but some of it they seemed to feel more comfortable asking Camille and Robbie on the sly. On more than one occasion, Camille helped one of them draw a map of the area that included their house, the railroad, the river, and as many roads as she could remember.

Even then, Camille guessed that Hunter stood apart from the others and had merely gotten mixed up in the rebellion. There could have been a girl, she thought, or it could have been as simple as drugs and lawlessness. Perhaps he had stumbled into their network, cagily knitting himself into its fabric, masquerading as a believer. In the end, it didn't matter much how it had happened; he had done some things bad enough to worry over, and so, like the others, he ran. The amazing thing was that he had remained at large, because he was sloppy and seemingly untrained.

When he was sent to them that winter he had the same credentials as the others. Things with him were different from the first day, however; the car he was driving had broken down just south of Twin Ponds, some thirty miles from Shallsville, and he said he had walked the rest, sleeping along the way in a barn under some horse blankets. He came to the door a full day after he was expected and told them what had happened, that his car sat on the road along US 33. They could do nothing about it, she overheard her father tell him. Hunter claimed that it was his and not stolen, but her father had been insistent: they had to leave it. They just couldn't risk rescuing it. And so Hunter had no car.

He was a handsome figure, tall and lanky with rippled arms that fit snugly in his two Western-style shirts. He had a drawl that was not quite Southern, but perhaps Texan or Arizonan. His lips, Camille thought, were redder than normal lips, a striking thing on a man, almost as if he wore a subtle lipstick. His long, sandy hair curled slightly at the neck, and he wore a beard, though nearly all of the men who came to the house in those years did, the thinking being that it hid their features.

Hunter slept in the small shed, stoking the stove with wood that Camille and Robbie had helped their father poach from the national forest. It was tight quarters in there, but most of the visitors seemed to prefer it for its privacy. In other houses and apartments in other states, she imagined, things were probably awkward with shared bathrooms and bedrooms. Here, you could be rid of the whole world; you could disappear into your tiny bungalow and never come out except to use the outhouse back at the edge of the woods.

The one thing she knew about Hunter was that he had a tape player on which he listened to someone's speaking voice, perhaps some sort of a book. He used an AC adaptor for it in the shed—the light fixture had room for one plug-in—but he sometimes carried it out in the woods with him, running it on D batteries. She could not tell what the recording was, but the reader of the book—she had overheard the tape several times, because he played it loudly—was old and certainly not a professional: he coughed and stumbled over his words, seemed to include asides of his own and apologies for his performance. Likely it was someone in Hunter's life who had recorded the book for him, if it was a book. It made her wonder if Hunter was perhaps illiterate. She didn't know anyone who was, and the idea seemed unimaginable, historical, as if living among them was a character from Mark Twain or Charles Dickens. She was dying to know what the book was and had considered stealing into his quarters to see if the title was scrawled on the tape.

In truth, she had had but a few encounters with Hunter during his stay—a brief greeting one evening as she was bringing wood to the shed, and another one frosty morning as she was on her way down the lane to the bus. It was easy to avoid the visitors if she wanted to; they were there for a short time and tended to be private people. But as the winter of 1972 dragged on—snow coming just an inch or two at a time, but never melting and gradually mounting depths of nearly two packed feet—this strange boy seemed to grow increasingly erratic. He came out of the shed more and more, wandering around the yard and the forest, apparently inspecting things or looking for something. She saw him in the house a few times, talking wildly with her father and, once, surprisingly, with her mother.

By the first week of March, it seemed that neither winter nor Hunter would ever move on. She overheard a conversation between her parents about him early one morning that week. They were in their bedroom with the door closed and she only knew it was about him from their tone; she couldn't make out any words. What else could they have been talking about with such muffled bursts of language?

The following Saturday, at the laundromat in Rush her father did something she'd never seen him do before: using a number from memory, he dialed the mysterious disembodied voice.

This is Harlan, he said when a voice answered. She'd never heard the name in her life. We have a problem with our last shipment, her father said.

The voice said some things that registered to her ears not as language but syncopated static, and then her dad said, It's time to reship. Yes, he said, answering a question. Another yes. Transpo not available until next Saturday? He was quiet. Sooner would be better.

There was a very long silence then. Okay, her father said. Saturday.

He hung up and looked at her. There was an exhaustion in him she hadn't noticed before. He glanced around the room. The owner came in late in the morning to empty the coins, but otherwise, there was no supervision in the laundromat. On this day, the room was empty but for one woman who was using a bank of four washing machines and holding an infant as her toddler tried to get into a trash can.

Her father looked down at the phone, which he still held and which was now beeping with a disconnect signal. He glanced at the woman, who was paying no attention to them, and then unscrewed the handset and looked into the mechanism.

Come here, he said.

She approached and looked at it.

This is the transmitter, he said, pointing to a cylindrical device with a pencil he pulled out of his shirt pocket. And here is the power and the outgoing line. Do you notice anything strange?

This? She was pointing to a bulky green square with a miniature coil and a tangle of wires soldered to it, one of which was grafted onto the red power source. It was all very messy and haphazard.

Yes, he said, shaking his head. That.

He didn't remove it, but screwed the cap back on.

Are the clothes dry?

Yeah.

On-y-va, he said. *Let's go.* He had a bit of French from his childhood he still used. She used this one, too.

Walking along the street toward the truck, her father hefted the U.S. Army laundry bag full of clothes. It dawned on her only then that this had been her Uncle Stephen's bag.

He shook his head. What a world, he said.

He stole a quick glance at her, smiled. My father, he started to say. She'd never heard him mention his father. She knew then very little about the man, only that he had died in 1960.

Well, he said. Somebody oughta write this stuff down in a book. You couldn't make it up.

She said nothing.

You'll probably do that one day, he said.

She laughed. I can barely get my book reports done on time, she told him. And anyway, I wouldn't even know what I was writing about.

He nodded and then a moment later shook his head, smiled again.

—

Things moved quickly then, as if from some force outside of them. First, Hunter disobeyed the fundamental rule of the house and wandered off the premises, the very next night. Camille saw him go. She sat just after dark staring out of the icy dormer window in the bedroom that she and Robbie still shared then, and watched as he left the shed and trudged through the snow down the lane and toward the road. For reasons she couldn't name, she sat and waited for him to return, thinking he had maybe simply gone to check something in the woods that bordered the lane. Time passed. Hours, eventually. She thought often about waking her father. Why she didn't was a mystery to her and, she knew, a betrayal. As the baby grandfather clock in the living room downstairs rang out the early hours, she continued to sit at her perch. Robbie breathed heavily, as he always did in sleep.

Sometime not long after three, snow blowing around the yard in gusts, she crept down the stairs and out the back, careful to shut the door behind her softly. She wore only a ratty Ohio University sweatshirt, a pair of jeans over her pajamas, and some slipped-on snow boots. At the shed, she peered into the single thick-glassed window. There was no light, no movement. She saw no sign of Hunter, no footprints in the nearly inch of snow that had fallen since dusk. The whipping wind stung her face.

But as she turned to go back to the house, she was startled by Hunter's boots crushing the snow behind her.

What the shit you doing out here?

She turned to see him hunched over against the cold, ice in his beard.

Dad asked me to make sure you were okay, she thought to say. Because of the cold.

Your dad didn't send you out here.

And so he wasn't a fool, she thought. Buried in his statement was the insinuation of something she knew to be there and not there at the same time.

I didn't see any smoke from the chimney.

He smiled, came a half-step closer, as if to lean in and tell her a secret. The smell of alcohol was strong enough to reach her through the cold and flurries.

I was just starting a fire. Come inside.

She recognized the invitation from a hundred books.

The snow crunched beneath his boots as he shifted his weight, feigning indifference, above them a full moon obscured by clouds.

She neither said nor did anything for a moment as he pulled the tarp off the wood pile.

Why is it not Kuh-meel? he asked, picking up several sticks and then pulling open the rusty hinged shed door.

It's my grandmother's name, Camille said, making a decision to follow him inside. She was French.

Inside, he began messing with the old stove. One 60-watt bulb hung from the center of the room, which ran to a single wire that traced back to the corner of the house, supported along the way by two bamboo poles spaced fifteen feet apart.

French? he said. And you get the folks around here to say it that way?

French-Canadian, I guess.

Well that's different, ain't it?

She watched while he swept out the stove, which was choked with ashes. She stole a glance toward the house through the window.

People say it Cammy, she said. Which is close.

He lit a sheet of newspaper beneath some frosty twigs.

What do you know about all of this? he asked obliquely.

Probably about as much as you do, she said. She was a pro at this information game. Her father had taught her over the years by example. On many occasions, she had seen him deal with men whose land they were poaching on, crafting not lies, but subtle occlusions of the truth.

More, probably, Hunter agreed. It's odd, though, ain't it? I bet it's odd living here.

She figured he was dying to tell her something, to unburden himself of some heavy piece of knowledge. Or perhaps it was simply that he couldn't see beyond himself and was asking her for some verification, something in which he could believe and find grounding.

She wasn't interested in any of this, though.

Not really, she said.

Those other people who stay, Hunter said. They're nuts, aren't they?

He seemed desperate to find accord on this point.

Why would you say that? she asked.

He watched her, shaking his head. Why am I talking about this stuff to a little girl?

She was supposed to protest this, she knew, but she did not. Some men, she had already gathered, marshaled all of their resources in order to get women. Girls.

She was from Montreal, she said. My grandma. But she was born in Bretagne, in France. My dad grew up in Montreal until he was six.

Canada, Hunter said pensively. Doubt I'll ever make it up there.

The fire was popping now, eating up the dry wood. He pulled off his jacket, even though it was still very cold in there. It wouldn't take long for the fire to warm the small room.

Take your coat off and stay a while, he said, getting up now to fetch some more wood. She looked at the single bed against the wall for the first time. Now is the time to go, she thought.

When he opened the door again to get the wood, she was on his heels. Before he was even aware of her there, she was past him and ten feet toward the house; he was leaning over, picking up wood.

Goodnight, she said.

He stood and turned and just watched her go.

From the darkness of her room, she looked down once more at the shed, wisps of smoke issuing now from the stovepipe jutting out at an odd angle from the roof. The thermometer out her window read 4 degrees.

—

Over five years passed between the funeral of her Uncle Stephen, in December 1965, and the arrival of the visitors. So the connection between these events was not readily apparent to Camille at first. She was only seven when Stephen's body was shipped home from Gia Lai Province, where he had caught a four-inch piece of shrapnel in his jugular during a nighttime firefight. Camille was too young to make any sense of the strangeness of Stephen's being gone and why—or her father's reaction. Stephen had been his little brother, nearly a decade his junior—more like a son, she later came to understand, so involved was he in Stephen's upbringing.

The truth was her father was a strange man, an outsider, long before Stephen's death. His record of employment revealed this from her earliest memories, when, for a time, he worked rebuilding lawnmower engines for a hostile old man named Tallmadge whose shop was little more than a junkyard for small-engine flotsam. Even this work was sporadic, and then one day her father and Tallmadge had a fistfight—over what, Camille never knew—that ended his employment at the shop.

There were a number of years when he did not work for money at all, the years just before and after Stephen's death. That was the period in which he had begun to trap and hunt and fish—most of it illegally—to support the family. Though unemployed, he was far from idle, always busy in one of the three sheds that sat on the back lot of the small house they had inherited from her mother's father when he passed away. Among other things, he was tanning the hides he had hunted and trapped, canning tomatoes, cucumbers and beans, making syrup, even for a time forging nails that he sold to the Museum of Eighteenth Century Settlers in Mason.

The last steady job he held before the visitors began to arrive, before things began to unravel, was as a paid-under-the-table lathe operator at Shallsville Foundry, a dilapidated nineteenth century structure that butted up against a defunct lock factory. He had once taken Camille there in the middle of the night to watch for cars while he machined a blown head gasket for his '54 GMC, a truck that by 1968 was more rust than steel. She was just ten that night, but already, against her mother's fervent protestations, her father's trusted assistant in his many operations.

They'd gotten into the building through a torn-away section of aluminum siding hidden behind two oil drums he'd rolled out of the way. First he'd lain down on his back on the damp concrete and shimmied through the hole and then she'd done the same. Inside, they used none of the electric lights, but navigated by the spare glow of a small mining headlamp her father wore. He stationed her at a large window facing the empty parking lot; there were probably two or three hundred square panes, though the glass was missing from many of them and had been replaced with rectangular sections of plywood. He found her a bench to sit on while she watched for movement.

I'm there, he said, pointing. If a car comes into the lot, don't yell. Come and touch my back.

She nodded.

Camille remembered little of the noise of the lathe from that night in the foundry or the danger of getting caught; she was already accustomed to danger. Mainly, she remembered the heavy smell of petroleum in the air and the strange darkness of the place and then the long walk through the woods afterwards, next to her dad, who carried the refurbished head gasket in a rucksack he frequently brought along on excursions. They walked back across the highway to a borrowed car parked on a side street near the Bryant River.

—

Two days after the night in the cold, Camille woke with a fever and achy bones, a throat on fire. Whether or not it had been her early morning trip outside in only a sweatshirt that gave the bug its in was impossible to say. When her father entered the room to wake her and Robbie for school that morning, he turned and left almost immediately, coming back a few minutes later with some cold medicine for Camille, as well as some toast and orange juice and a pack of cards. He knew she liked to play solitaire. She hadn't said anything of how she felt.

Rest, he told her. I'll check on you in a bit.

She closed her eyes and was only marginally aware of her father coming into the room every minute or two to harass Robbie, who kept crawling back into bed. After he had finally cajoled Robbie into getting dressed, he knelt beside her again.

If you are better by Friday, we'll check the Snake Creek lines. It was Tuesday morning.

Can I come? she heard Robbie ask from his side of the room.

On-y-va, Robert. School starts in an hour.

I want to come trapping, he said again.

We'll see, her father said on their way out the door, which almost always meant no. By Robbie's age—he was nine that year—Camille regularly went along with him everywhere, but Robbie was a different sort of kid. He was emotional, sometimes petulant and sullen, but also given to moments of wildness. He had never totally left the terrible twos behind, falling into fits on the floor of the grocery store if his body chemistry hit some low point. He was a good kid, a smart kid, but just too unpredictable.

Because the vent in her room was right above the kitchen, Camille could hear her mother coax Robbie toward his oatmeal; then in the small mudroom off the kitchen, their voices now muted, she helped him into his coat and hat and gloves for the long walk down the lane toward the spot along State Route 28 where the bus picked them and the Smolt children up.

After Robbie was finally gone—her father had quietly left before, though she didn't know to where—the house was still. Hunter was no doubt holed up in his shed. Sometime late in the morning, a knock on the door woke her with a start. It was rare that someone showed up at their house.

She heard then her mother's chair in the kitchen scoot back; she had probably been doing a puzzle or crocheting, something while she smoked. Camille tracked her movement across the kitchen's old hardwood floors to the mudroom, which led to the only door that they had shoveled a path toward. There, she could hear her mother greet the visitor familiarly. That it was a woman was all she could discern, their voices muffled. The woman and her mother spoke for a minute and then made their way back to the kitchen, where she could hear every exhaled breath and clanging spoon. Her mother poured them both coffee, which sat on the back of the gas stove warming every morning.

I'm sorry to barge in on you, Mrs. Mills, the woman said.

It's okay, Lana.

Camille didn't know anyone named Lana. Sometimes it felt to her as if all the world was a web of secrets that everyone was keeping from everyone else.

I didn't want to come, but Mom said I should.

Camille's mother said nothing to this.

Your kids doing okay? Lana asked.

They're doing fine. Camille is on the honor roll always. Robbie's thing is more physical. Basketball these days.

Camille thought it curious that she hadn't mentioned her sickness, her presence in the house.

It's amazing how they grow up and become these little people, Lana said. My little Ryan is already four.

It's something. Her mother's tone was still warm, but becoming less so.

Camille's thoughts returned to the shed, to Hunter. She doubted he was up, so the chimney probably wasn't smoking.

Well, said the woman. I know it's sort of a strange thing to show up on your doorstep. I have something I need to show you.

She dug around for something in her bag while she explained. You know that I'm working as a secretary at the sheriff's office.

I'd heard that.

It's just for a while, until Van can get back to work.

Sure.

Camille guessed that Lana was probably the daughter of someone at the Catholic church in Shallsville, where her mother alone went to Mass on many Sundays. Lana found whatever she was looking for, presumably setting it on the table.

This is from the new xerograph machine the department has. It's sort of like an APB. Do you know about those? It stands for All-Points Bulletin.

I'm familiar with the term.

I never knew it until I started there. You're always hearing it on TV shows, but no one ever says the whole thing.

What am I looking at, Lana? her mom said very calmly.

We saw this man at Lehman's two nights ago, she said. Van and I went down there for a while. Mom was watching Ryan and we went down to Lehman's to celebrate our anniversary. It was our fifth. A big one, right? We were out pretty late.

Her mother was silent.

It's none of my business. I am not judging anything. But at the station, I see all this stuff that comes in. Ten Most Wanted and all that. And I remembered this one because, well, this boy is hard to forget.

So you saw the boy in this picture? her mom said. What about it?

Do you see why he's wanted? There?

Yes, she said. Terrorism. Murder. It's hard to miss. I understand all of that. What I don't understand is why you're bringing this to me.

That's the thing. Terrance Cotter said that he passed this boy after he left the bar on Sunday. He said that he saw him turning up your lane late that night.

I don't recognize this person, Lana. He could've been running into the woods. He could've been going to the Smolts'. He could've been doing any number of things. If it was even him.

The Smolts, Lana said. I didn't even think of that. That's a more logical explanation, isn't it? It's just that Terrance thought it was your lane. God knows what they might be doing over at the Smolts'.

God knows, her mom agreed.

Camille drifted off then and did not hear the door shut when the woman left. Her mother was at her bedside not long after.

How you doing? she asked her, pulling Camille's hair out of her face.

The fever was coming on strong now.

I'm okay, she managed.

We had company, her mother said.

Camille said nothing, drifted toward sleep even as her mom spoke.

Her mom's hand was on her for a very long time, too long, but she was too weak to say something, to address her. Later, she thought her mom was crying, but there was the fever, too.

—

That evening, her father came up the stairs carrying a cup of hot tea for her. He'd been ice fishing, he told her. She knew just where, a lonely pond just to the west of the forest. They'd gone there a month back. It was very hard to get to, which was why he liked it. The farmer's name was Woolton, an old cuss that her father actually knew from somewhere or another. His farming days were over, though, and he just sat around his cold house and nursed old grievances toward people no longer living. His land was safe to use because though he would never give anyone permission to fish or hunt, he also would never be able to check on his back 40.

Her father didn't mention anything about the visitor from the morning, but she could tell he knew. There was some muted apprehension.

He asked her if she needed anything, and she said, No, just sleep. He left her and turned out the lights again.

That night, Camille's fever broke. She got up to change her drenched sheets very early in the morning, weak from the battle. Robbie woke and in a rare show of maturity, made her sit in a chair while he found clean sheets and put them on her bed. He also dug out some pajamas. Thank you, was all she could say. As she drifted back to sleep, she was thinking about Hunter, a venom rising in her.

By morning, she felt well enough to finally look at the homework Robbie had brought home from her teachers—more difficult biological processes coupled with some algebra and five more chapters of Anne Frank's diary. She made some slow headway, before drifting off to sleep again. At various points in the day, food was brought to her—once by her father, twice by her mother—which she was regaining an appetite for. After dinner, she was well enough to stand without fear of falling over, and she stood and looked out on the shed. Smoke billowed from its stove. Saturday, she thought.

On Thursday, she dragged herself downstairs early in the morning. She knew that if she didn't, her mother would use it against her on Friday.

Uh-uh, her mom said when she saw Camille come into the kitchen.

I'm fine.

Back to bed.

I can't miss any more school.

The mind is always working, isn't it? she said. You two are of a piece. You see where it gets you, I hope.

She poured herself some cereal, ignoring these allegations.

Sit down, her mom said. I'll make you something. You can't make it to lunch on Cheerios, on top of being sick.

They're not actually Cheerios, she said, setting the generic box back on the table.

For that, she got a very cold look, as if in this comment she had criticized her mother's entire life.

—

Of her father's many sidelines, trapping was by far the most lucrative. He had a man in Quebec who bought the pelts at a good price—apparently there was a market for them up there. God only knew what they did with the things. The contact was an old friend of his parents, she later learned. She liked imagining how this arrangement had been formed.

But her father cleaned, skinned, stretched, and dried them in what he called Building #4. The joke was multilayered. He was making fun of his production-line livelihood—the syrup and tomatoes and nails. Also, then there were only the three outbuildings.

When he had enough pelts, he packaged them in a box that indicated suction lines and other oil-drilling implements and he mailed them north, stamping the box with an oil company logo and return address of his own devising. He drove to Hamden to mail these packages, a small city big enough to be anonymous in. Nobody bothered oil-drilling supplies at customs anywhere. That her dad would have known this was indicative of the type of knowledge he seemed to have been born with—knowledge not useful to most people, but for him, an entire cottage industry could be formed around it.

In the evenings, he ran traps out in the hills, the southern Ohio landscape thick with streams large enough to sustain beaver and mink. Sometimes he did this in one of the two massive sections of Bryant National Forest that filled a great swath of their corner of the state, though frequently it was on private land, the back lots of large farms left unattended like Woolton's. Rarely did he have anyone's permission—neither government's nor farmers'—and since none of it was aboveboard anyway, he didn't bother adhering to the Department of Natural Resources' limits. The government owed him one little brother, she later figured his thinking was, which no pile of pelts, however high, would be able to pay him back for. It was less clear how he justified the trapping on private land, except through an unarticulated though deeply felt philosophical ethos about the boundarylessness of the natural world.

For her part, Camille cherished the evenings with him in the hills, where it was almost always just the two of them in the one place they both felt most comfortable, the caw of crows drifting along the dusk treetops, the sun truncated early by the steep rise of the hills out of the narrow glacial finger valleys.

—

When he showed up on Friday to collect her after school, many of the buses hadn't returned from the high school run yet, so the kids from Chelsea Junior High School milled around in the snow and on the salt-slush of the sidewalk in front of the decaying building.

Usually, he would wait in the truck for her to come find him on Maple Street, but today she saw him wading through her loitering classmates. She did a double take as he approached where she was leaning against a wall, talking with a few friends.

Dad, she said. I didn't see you pull up.

He raised his eyebrows, tilted his head. There was a reason for everything, that gesture meant, most of which will never be explained to you, by me or anyone else. Like so much else, you will have to figure it out for yourself.

At moments like this, when he was on display in front of her classmates, she knew that her shaggy, underemployed father was supposed to be an embarrassment, but she felt no such thing. Quite the opposite; she felt a kind of pity for other children who had to go home to a different, lesser father each night.

The jalopy of a truck alone would have been enough to elicit ridicule toward another kid, but, save the three girls she was now talking to, the seventh- and eighth-graders of Chelsea Junior High School kept their distance from her; she was dangerous somehow, a cloud of mystery about her. Her father was perhaps a part of that danger and mystery, though its main source was really Camille herself. In a world dominated by physicality—something in which she could, in any case, match just about every classmate, boy or girl—she possessed a kind of superpower of reason and verbal ferocity. She was in effect a grown-up with respect to wit. She had, for instance, recently diminished the junior high wrestling team's heavyweight class starter, Bill Gough, to a sullen retraction of an insult about her homespun clothes. She belittled his intelligence so swiftly and profoundly, it was clear to everyone in the study hall where the exchange took place, that he hadn't even understood most of the insult. When the bell had rung afterward, he approached her, chastened. I'm such a idiot, Cammy, he'd said. I'm sorry. I don't know why I would say that. I really don't. I actually like your dress.

She had shrugged, neither comforting him nor taking the opportunity to explain the lesson.

Girls, her father said now to the small group.

Hello Mr. Mills, they said. The girls mostly looked at his shoes.

I gotta go, Camille told them. See you Monday.

On the way down the long block, they passed the turn for Maple Street and it dawned on her what had happened.

You have the man with you, she said. She didn't know why she couldn't use his name. Probably because it wasn't actually his name.

I have to keep an eye on him until tomorrow.

Someone will come to the house to get him?

He shook his head. I'll drop him at a spot. Later, they'll pick him up. He will be the last one.

We're still checking traps?

We are still checking traps.

He'll come with us?

All she could think was she'd have to ride out to the county with her legs up against his in the front seat.

I've already talked all of this over with him, Camille. He'll stay in the truck. How are you feeling?

Much better, she said. She was some better, not much better.

As they approached the red pickup, she saw his profile in the passenger seat, his uncut hair wildly curled. She stood outside the door and waited for him to open it and get out so that she could climb to the middle. She was sure he would not be willing to ride on the hump.

Hunter probably should've been embarrassed by the trouble he was causing them, but instead he was looking around the town of Shallsville like he had just arrived back from ten years at sea, apparently amazed at the place, the people going about their law-abiding lives. He probably knew, as Camille and her father did, that his time was short. They would keep him safe until tomorrow, but after that he was back in the real world, on the run with his faulty credentials and id-driven life.

They were silent on the drive. The radio played the Beach Boys then Carole King. After that, there was news. A conflict of some sort in eastern Pakistan. An ROTC cadet and some police officers killed in Puerto Rico during a riot about the presence of ROTC on a campus. A massive snowstorm in Quebec and the maritime provinces of Canada that had closed down that part of the country.

Quebec, Hunter said, looking up, pronouncing it the American way. You have people there, right?

Her father, a warm man full of concern for the world and the people in it, would never ease the way of someone who had crossed him. He did not acknowledge the utterance, though Camille was sure he had noted its specificity and had already calculated its provenance.

Just making small talk, he said to himself. Jesus. And then he returned to his landscape watching.

The drive to Snake Creek followed a series of county roads, the snow plowed into dirty, crusty piles along their edges. Beyond the piles lay the small tributaries responsible for carving out the valleys through which the roads ran. Farther out from Shallsville, houses were scarce, crowded into small clearings or built in the flood plain. Snake Creek itself ran through a broader valley, nearly a mile across, filled mostly with bottomland farms, here and there dipping along the borderlands of two properties, through a copse of renegade cottonwoods or birches.

Her dad had a well-concealed pull-out up a lane that had probably once been the head of a logging road, but was now overgrown with oak saplings and multiflora rose. But first, they did a lengthy check of the area, up and down a two mile stretch of road, assessing the houses and any movement, looking for hunters, though there shouldn't be any in March; her father was a great one for surveillance, and sometimes they would watch a building or farm for hours at a time. After half an hour of this, as the sky finally began to darken, he slowed the truck to a stop in the middle of State Route 12 and backed it up the lane, its engine grumbling about the last bit.

Camille was happy to be able to get out—they'd been in the truck nearly an hour—and she was looking forward to getting away from Hunter and into the water. It had begun to dawn on her that his arrival at their house two months back had been the beginning of a steep drop from a great height for their family. She'd never seen her father so troubled. His confidence in the world—his sheer ability to produce for them, to light the world for them—had never felt so shaky. She couldn't see into the future, and so didn't know how fully it was in shambles, but she read people and situations well enough to know that the stakes were now very high. So high, in fact, she couldn't really bring herself to name what could possibly be lost.

Hunter peed in the weeds as she and her father fished their tools out of the bed of the truck, a feed sack, a Bowie knife, and a pair of shabby waders for each of them.

This is some real backwoods shit, Hunter said, rejoining them.

He might as well not have been there, as neither of them were willing to acknowledge him.

Her father got into his waders first and waited while she struggled against the vulcanized rubber. He absently checked his watch and the sky and a small thermometer that was safety-pinned to the sleeve of his coat.

Tu es pres? he asked when she looked done. She nodded.

How long's this going to take? Hunter wondered.

We'll be back in no more than an hour and a half, her father said.

Jesus. An hour and a half? It's too cold in that truck without the heater, he whined. You gonna leave me the keys?

If we can be in the river for that time, I think you'll be okay here, dry.

He pouted and swore under his breath.

Her father nodded for them to go. As they descended the steep path to the road, Hunter stood in front of the truck and watched them, yelling after them when they were almost to the road. This is bullshit!

Soon, they were away from him, and Camille felt a burden lifted.

They listened for traffic and when they were sure it was quiet, they crossed the road and then hiked about a quarter-mile through a fallow field and into the trees of the flood plain. They were silent except for the heavy breath Camille exhaled, her respiration still strained from the sickness.

Near the creek, they stopped and her dad pulled from an interior pocket a thick plastic packet of handwritten maps he kept of all the creeks he worked, each with the locations of the traps they had out. He found the right one and compared it to where they stood. Snake Creek ran almost north to south here. She knew he knew exactly where they were, but he was very careful always, very thorough.

They traced a deer path along the banks of the creek until they came to the first trap and then they lowered themselves into the water and began to tend the long lines scattered from this point north for nearly a mile, climbing onto the bank where it was convenient, but mostly moving along the edges of the water. Camille's waders had a hole just below the crotch, which was a problem when she had to maneuver through the center of the creek, where the water could be deeper and rise to her hips. She'd tried to duct tape the waders a number of times, but the water always found its way in. She knew her father's were even worse.

As he tended a trap, she moved ahead to the next one, and in this way they moved quickly. He had taught her how to safely locate the trap, and how to remove the dead animal and reset it without endangering her own hands or damaging the pelt. As with all else, she had mastered the system.

When they'd been in the water for forty-five minutes—enough time to collect a male beaver and, unfortunately, a juvenile mink—they heard some voices nearby. Her father handed her the mink.

Stay here, he said. She watched as he maneuvered around a birch branch, now empty of leaves, dipping into the water. She could see down the creek channel to where it bent, perhaps fifty yards distant, where, for an instant, she saw a dim flash of orange. A hunting cap.

She slid back, very slowly, toward the bank, underneath the tree. She could just make out her father in the dusk, using the roots to climb up the bank to get a better look. After a moment, he came back down and very cautiously moved to where she waited. He raised his index finger to his lips and grabbed Camille's arm and he directed her further under the tree and deeper into the eddy, where water flooded into her legs through a second, higher hole at her waist. Her head felt light with the cold.

The voices above grew stronger. Closer by, she could see one of the men crest his head over the bank and look into the channel. It was dusk and hard to see much of anything. Hard for her, harder for them, since everything in the creek bed was dark, including their coats and hats and waders.

They gotta be out here somewhere, the voice said, frustrated.

You know goddamn well they are, another said. I seen that old truck poking around here fifty times if I seen it once.

A minute later, she could hear boots along the banks above them, crunching the snow and winter-dried leaves and fallen tree branches. Her father was looking directly above himself, as if toward God. Her legs were now numb.

The men moved downstream. They waited five minutes more, and then they pulled themselves out of the water and sat on the bank for a minute while her father again consulted the map, this time with a pin light inside his jacket. While he did this, Camille reached down to the water and cupped a handful and drank it.

One day a couple years ago, her father began, studying his map, a man called the house and told me he'd been a friend of Stephen's at Kent State. You may not remember that Stephen had gone to college for a few quarters. Your Uncle Stephen.

He glanced up at her.

His name was Brian and he said he'd been to Mom's house with Stephen one weekend back then. I remembered him.

She was trying to concentrate on the story, but all she could think of was getting dry.

He told me he had some things of Stephen's. I thought it was strange after nearly three years and I asked him what, because it was probably okay for him to keep them. He said I would want these things, but when I asked again what they were, he said he couldn't talk about it over the phone.

This sounded strange, made me worry some. I couldn't imagine what the items were. But I agreed to the visit. And I wondered all that week how he had found me, since our number is unlisted, and back when Stephen knew Brian we didn't even live in Shallsville.

But when he showed up, I saw immediately that he was there for some other reason. It was in his face, you know. All of these people have that look. I expect I do now too. But he came to the point quickly, right on the stoop. He said he was involved in an organization, a sort of resistance. Do you understand? He looked at her again. He was folding up his map now. She nodded.

They wanted my help, he said. They were trying to end this thing, the war that took Stephen. This was in early 1970.

She was silent, the cold gone for the moment.

I told him I couldn't do it, whatever it was, because, well, I had more than myself to think about. We talked about it a little more, but in the end he said he understood and he asked me to forget about the conversation. I said I would. He left and that was that.

He had put the map back and he got up and crouched on his haunches. She could hardly believe he was choosing this moment to tell her all of this.

Then, well. It's odd. Stephen came to me, Camille. Perhaps it was in a dream. I don't know. We talked for a while—not about anything special, our boyhood and people we used to know, the way our father did certain things.

He looked out into the stream, perhaps embarrassed, perhaps baffled still by that visitation.

It stuck with me. I just couldn't shake it, the things he had said.

And a few weeks later, I called the number Brian had left and told him what I would be willing to do.

This is the man you speak with on Saturdays? she asked.

He shook his head. That is someone else, possibly several others. It's very secret, this organization. It has to be. I am very sorry to have involved you and Robbie and your mother. I can't explain to you how sorry I am.

It's okay, Dad, she said.

You couldn't understand—I couldn't expect that you would—because Robbie's so different from you. But sometimes your brother is more than just your brother.

I think about that moment a lot. I wonder why this boy thought he could come to my house and invite me to participate in treason. Why did he think I wouldn't just get on the phone and call the sheriff?

Camille was silent, but she knew the answer to that question at least. There was probably more than one, in fact. Even in her earliest memories, Stephen's presence in the house brought about a shift in her father, a lightness. Everything about him changed in those moments; he was no longer brooding or embattled. Stephen, she had surmised, was someone who even more than her father saw the hidden alignment of the world, like a man armed with a chest of tools for peering into mystery. Including an ability, she guessed, for understanding his older, misfit brother.

Also, one look at her father and you knew there were almost no circumstances over which he would ever go to the police.

We should go, he said.

Once they were walking, she wished she'd pulled the waders off, but now there didn't seem to be time. They hugged the eastern bank of the stream, staying amidst the bushes there, keeping a safe distance from the men by heading north, though this also took them away from the truck. To their right, the bottomland fields were full of stubs of cut corn stalks poking through the cloddy soil, here and there a kernelless deer-eaten cob on the ground, barely visible in the gloaming.

They moved a little at a time and then stopped while her father surveyed ahead. Finally, they crossed the field toward the road, keeping low, just in case. At the road, over which only a very occasional car ever travelled, they were especially cautious. By Camille's reckoning, they were probably nearly a mile north of the truck.

The hills rose steeply here, and they scrambled up the bank until it crested and then they turned south. Unable to find any deer paths, they mostly scudded along through briars. Camille's legs were numb now—her body, she guessed, on the verge of hypothermia. The going was very slow, up and down rises in the hills and through the sometimes thick undergrowth.

When they'd been walking for nearly thirty minutes, her father stopped them on a sandstone outcropping to listen. As they stood, the chatter of her teeth was audible.

Camille, he said.

My legs are numb, she admitted.

Numb?

I can't feel them. She couldn't help it. Fear was creeping in.

He felt her body. You need to take these off, he said, pulling at the rubber of her waders.

She did as he said. Beneath them, she wore wet jeans.

The pants also, he said. He wasn't whispering, but talking very softly.

While she did this, he was pulling off his own waders and then his jacket and sweatshirt.

How far up are you wet?

Just my legs.

Take off the underwear, too.

Soon she was naked from the waist down and her father from the waist up. She was glad for the darkness, because though their relationship was extraordinary for a father and daughter, she had begun to feel the inevitable awkwardness about her ascension into womanhood. She knew that this would eventually alter things.

You need to get into the fetal position, he told her.

When she was on the cold rock, curled up, he took his dry sweatshirt and fit it over her legs—it was very large and her body slight—and then he covered her with his coat. Camille felt his body's warmth still in the fabric.

I'm okay, Camille said, breathing quickly.

She couldn't see him well, but she knew he was very concerned.

He paced. They waited, listened, Camille deep in her own mind. Her father eventually sat down next to her, shirtless. It was maybe 35 degrees Fahrenheit, but dropping.

Don't worry about me, Camille managed to say, her speech interrupted by a burst of teeth chatter.

It was then that they heard the unmistakable guttural whine of the GMC's ignition engaging, and then the pop of it catching.

Her father torqued himself off the ground and ran a little way up a promontory to see what he could. They were close, it turned out—so close that they could hear the truck's wheels knocking over saplings as it rolled down the hill. When the truck made it to the pavement, they could see faint lights come on through the trees and then a brief screech as Hunter tried to put it into first while it was still rolling, but then he clutched again and found second. The exhaust coughed loudly as he accelerated. He was heading back in the direction of town, which was also the direction of the highway. She knew they would never see him again and, oddly, the first thought that came to her mind was that she would be able to go into his shed and discover what it was that he had been listening to on his tape player.

They heard the report of two shotgun blasts then.

What's happening? she asked.

They shot at him I think, he said. Or maybe just at the tires.

As the truck's engine noise diminished into the night, they could hear the men yelling below. There must have been at least two parties, as the voices were coming from both far-off and nearby.

She watched her father in the dim light weighing the various options, none of them good.

The yelling continued among the men. We're over here, one was barking.

Let's go up, she said to him. We'll find something. She meant to disappear farther into the hills to look for an empty summer cabin. They'd done it before once, when they'd over-extended Camille's walking range while hunting. They had come upon a two-room place, neatly kept, a long, steep, rutted driveway connecting it to a county road in the valley below. Her father had jimmied open an ancient window and crawled in and then opened the door. They'd lit a fire and warmed up in front of it for a few hours, had cups of tea and some saltines he'd found in a cabinet. Afterwards, they washed the dishes and cleaned out the ashes from the fireplace and dumped them in a small creek running nearby.

She knew the problem with this plan was her state.

How do you feel? he asked.

I'm fine, she lied.

He exhaled. We've got to move then. Wrap the jacket around your waist and get your boots on. I'll take the shirt back.

What are we doing?

We don't have a choice, Camille. We can't risk being out in this weather tonight.

Dad.

Come on, he said.

He ditched the animal carcasses and waders in some bushes and then they started off up the small promontory. Below them a wider geological feature opened up, the tributary through which the logging road ran. The moon lit the place poorly through some clouds that had set in, but just enough for Camille to be able to see her father's back and shaggy black hair as they made their slow way. They skied down the bank toward where the truck had been, and then followed the logging road down to the valley floor, where they walked in the direction of the voices, which were all congregated now beside the road several hundred yards from them. One of them had a gas lantern, the rest flashlights.

Whoa there, someone yelled when they got close, swinging a shotgun on them.

We're not armed, her father said. We need help.

Who the hell are you? the man wanted to know.

My daughter is hypothermic, he said, ignoring the question. She needs to warm up now. Can you take her to your house and get her dry?

She was shivering uncontrollably at the thought of dry blankets and the coal-fired stove these men no doubt had.

Are you kidding me? You come onto my land and steal from me and then expect my help.

Please, her father said. Just take us to your house. She needs attention. I will tell you what you want to know. You can do whatever you feel is necessary.

The man seemed to think for a minute.

No, he said. I won't help you. But the deputy sheriff's car probably has a heater in it.

There was a silence as his words hung there. She could see the rough calculus going on in her father's mind.

It's going to take a deputy a half-hour to get here, at least, her dad said.

Come with me, another man said. Jesus Christ. You're an asshole, Ray.

Do not help these people, Ray said.

You do what you want on your property. This here is mine. I'm not going to have this girl go into shock while we stand around and jaw about this. Come down if you want, Ray. I'll have Cora call the sheriff. I think me and the boys here can handle these two.

There were five of them, total: Ray, the one who was helping them, another man who appeared to be with Ray, and then two teenage boys.

We must go now, her father said.

Christ almighty, Ray said, pointing his gun back toward the earth. Let's go then.

It was a half-mile to the house probably, nearly a ten-minute walk. Camille's father wrapped his arm around her for a while, but it was clear that they could go faster without that.

Along the way, Ray complained to no one in particular about poachers and about the state of the country. He would have a seizure, Camille thought, if he only knew the truth of who they were, and who had driven the truck off.

When they got to the house, she was set up next to a stove and covered in blankets. A middle-aged woman brought her tea.

What kind of man drags his daughter into something like that? she heard the woman ask in the kitchen. Eventually, Camille was brought some pants and a heavy shirt. Her father was given dry clothes, too, while Ray grumbled loudly about the royal treatment they were getting.

Her father sat on the couch across the big room and fielded questions about his operation, about who the other man was. He told them he'd trapped a few animals in their stretch of the creek, but that he had been confused about the boundaries. He had thought he was on state forest land.

Ray laughed at this notion. Jimmy says he's seen your truck fifty times out here, always at dusk.

Jimmy exaggerates, her father said. And dusk is when I have time to do this work.

Jimmy scowled. Ray coughed up the word "work."

What about your accomplice?

Accomplice? her father said. I don't follow.

Who was the third guy? The one in the truck.

There was no third guy.

So where is your truck then?

That's what I'm wondering, too. Someone hot-wired it, as best I can tell.

I saw you pass by earlier. There were three bodies in the cab.

I don't think you would've seen three people in that truck today.

You're a liar.

Her father didn't shrug, but gave the men the same turn of his head and slightly puffed cheeks that he had given her in front of the school earlier. You'll have to figure this out for yourselves.

The deputy was taking a long time.

I need to use the bathroom, Camille told the woman when she returned to check on her.

I'll show you, the woman told her.

The bathroom was off a hallway. On her way across the room, following the woman, she caught her father's eye. She squeezed her own eyes shut for a very long moment. When she opened them again, he gave her a nearly imperceptible head tilt. It had come down to this, an almost animal communication, so subtle and freighted. They had been through many scrapes up to this point. She wondered, as she disappeared down the hallway, if they would have the chance to go through more. If they could manage this, the odds were good. She felt recouped.

Inside the bathroom, she listened as the woman's footsteps traced a path back into the kitchen, and then she cracked the door open and slid out. She grabbed her boots as well as a sheepskin jacket that hung on a hook. Very carefully, she opened the door to the outside and slid past the threshold, squeezing the knob tightly as she closed it.

In the pines up the hill from the house, she waited for her father's escape.

Above the Factory

WHEN THEY MOVED FROM OUT WEST, they decided on a place far outside the city, near a small town. It was just a hamlet, really. A sign at the edge of it said, *Annecy, Ohio,* and below that, *Population: 800.* It wasn't even on one of the maps they had of the state.

This is what they wanted, they discovered, after long discussions about it, after making lists of their wants and needs and reading about the area in two guidebooks from their branch library.

Annecy had been the site of some important peace talks with the region's Indians in the eighteenth century. There were two different monuments in town marking the event: one at the sandstone town gates—a small plaque nestled there among some unruly junipers—the other on the side of a two-hundred-year-old building—once the home of a state senator—that was now occupied by a microbrewery. The town had later been the birthplace of a small but important nineteenth century publishing house, which was now more or less defunct, though people still recognized its name. The town name itself had come from a group of French Huguenots who had spread north from a busted land deal on the Ohio River.

Somewhat fortuitously, the town was named after the wondrous French town at the foot of the Alps where they'd once vacationed on an extended junket from Geneva, all on the tab of Nicholas' architecture firm. Of course this made the town and the farmhouse nearby that much more appealing on an emotional level and affected their decision more than either of them would have liked to admit.

Nicholas would drive to C— for work, they planned; it was only about forty-five minutes. They would plant a garden. They would get some chickens. Sharon could use a small outbuilding on the grounds, after they did a little work on it, for a studio in which she could get back to throwing pots. La Vie Simple, Nicholas said.

I love it when you speak French, Sharon said, kissing from his hand to his shoulder.

So they would get out of the rat race and, hopefully, a year down the road, they would have a little boy or girl—they both professed utter indifference at which, though Nicholas secretly wanted a boy; he assumed Sharon wanted a girl.

They didn't exactly buy sight-unseen, but it was a quick weekend visit and they were so taken by the little village with its square and gazebo and the river running through its center, with the charm of the bookstore on Main Street overstocked with excellent books on everything from coffees of the world to organic pest control. It was, to be sure, everything their bustling, sprawling, anonymous Western metropolis was not. The barbershop just off the square had been doing business uninterrupted since the Great War, a sign on the side of the building informed them. During the Great War, Nicholas noted to Sharon, their city had been a wide spot in an arroyo, not more than a couple thousand people squatting in the heat and praying for rain.

And so they swept through the house at the showing and didn't pay much attention to the details. They missed, among other problems, the badly caulked bathroom and the fact that the roof leaked in the garage, right onto the workbench area, where Nicholas was supposed to build some custom bookshelves for the nook in the hallway. They missed the fact that all of the upstairs was on one 110-V circuit breaker and when one thing blew, the entire floor followed.

These were the types of things missed by young couples buying their first real home—they had owned a condo out West, but that hardly counted. They were things, too, you could compensate for. It was not hard, with a little know-how—even with a borrowed library book on the subject—to re-caulk a tub. For that matter, it would be easy on Nicholas' salary at Finissons, Inc., the firm in C— he'd landed the senior architect position with, to call up a roofer and have him come out and do something about the garage.

The thing that was less clear how to handle was the factory in the basement.

They were at a loss for how exactly they'd missed this during the visit and in the paperwork. But they most certainly had—the result, apparently, of the distraction brought on by a major purchase. Or perhaps just the exuberance of youth. Or maybe Nicholas and Sharon were just not as detail-oriented as they thought they were.

Whatever the reason for the oversight, there was indeed a factory in the basement, and this had simply and inexplicably slipped under their radar. And the fact that they had arrived on a

Saturday—by car, after a four-day trip across the high desert and through the panhandle of Texas and the Ozarks and then one long day from there—prolonged the ignorance until Monday morning. That was when the employees of the factory started showing up for work.

Sharon was running the shower that first morning—it was October, the heat finally abating, the exquisite Midwestern dawn coolness between the dog days and the gray and blowing chill of November—when the gravel driveway to the west side of the house began to fill with cars. They'd had, in fact, a conversation about the size of the driveway—it seemed awfully big—but the conversation had been changed for some reason—perhaps it had been to discuss what furniture to put in the solarium—and the subject forgotten, another clue missed.

The workers entered through the back door, which led to a landing from which you could take three steps up into the kitchen or descend into the basement. Sharon watched from the small window above the toilet in the master bathroom on the second floor as the first of them made his way to the house from the driveway. She called out to Nicholas that there was someone at the door. Nicholas, though, was still sleeping—in the middle of a dream, actually, about an ultra-light flight between C— and Chicago. He reckoned in the netherlogic of his sleep that the flight would break the unassisted ultra-light distance record. He didn't in his waking life own an ultra-light, nor had he ever flown in anything without at least two and preferably four jet engines each providing 4,000 pounds of thrust per second—or more. Also, the distance between the two cities was four times what an ultra-light could legitimately fly. But it was the kind of hobby he imagined to be popular here, and one suitable for his sense of adventure, and anyway, it was his dream and did not belong to reality or to what was possible.

Sharon—they'd been married just three years and had dated, sometimes on, though mostly off, for nearly six years before that; he actually still called her father Mr. Keller—now standing under the ample stream of a Midwestern shower head (none of these low-flow jobs were necessary here where the rivers were all bloated) was calling to him, dragging him from the heroic landing at Meigs Field, where many Chicagoans—colleagues, he figured, from firms in the Windy City—had come out to greet him.

He lay in the bed for a long moment, just lay there, allowing the real world to seep into his senses.

Nicholas, she said again.

Yeah, he said.

I think there's someone at the door.

He closed his eyes, not really awake, still with one foot in the dream, recalling that there'd been a stiff southwesterly wind coming off Lake Michigan, making his approach tricky. He smiled at the preposterousness of it. He knew nothing about wind shear.

He got up and made his way downstairs. There was nobody at the door, though there was someone messing around in the basement—he could hear clangs of metal on metal, which, in his groggy state, he took to be Sharon fiddling with the washing machine, never mind that she'd been in the shower upstairs, had in fact been the one to ask him to go down and check the door in the first place. Never mind that the washer and dryer were conveniently located in a hutch just off the kitchen, which had been another thing they'd both really liked about the place.

He made his way back upstairs and found her in the bathroom, and stood there confused for a very long moment.

Who was it? she asked, and then the fog started to lift a little. He made it back downstairs in time to meet a second employee coming through the door. A middle-aged woman was taking off her jacket in the small mudroom.

Who are you? he asked. Nicholas was wearing his pajamas, which were covered with dozens of the orange and blue logos of the pro-basketball team of their old town. Their new town—the city forty-five minutes distant where Nicholas would be working—had no basketball team, but did have a new hockey team, which meant that Nicholas would probably have to learn the rules of the sport, as he had with basketball in the first year of his old job. Though to be fair, he'd come to love the game of basketball and had checked with the office manager every gameday to see if the corporate tickets had been claimed.

Edith, she said.

What are you doing, Edith?

She screwed her eyes up at him, as if she were measuring whether or not he was pulling her leg. Finally she seemed to decide he was not.

I'm not even close to being late, mister, she said.

He stared at her in utter confusion. She disappeared down the stairs. The door opened again and a large man came in, a couple stray leaves blowing behind him.

Morning, the man said.

Morning, Nicholas said. He would take a new approach, he figured. When the man went down the stairs, Nicholas followed him. Halfway down, the man turned. Um, you can't be down here like that, he said. OSHA'd be on us like flies on stink.

Nicholas nodded. OSHA?

Steel-toed boots, the man said, seeing that something wasn't registering for Nicholas. No loose clothing. Lookit. You're wearing your kid's jammies or something.

Nicholas looked down at his New Zealand sheepskin slippers. He'd bought them for himself at the Auckland airport on his way back from some business in Brisbane. Back upstairs, he began digging in one of the unpacked boxes in the office that read "lawn

darts—backpack—softball glove—hats—winter boots—porn."
His friend Kent, who'd helped them pack, had added "porn" to
the list while he was helping box things up. What a freaking
comedian, Nicholas was thinking, now more or less awake.

Inside the box, he found the boots he'd worn at a summer job
years before—work boots, but hardly used. He sat on the bed and
put them on. Sharon was dressed now.

What's going on? she asked.

I don't really know, he said. But it seems like there's a party or
something going on in the basement.

What do you mean?

He looked up at her. I'll tell you in a minute.

In the basement, he found several discrete rooms of industrial
machines whose purpose might have been anything from molding
plastic silverware trays to forging bolts or bombshell casings. He
couldn't believe his eyes. He didn't remember any of this stuff
being here in the walk-through. But in truth, he didn't remember
much about the walk-through.

The employees were congregated in a small break room,
smoking and drinking coffee. Smoking? Nobody had asked him if
they could smoke. Sharon could very well be pregnant any minute.
He nearly said something about that, but then the employees
seemed to become aware of his presence. One of them, the
foreman apparently, came forward.

You shouldn't be down here, Mister...

He trailed off as if he had known Nicholas' name but had
forgotten it.

It's Nicholas Dawson.

Mr. Dawson, the man finished. We agreed with Mr. Pollock
that he wouldn't bother us and we wouldn't bother him.

Pollock, Nicholas remembered from the paperwork, was the
man who'd sold them the house.

I'm not Mr. Pollock, Nicholas heard himself say. He was looking around the room. What's going on here?

Look, Mr. Dawson, the man said.

Call me Nicholas, Nicholas said.

The man exhaled, frustrated, apparently tired. Probably he'd been up late, Nicholas caught himself thinking, knocking back longnecks at one of those windowless places along Raccoon Road.

Nicholas, the man continued, we've got quotas to fill—a shipment to go out this afternoon, actually. Here he looked at his watch and then turned to the employees who had continued talking, though they were obviously also eavesdropping. Okay, folks. Time to get on the ball, he said to them.

What's your name? Nicholas asked the man.

Kendrick Hampton, he said.

And what, Mr. Hampton, do you make here?

Look, Nicholas, he began. You could see that he didn't feel quite comfortable with the familiar address. I'm sorry. I just don't have time to chat. I assume Mrs. Holtz will be in touch with you regarding some recent purchases. You two can sit down and hash out all the details.

Details, Nicholas said, vaguely, part question, part statement.

Oh yes, there are always details, Hampton said profoundly. With this, he turned to board a small electric forklift, and then took off with a load of medium-sized cardboard boxes, Korean or Chinese characters printed across them, a small beeping noise marking his path.

—

At breakfast, Nicholas and Sharon talked it over and then called the real estate agent, Emily Calder. She confirmed that there was a small factory on the grounds, now that they mentioned it—she'd had so many properties coming and going lately. Would it be a problem? she wondered.

Yes, said Nicholas, as calmly as he could muster. He was practiced at phone manners from six years of dealing with clients—some of them occasionally irate at how far over-estimate his firm had come in or at how the windows the firm had argued for were hard to slide shut.

It is, actually, a problem, he said.

Well I don't know what to tell you, she said. It seems like a good second income to me.

You mean this is our factory? he said.

He looked at Sharon's face as he said this. Her expression changed some.

Of course, said the agent. Who else's would it be?

He held the phone to his chest. Did you get that? She says it's ours.

I heard, she said, nodding.

But in our basement? he said to Emily Calder.

You could build a pole barn for it, I suppose, or move it off the lot entirely, the agent said. But the basement is the current location. And a pole barn doesn't hold heat well in winter. Another location would be costly, of course. The move alone would put a big dent into the earnings of a company that size.

—

After some oatmeal and two cups of coffee, Nicholas got ready for his first day at Finnisons, Inc. He kissed Sharon goodbye on the expansive wraparound porch.

We'll talk about this? Later?

Agreed, he said.

He drove through the bucolic countryside toward the city,

which popped out of the flat plains like a volcano's conic summit. It was all new to him, and he drank in the sights, the farms and small towns and little vegetable and pottery stands.

His first day was filled with introductions and meetings and a long lunch in a restaurant forty-five floors above the city, from which he could see the flatlands stretching out in all directions like the sea itself, filled with crowded suburbs that had, he knew, good high schools and excellent department stores, but were too close to the city for Nicholas and Sharon. Let everyone else deal with the inconveniences of wall-to-wall people, he thought. He was tired of sprawl; he'd lived his whole life in it and around it, and he was done. He felt a sort of inner rightness at their choice—to move here and to live out, away from all of it, in their revolutionary-era village.

Though the factory was never far from his mind, he was able to let himself take in his new life, meet his new colleagues, make small talk about TV and sports. He had a corner space in the open-plan office, not a single gray cubicle wall to be found. Instead, he had a large oak table, a single floor lamp, a trash can which said *Métropolitain* in the style of the signs that hung above some of Paris' metro stops. Nearby was a man named Roger Brass, a project manager, he learned. He was maybe a few years older than Nicholas and wore a stylish orange and white shirt with a very wide collar. He was over to Nicholas' office a number of times during the day, checking on him, offering him coffee from, first, the drip machine in the break room, and later, from a new café on street level. Nice guy, by all appearance. Nicholas tried to settle in, organize his office, find the stores of paper and pens, figure out how to log into the printer. There was a lot to do to get going, and he also had to figure out a completely different software suite than he was used to.

He thought of Sharon at home, unpacking, a powerful love

inside him. He was happy, he realized. Whatever the deal with the basement was, they'd get it settled.

When he returned home that evening, the driveway—he might as well go ahead and call it a parking lot—was empty. Sharon, who had been unpacking most of the day, said the workers had left at 3:30. Nicholas took off his tie and opened a couple of beers and the two of them went downstairs and snooped around the factory.

Even upon closer inspection, they couldn't really figure out what was produced here. They found a desk in a corner that appeared to act as the foreman's office. On it were hardware manuals and shipping schedules. The goods, whatever they were, were apparently sent all over the Americas—one invoice said San Juan, Puerto Rico, another Guadalajara—and small allotments seemed to be on their way to Austria, Japan, and even Madagascar.

This is very strange, Sharon said.

Isn't it? he said.

Like something out of a children's story.

He shook his head. It's just really weird.

I never really wanted to be in a story, Sharon said. For the same reason I didn't want to be in *Damn Yankees!* in high school.

I don't know, he said. I'm not sure how to feel about it.

Later, they went to have dinner at the small German restaurant in the village—they'd read the menu during their visit a few weeks before. It turned out, though, that the ownership had changed recently and the restaurant was now specializing in American cuisine, and so Nicholas had meatloaf and scalloped potatoes; Sharon had some fried chicken. They talked about their new home and marveled that one could live in a country big enough to live thirty-four hours east of your old home. They talked about the long drive.

What about that old man selling the chilies in New Mexico?

He was so sweet, Sharon said.

Nicholas knew the factory was something they needed to deal with, to square, but it was so much more pleasant to talk about other things, to focus on their new life and feel the joy at having escaped something.

Each day that week, the workers arrived at seven and disappeared into the basement. The house had apparently been well sound-proofed, and Sharon was able to go about her business of getting things into shape without much notice of the six people in the basement. And at night, Nicholas and Sharon would go down to the basement with beers from the Annecy microbrewery and they would stroll around the place as if they were inspecting a garden they had planted and were now expectantly awaiting the fruits of.

—

Early the next week, Nicholas returned home from work in the afternoon a little early. Dozens of cardboard boxes were broken down into bundles on the porch, wrapped in bands of twine. Nicholas was to be responsible for taking them to the recycling center in the county seat, he knew.

He walked around the first floor of the house, looking for her. She had gotten most of the downstairs set up and it was pretty tidy. He loved the old wooden floors of the place. They were nicked and scratched in just the right way.

He found Sharon upstairs in the room that he knew they both thought of as the future nursery. They called it the library. There was a third bedroom upstairs—besides this one and the master bedroom they were sleeping in—where the books could be shoved if a baby were to arrive, but in the meantime, it was a psychological hedge to not talk about this room as the nursery.

They had read that the more couples fixated on the topic—the more they talked about it and planned for it, bought things, painted things—the harder it became to actually conceive. It was a weird phenomenon.

He found Sharon sitting on the floor. She had a pillow behind her back and she was reading. She looked redolent in the afternoon light, he thought, her long auburn hair with just a touch of curl to it, her strong chin, her upright posture, even there on the floor.

Hey baby, he said.

She didn't look up immediately.

Sweetheart?

Oh, she said, pulled from her trance. I didn't hear you come in.

What've you got there, a crime story or something?

She held up a worn paperback. It had the look of a classic, even from across the room. No, she said. *Das Kapital.* Have you read this?

Das Kapital? Nicholas said. That's sounds boring. Philosophy, isn't it?

Yeah, dummy. It's Karl Marx.

Oh, that. In English, we just say Capital. Das is German for something or other.

Yeah, she said. It means "the."

Why are you reading that? It sounds awful. I think I was supposed to read that for a political theory class.

I just came across it in one of these boxes. I don't know.

How long ago did that happen?

A while. I just opened it up and looked at it a bit.

Did you learn anything? I can think of better ways to spend an afternoon. You know there's a state park not three miles from here.

It's a reservoir.

Still. There are hiking trails.

Well. There are trails. Hiking is probably a stretch.

Or the farmers' market in town. This weekend, I'm going to clear out the shed so you can get set up in there.

Why can't I sit here and read?

You can do anything you like, sweetheart. But sitting around reading Karl Marx seems...

He searched for a non-offensive word but couldn't think of one, so instead he changed tactics.

You know that Marx was supported by what's-his-name's dad, who had a factory of his own.

Yeah, I know. Engels, she said. It's all right here in the introduction to your book. And you know that doesn't disprove anything they had to say.

Maybe not. But it makes me trust it all a little less.

Listen to yourself, she said.

Did you not see the footage of the Berlin Wall getting smashed to bits? Or that guy—what was his name?—the kingpin guy in Romania—getting shot? McDonald's is in Red Square now.

I think you're missing the point, Nicholas. These guys had no way of knowing about Stalin.

Okay. But cher, we're not really industrialists. We're just middle-class Americans. This means of production business seems to be intended for a much larger scale of operation. Like General Motors.

These are all just rationalizations.

Let's get some dinner, Nicholas said. Decompress a little. I'm starving. We can talk about it more then.

Sharon was nothing if not reasonable, Nicholas knew.

Okay, she said. I'm pretty hungry. I guess I missed lunch.

You've been here since before lunch?

I guess.

Well. Let's head 'em up and move 'em out. And give me that.

She handed him the book.

You can't control what I read.

I know. I'm not. I'm just holding this for a short time-out.

She rolled her eyes. As she was getting ready in the downstairs bathroom, Nicholas saw a note on the kitchen table, a phone message. Who's Margaret Holtz? he asked.

Oh, she said from the bathroom. I forgot to tell you. Margaret Holtz is the accountant the old owners of the house used. Anyway, she's the one with the lowdown.

What did she say?

Nothing. Her secretary said that she would come out and talk with us. I set it up for Saturday.

Saturday? We were supposed to go to the Amish Country.

It was the only time she could do it.

Saturday then, Nicholas said, looking for a snack to tide him over.

Ready? she said, appearing in the hallway.

You look great.

She curtsied. How was your day at the office?

Before he could answer, Sharon said, Wait.

It's okay, June, he said, and smiled. This smile, he knew, was disarming for people, especially for Sharon.

This is all getting weird, she said.

No, he assured her. It's our new life. We're just retooling.

She puffed air out of her cheeks. Retooling is hard, she said. I'm not sure I care for it.

It's all in the service of a greater good.

I'm going to need a reminder of the details of that greater good, she said. I miss my friends.

You'll make new friends.

You sound like Mom.

Sorry, he said. I don't want to sound like your mom.

—

Margaret Holtz was on the cusp of elderly, though she was still sharp in what Sharon told Nicholas later she thought of as a Midwestern way, snapping wry witticisms about the weather and state politics, the latter of which was lost on them. In truth, they hadn't followed politics in their old state, either.

They met in the Dawsons' kitchen on Saturday morning and she pulled out a squeeze-box file system and strew paperwork over the table. Nicholas and Sharon swam in the information. There were invoices and quarterly tax forms and letters from lubricant distributors. Neither of them had run a business or even knew anyone who had, but they both had a mind for the task, and they quickly made some order out of buying and selling, shipping and receiving.

Gradually, they got a picture of the financial situation of their factory. It was not bad. They made some sort of part that fit onto some other part of an apparatus that went into metal detectors. Metal detectors were doing pretty well recently, since everyone seemed to believe they should be allowed to have a gun, and kids were taking them into schools and shooting other kids and some teachers. To say nothing of what crazed terrorists were trying to take on planes. Metal detectors seemed like a pretty good thing to be making, morally speaking.

The company was called Ptolemy Industries. Nicholas really liked the sound of it; he'd always been strangely fascinated with silent letters, he told Sharon.

Wasn't Ptolemy the one with the idea that everything revolved around the Earth? Sharon asked Nicholas after Mrs. Holtz left.

Like you've never thought anything at least that crazy, he said. And probably it was what everybody thought; he just got the blame pinned on him by the half-baked research of later historians.

She'd shrugged. Nicholas' argumentation style frequently veered toward plausible exaggeration, which he knew frustrated Sharon.

But who runs the company? Sharon had thought to ask Mrs. Holtz. I mean, doesn't a company need a business office?

Mrs. Holtz shrugged. A company like this, not really. The contracts are through this metal detector company. There's no need for advertising or public relations. It's all pretty much residual from some guy, the founder, fifteen years ago. His name was Plank. Anyway, it pretty much runs itself. Kendrick does the shipping and receiving and he passes all the invoices to me once a week. I pay the employees and myself. And you.

That afternoon, they watched some television—the state university's football team was playing and Nicholas felt like it would be smart to have seen the game—and they ate some popcorn, but they were feeling fairly keyed up about this whole factory business. It was so absurd on one level; yet, already it was becoming a sort of natural thing, a bizarre fact of being alive not so different from other bizarre things people did, like having one's teeth cleaned or worshipping a god or drinking whiskey until one can no longer stand. Being alive was itself a bizarre business, he reasoned, and as rational as we attempted to be, we participated in all sorts of strange customs and behaviors. Owning a factory— even living above one—was no more or less strange than the next thing on the list. You know, Sharon said. I saw on a documentary once that Thomas Jefferson had a nail factory at Monticello.

He did not, Nicholas said.

It's what they said on the documentary. I don't know.

Wow, Nicholas said. See. Right there. Thomas Jefferson. You don't get more high-minded than that guy. We had to read a part of *Notes on Virginia* in a history class in college. Amazing stuff.

I'm surprised you read it.

I didn't say I read it.

You're shameless.

I got the gist from discussions, he said.

I'm starting to think my dad is right about you.

Thomas Jefferson, he said, ignoring the reference to long simmering tensions with her parents, whom Nicholas had happily left back in their old city.

I've got to pee before we go, she told him.

A Founding goddamn Father, he said.

———

A week or two passed uneventfully, and then, one evening when Sharon was at a yoga class just outside the city, Nicholas got bored with TV and pulled out the copies of the statements Mrs. Holtz had left with them. He put them all out on the kitchen table again and pulled out his laptop and created a spreadsheet of his own and made some projections, based on the company's past performance and on some optimization of it; he funneled some money into an account for exploring other markets.

A few hours later, he had printed out a number of scenarios. When Sharon walked in carrying a bag of groceries from the organic grocer near the yoga studio, he told her he thought it possible that he might be able to leave his job at Finnisons in a couple years—if they were able to cut back on some of the extravagances of their lives, like, he said, buying organic produce (here he took a quick glance at the cloth bag on the counter) and French Syrahs and bottled water.

We can drink Shirazes and risk the toxins of grocery produce and well water with the rest of America, he said.

They'd have to do things like change their own oil and wash their own car. And there would be less trips abroad—there would be no company junkets, obviously—and there would be even less trips on this continent—not the ones they'd been talking about taking to Glacier National Park or to Mardi Gras. At least for a while.

But if they did these things, Nicholas went on, he could probably start working as a consultant and then, eventually, he could go back to pursuing his own art. Nicholas had shown great promise in his senior show years before, a series of images of cacti-like people with startling expressions of anger and contempt and joy; that was before he had graduated and worked at a coffee house for a miserable year before going back to do a masters in architecture.

I would love that, Sharon said, clearly excited at the thought of having Nicholas around. Even though money would be tight, they could take trips in the country, get to know their neighbors, find a tavern to play softball for. She'd only ever played softball in junior high gym class, but she thought she'd like it.

Nicholas, she said later. Do you think I would make a good shortstop?

He looked at her with a grin. Athletic sort like you? No question. I remember the way you dominated those hussies in the intra-dorm flag football game.

She screwed up her face at him.

Speed kills, he observed.

I never know when you're being serious.

Did you mean in the majors?

You're a jerk, she said. I meant for our bar.

Sorry. I didn't know we had a bar.

We're going to, and I'm going to play shortstop for them next summer.

I bet they need a sexy redhead over at short, he said.

—

Because of this new perception of their future, Nicholas grew ebullient at his job. So much so that some of his new coworkers noticed. Nobody they knew had ever been so happy to land in the Midwest—particularly coming from the Western state he had left. And so they talked about him outside in the small piazza where Finissons had brought in a university professor's monumental sculptures of enormous fish seemingly having sex. These fish still caught the eye of passersby on their way to the nearby market, though the employees of Finissons had long ago grown inured to the provocation. They simply snuck cigarettes out there on long, Stalinistic marble benches and enjoyed the sun when it showed itself, and now, they talked about the new guy, Nicholas Dawson.

Roger Brass made the bold proclamation that he was going to investigate the matter. No one walks around this job with so much happiness in his heart, he proclaimed. He said it grandly, facetiously, but everyone could hear a hint of seriousness in his voice and could see that he meant it a little. And the truth, Roger Brass knew, was that he did mean it.

Over the following weeks, Brass developed a strong interest in the new guy. He had been at Finissons as an analyst first and eventually as a project manager for what seemed to him a long time—eight years—and he felt he had a pretty good handle on the psychology of the place and the people in it. He felt quite confident with his understanding of this world. He knew that there were people in other walks of life whom he understood no better than he understood *Beowulf*. But his office—floors one, two, and three of the Martin-Ellis Building in downtown C——: he was pretty sure he had a firm handle on that.

And so his fascination and curiosity with Dawson, at first idle and relatively harmless, grew, slipping gradually toward—eventually, there were weeks and months involved—something closer to, in the words of Bill Cray in marketing, a fanaticism. He would report to people from the office through short emails or out on the piazza at lunch, or after work at the IRA, the pub on Waters Street next to Finissons where many of the firm's employees not yet engaged at home with families and children sat around after work and drank Malbecs and single-malt Scotch and thick dark Irish beers and bitched about the decisions of corporate—the firm was actually based in Minneapolis—and also, usually, about the hockey team.

This Dawson fellow was a mystery, and if fanaticism is too strong a word to describe what eventually took hold of Brass' mind, it is only barely so. Roger Brass knew people could be truly happy, that people were capable of such a thing. He'd known happiness in his own life, and he was no scrooge; nor was he a misanthrope, despite what one ex-girlfriend, Tara Kelch, had said; he didn't wish unhappiness on others. But the truth, the bottom line, was that he didn't really know many happy people. And this Nicholas Dawson seemed to be one. Who wouldn't want to understand that?

Charlotte Colson, a technical writer with the firm, whom Roger had known for most of his tenure there and with whom he'd once had an awkward date that had ended with the two of them making out while parked in the lot of her apartment building—an event they both had since pretended had never happened—told him in so many words to put a lid on it. Sometimes, she said, people are just happy. They just are, Roger. She pronounced "Roger" as if it were "shithead."

Don't mess with it, she told him.

For Roger Brass, though, this was no kind of explanation.

You know and I know, he told her, slurring his words almost imperceptibly. We both know it. Something is amiss here. We both know this guy is probably hiding something.

I just wonder what makes him tick, he found himself saying to friends, some of whom told him what he already knew was in its way true: he was not the befriending type.

Damn the torpedoes, he told them. And anyway, he added, he had a good idea about the source of this happiness. Most of all, he said, he wanted to meet Mrs. Nicholas Dawson.

When he did finally meet Sharon Dawson, at a company event early in November, he found her to be perfectly average—not particularly the type of partner to inspire widespread joy. She did not seem so full of life as he thought she might, but he had to admit—even though they'd spoken for only ten minutes or so, near a speaker blaring some nostalgic music popular when most of the people in the room were in junior high school—she did seem to possess some ineffable quality, a sort of harmony, the female version of what Nicholas himself had, come to think of it, though perhaps somewhat muted by comparison.

Roger Brass pressed on. He invited Nicholas and Sharon to a hockey game. They were lucky to get the company seats and it was a good game, though afterward, Roger couldn't say he felt much closer to understanding anything. He had to spend a lot of the game explaining the rules to them both, so he lost a lot of time during which he might have been able to slip in probing questions.

A week later, he invited them to a friend's party, which they stopped by dutifully, but only for forty-five minutes or so. They said they had to get home, that they were taking care of a neighbor's dog. That sounded like a story to Roger, but he told them that it was good of them to come at all.

Eventually, after suggesting a few times that he'd been meaning to get out to their little hamlet—ostensibly to eat at the microbrewery that everyone seemed to agree was so charming—he got Nicholas to suggest they meet up there some night.

Well you should come out to Annecy, Nicholas had said. We could have some food at the brewery. It's a great little place. Annecy is a great little town.

Perfect, Roger said. Let's do it. Sunday? Maybe I'll bring a date. Is that okay?

Of course, Nicholas said. Of course.

The best way Roger could think about Dawson, about his fascination, was as some awful urge—like the desire to binge eat that some people had. Or, if he were being honest with himself, it was probably more like a sexual desire. He felt a kinship with the furtive movie stars who got caught with some tart in their arms at an hourly motel. Nothing, he realized, is ever so gratifying as the thing you know you shouldn't do but do anyway. That's what this thing felt like.

And each contact was a step closer. It was all a step closer and another step closer. Because his discussions with Nicholas had not yielded much, he felt a need to get to the place Nicholas called home. There, he could get a better fix. There, he reasoned, he stood a better chance of getting a glimpse of the wellspring from which this apparent joy ran.

—

On a cloudy Sunday afternoon in mid-November, the leaves all but gone from the trees, Roger Brass finally drove out to Annecy, to the Folsom Plains Brewery. He brought along an old college friend, Meredith Schultz. Meredith, like Brass, was thirty-one, single. The two of them had a longstanding arrangement that started when their college friends began to pair off: when one of them needed a date—it was almost always for a wedding—the other would fill the role. There was nothing between the two of them, though. Besides a few self-destructive weeks of sex not long after college there never had been anything between them.

Roger picked her up at the bungalow she had bought in a gentrifying neighborhood on the north side of town. She was wearing a long purple dress, and heels. Roger himself was wearing khaki pants and a long-sleeve polo shirt. They were after all going to a brew pub, which he was sure he had told her. But he decided not to razz her about being a little overdressed and instead told her she looked nice. Everything was going according to plan, as far as Roger was concerned.

But then on the way out there, Meredith was in a mood. She sat in the passenger seat with a compact doing her makeup for a long time, silent.

I thought you said this was a wedding? she said to her mirror.

No, he said. But then, he wondered. Had he?

He changed the topic. He tried to talk to her about mutual friends, her job. She was not having any of it. And then something—he couldn't even figure out later what it had been— triggered a sort of dormant rage in her, and she wheeled on him. She told him that she was sick of him and that she didn't want to see him anymore.

Taken aback, he joked with her. Well Schultz, he said. We haven't been dating for the better part of a decade.

After this, she said firmly, calmly. I don't want to see you again. Ever.

This was the strangest twist he'd experienced in a while. With the exception of this Dawson business of course. He hadn't even suspected that he could elicit such a thing in a woman. He'd had a lot of girlfriends over the years—most of them, admittedly, so short-lived as to not quite qualify as girlfriends—but none of them had ever said anything so toxic. And as a rule, Roger Brass was a relatively stoic guy—not exactly impervious to the reversals and minor difficulties of the world, but difficult to ruffle. For this reason, he'd been a clutch free-throw shooter in high school, standing there at the line with three seconds on the clock, as if he hadn't noticed how much time was left or the score or that there were 2,000 people in the stands screaming at him to miss. Clutch, they had called him, but for Roger Brass it had been easy; from his perspective, it was like shooting free throws in his driveway.

But this from Schultz, this—especially coming from these quarters; she was essentially his oldest friend with whom he still had contact, not counting Shane Woodruff, whom he always visited on his trips home to the small town of his youth down in the hills of the southeastern part of the state. Schultz was a dependable friend; the female version of himself, he realized he thought of her as—the only one left of his old college gang, the lot of them ten years down the road from those days, now a diaspora of sorts, strewn out through the suburbs and back to their own towns and off in Pittsburgh (that was Claire Williams, the one who got away) or down to Atlanta. Other places. Who knew where they all were now. The fact was, they weren't here in C— anymore, except for the ones out beyond the outerbelt, with their new 4,000-square-foot houses and their wide-screen televisions and outdoor kitchens and their chain coffee and sandwich places a mile down the avenue. And he and Schultz didn't talk to them. It was just Roger and Schultz still standing.

Goddamnit Schultz, he thought. Not now.

He was quiet for a long time and then said, This is a bit of a shocker, Schultz.

I don't want to talk about it, she said. I want to get there and be done with this.

The thought of calling up Nicholas and canceling never occurred to Roger. He had the phone number in his wallet. He could've pulled over and rung Nicholas and said that something had come up. He could've said, Nicholas, how about another time? For that matter, he might also have pulled over and tried to talk this through with Meredith, smooth things over, whatever it was. She was probably just having some monthly hormonal issues, he figured. Or perhaps things at the university, where she was an administrator, were not going well. Lots of places up there were experiencing cuts, he knew.

In any case, he didn't do these things; he watched the road and kept quiet, rolled his eyes a little for his own benefit, forged on, Hannibal in the Alps.

He was thinking, though, that he'd obviously made a miscalculation with Schultz. He should've come alone. He could see that now. This could turn into the worst of all possibilities, to be able to get so close to Nicholas and Sharon, to finally get behind enemy lines and see how the operation worked, and then to have it all blown out of the water by a moody Meredith Schultz. That was a disaster scenario.

—

They arrived at the brewery right on time and he turned off the car and swiveled in his seat so that he could see her better.

Are you okay? he asked her.

I'm fine, she said, unbuckling her seatbelt and opening her door. Standing outside, she bent down and added, You know what? I've never been better.

He had no choice but to get out of the car and follow her into the restaurant. Christ, he was thinking, shaking his head. But he collected himself, braced himself for the worst. Inside, he explained to the hostess that they were meeting some people, as Schultz inspected some nineteenth century memorabilia on the wall from the town's grist mill, reproductions of documents, bills of sale and invoices, the mundane stuff of commerce. Roger scanned the room for the Dawsons for a minute before finally finding them camped out in a cozy booth near a fireplace.

As they made their way back there, he had more than a little trepidation about what Schultz was going to do. Anything seemed possible. But after the introductions, he was pleasantly surprised—taken aback really—by how lively and charming Schultz seemed. He continued to watch her with uncertainty for a few minutes, worried that it was somehow a trap and that she still intended to dismantle the whole works. But after ten or fifteen minutes, he realized that she was fine, that she in fact seemed relieved to be in the company of the cheerful Dawsons, and was making a point of engaging with them. She talked to them about a tea house she liked in the city and then about a book on the Indians who had been chased out of the region in the eighteenth century, which had come up because of the plaque on the side of the brewery. But it also turned out that Schultz had done a master's thesis on the interactions between the European settlers and the Indians, which was news to Roger Brass. How, he wondered, had something like that escaped his notice? In any event, she did not pout, as he had feared, or behave badly in any way.

The food at the Folsom Plains Brewery was exactly the same as any number of bar-and-grills across the metro area, which was to say, it was fine; not bad, but nothing special. The beer, though, was good, better than Roger thought it would be, as if once beyond the outer belt, the recipes for strong stouts wouldn't translate. But this beer was superb. He ordered a second when the waitress returned to take their order.

Strangely, given how things had started in the car, dinner went well. Everyone seemed in good spirits. Roger, for his part, had in recent months most often found himself in good spirits when he thought he was close to some view into the life and happiness of Dawson. And at this moment, sitting across from the man and his oddly beguiling wife, he felt on the cusp of this knowledge.

True, he got a little loud from the beer. And when the check came, he made a show of covering the whole thing.

You don't have to do that, Roger, Nicholas said.

Nonsense, he boasted. Nonsense. He was digging around in his wallet for his credit card. We're just pleased as punch to get the chance to come out and see your beautiful little village.

Thanks, Roger, Sharon said.

You know what would be great, though? Roger said with less finesse than he would've liked.

Name it, Nicholas said. You want us to get the tip?

Nah. What would be awesome is if maybe we could grab some tarts at the bakery down the street and go sit someplace, maybe out on the porch at your house? And eat them? It's such a nice evening for November. You have a porch, don't you?

Nicholas was nodding, stealing a look at his wife. Yes, he said. Of course we have a porch, Roger. That's a great idea.

Roger could feel Schultz looking at him, staring at the side of his head. But he didn't turn toward her. He knew in some part of himself that he was on his way down and he was not particularly worried about who he offended in the fall.

And not forty-five minutes later, the four of them stood in the Dawsons' living room, each holding an apricot tart on one of the light blue Corning plates that Sharon had pulled from the cupboard. Sharon had also poured them each a glass of dessert wine from a vineyard in Upstate New York.

Fantastic wine, Roger said. They make some of the best dessert wines up around the Finger Lakes.

Sharon nodded.

They stood directly above the factory, looking at some of Nicholas' cactus paintings, which Sharon had hung on the walls in the living room. Nicholas hadn't thought about it until this moment, but these were, he realized, the first guests in their new home. And of course the thing on his mind was not Roger and Meredith and the formation of new friendships, but the strange second income downstairs, the appendage to their new lives. In this moment, the entire scenario seemed improbable.

And then Roger drunkenly said, I'm on to you, Nicholas Dawson. Which was startling because of where Nicholas' thoughts had been.

I know something here is amiss, Roger was saying, looking around the room and then, incredibly, sniffing, like a wolf, like he might have some heightened sense by which he was going to literally smell the thing that made Nicholas Dawson happy.

Nicholas looked at Sharon, frowning, and was weighing the possibilities of how to respond to this, but then Meredith, who had been ignoring Roger and looking at the images on the wall, spoke up.

What's spring like there? she asked. I've always wondered.

Sorry? Nicholas said.

Oh, she said. I was talking about these desert paintings. Is that where you lived before?

Yes, said Sharon. We both grew up in the desert.

I was just wondering what it's like in spring. I've never even seen a desert.

Nicholas pursed his lips, raised his eyebrows, as if to think.

What do you mean? he asked.

I guess it's kind of a strange question, she said. I think I once saw on *Sunday Morning*—the show that used to have Charles Kuralt, before he died—you know at the end, they used to have those two- or three-minute segments of sights and sounds of a place. This one that I saw once, they were in the desert and it was early spring. It's been ages since I saw it, but it's stuck with me, this one bird chirping, perched on a cactus, I guess.

A desert wren, probably, said Sharon.

Yes, I think it may have been a desert wren, Meredith said.

You've never been to the desert? Nicholas asked, incredulous.

No, she said. I guess I haven't.

Wow, he said. You should really go. You should definitely go. It's an amazing place.

I'm going to, she said. That's exactly what I'm going to do. I might even go next week.

Really?

Yeah, she said, laughing. I think I just might.

We can tell you some things to see, Sharon said.

That would be great.

There was a lull in the conversation as everyone looked at the paintings some more. Soon, Nicholas noticed that Meredith was looking down the hall, as if for something. Roger was oddly quiet in this moment, temporarily derailed by the desert conversation.

It's just around the corner, off the kitchen, Nicholas told Meredith. He took a few steps in that direction.

Oh, thanks, she told him.

When Nicholas turned back, Roger already had Sharon cornered. This guy, Nicholas was thinking, had a seemingly endless supply of questions. And he was beginning to realize that he didn't like the tone of some of them.

It couldn't have been so bad out there, Roger Brass was saying to her. He knew he was now officially at his endgame. The clock was running out. He may not have lined up all the pieces well enough to pull it off, but he saw that his chances were about to evaporate.

Who said it was bad? Sharon said.

But why move here then? Roger demanded. Nobody wants to move here.

Why not here? Nicholas said, approaching them. It's a great place. Up-and-coming. Also, it's a lot cheaper. And a great place to raise kids.

Nicholas immediately regretted saying the word "kids."

Oh, yes. That's true, Roger said, a smile, or maybe more of a smirk, crossing his face. Kids, he thought. Kids. He thought of those old friends out in the suburbs with their lawns full of four-wheeled plastic things and the shrieking noise issuing up and down the block. Was that all? A pregnancy? This was going to be a disappointment if it was a pregnancy at the heart of all of this. He took a very quick glance at Sharon's midsection to see if he could note anything approximating a bump there.

And cheaper, sure, he said. But a downgrade on the prestige scale. And anyway, how good are the schools out here?

They're not bad, actually, Nicholas lied, just as Sharon excused herself to go into the kitchen, thankful, he knew, to be freed. Roger sat down in a soft chair. It was dumb to have said "kids," Nicholas was thinking. He really wished he hadn't. Kids were the heart of the matter. For thirteen months, so far, they had been the heart of the matter, or the absence in the middle of it.

From his new perch in the cushy chair, Roger Brass could hear Sharon rinsing off the dessert dishes, an unambiguous sign that he and Schultz should be on their way. All but an invitation for them to gather their things and move on down the road.

Kids, Roger said ambiguously now. It might've been with scorn, it might have been to suggest, I have a few myself and can tell you about the hardships.

Well, Nicholas said, feeling obligated to explain his comment. At some point.

Sure. You guys are young. Young enough.

So, Roger, Nicholas said, understanding that this was going to get worse before it got better, understanding that as long as Roger was still in their house, he would have to be on the offensive. Has Finnisons changed much in your time there? You've been there a while, haven't you?

Eight years, Roger said. Then he looked up at the ceiling for a long moment. Changed? he wondered aloud, and then, Yes. The company's changed, I would say. And I wouldn't say for the better.

Oh?

For one thing, people never used to worry about losing their jobs. That's one change.

Are people worried about losing their jobs? Nicholas asked, smiling, assuming Roger was pulling his leg.

You should get out more, Nicholas. Come to the bar after work some time, get to know the folks on the ground. It's going to be important for you to know what's on people's minds if you're going to ascend.

Ascend, Nicholas said, not bothering to hide his annoyance. Who's talking about ascending?

Is that not your plan?

Roger, he said. I came here to work in a better environment with good people. That's the end of the story.

I didn't mean to make assumptions, Roger said in a way that was clear that he didn't mean it. Anyway, he added, you're probably a little insulated as a new hire, but the partners are always sending messages down through channels.

This also wasn't really true—the partners had never used rumors this way—but Roger reasoned that it might possibly open up some anxiety in Nicholas.

Just then, Sharon came back into the room.

Where's Meredith? she asked, a confused look on her face.

Bathroom, Nicholas said.

He peered down the hall toward the bathroom. He could see, even from where he stood, that the door was not closed.

Excuse me for a second, he said in the direction of Roger, an anxiety rising in him. At the end of the hall, he saw that the bathroom was indeed empty. He looked back down the hallway to where Sharon stood looking at him, her eyes big, saying, fix it, fix this. Behind her, Roger Brass was out of his chair again, eyeing those cactus paintings.

Just bang on the door, he yelled drunkenly, not turning away from the wall. She's probably just reading your magazines.

Nicholas looked on down the hall. This can't be happening, he thought. He walked past the bathroom, stepped down onto the landing that led to the basement, and descended the stairs. He had no idea why she might've gone down the stairs to the basement, but something told him that she had. There was a light on down there, he saw. Christ.

Meredith, he said in a low voice, taking each step cautiously, as if Meredith posed some physical threat to him. There was no reply. He said the name again. He crept into the second room and flipped the light on there. He half-expected to find Meredith crouched among the boxes of widgets, reading a shipment invoice, wondering what in the hell he and Sharon thought they were up to.

He wandered among the skids of product. Meredith, he said again and again. There was no answer, nothing. Nicholas had never been one to frighten, not by the dark or ghost stories or scary movies, not even by dangerous predicaments, like the time a man, probably on drugs, had accosted them on a train in Boston, aggressively asking for money. Nicholas had told the man to back off, and when the train stopped a moment later, he had whisked

Sharon onto the platform, where a crowd was gathered. But here he felt uncertain, a child's hesitancy.

What is the matter with you? he said quietly to himself. He turned and walked back through the basement, toward the stairs, turning off the lights and shaking his head as he started to climb.

At the top of the stairs, he could see down the hallway to where Roger Brass still stood; he hadn't moved. He was staring at one of the cactus paintings with a fierce concentration, as if he were trying to find something he'd lost in the thing. Sharon was back in the kitchen, again straightening up, clattering dishes. Nicholas, she said, apparently sensing his presence.

Yeah, he said.

Come here, would you?

Roger Brass turned finally to look at him down the tunnel of the hallway and Nicholas made an I dunno expression and walked around the laundry hutch and on into the kitchen. Just as he saw his wife, he saw, behind her, through the window, Meredith— there was no mistaking her, because of that purple dress, because of those heels—out in the empty soy fields beyond the lawn. She was already probably a hundred yards away, making brisk progress toward the woods back there that, along with the fields, belonged to a farmer named Frank Holly.

Roger, Nicholas said then.

Uh-huh, Roger said from the other room.

Can you come in here real quick?

Roger Brass didn't answer, but was shortly standing in the corridor next to Nicholas.

Um, Nicholas said, looking out the window.

It took Roger a minute, but then he saw.

Oh shit, he said. What's she doing?

Nicholas raised his shoulders. The three of them stood and watched her. She moved quickly, with purpose.

What do you imagine her plan is? Nicholas asked.

I don't know that she's got one of those, Roger said. I think something has happened. She's been acting strange all afternoon.

Shouldn't somebody go after her? Sharon asked.

I guess, Roger said. And then, Absolutely.

I'll go, Sharon said. She huffed out of the room to find her boots in the hall closet.

I'd go, Roger said defensively, but I don't think it would help anything. She's really mad at me.

Why's she mad at you? Sharon asked, coming back into the room and pulling the boots on while she balanced herself by placing one hand on the counter. Roger's strange behavior made Sharon's aggressive question not seem too unwarranted.

I don't know, Roger admitted.

Sharon looked at him skeptically.

Sharon, he said, a little too familiar. I honestly don't know.

I think you'd better go after her, Nicholas said to Roger.

Roger looked at him. He was trapped. Schultz had screwed him after all. If he was out there, he couldn't be in here. Out the window, Meredith continued to make progress through the plowed-under field, in spite of her footwear. Roger watched her. Godamnit, he thought.

Yeah, okay, he said. You're right. You guys don't really even know her.

They were quiet while they waited for Roger to go, but he stood there, alternating looks at them and then out the window at Schultz's diminishing figure.

Okay, he said, mostly to himself.

It was starting to get a little dark, but something about the material of her dress caused Meredith to stand out. Roger put his empty wine glass on the counter. I shall return, he said.

We'll be here, Nicholas said.

He opened the back door and walked down the four stairs to a small concrete pad and then across the half-acre that Nicholas had mowed on Thursday after work, probably for the last time this year.

A long morning rain had left the whole of the earth soaked and his feet sunk with each step, two inches at least. He was wearing Italian leather shoes he'd picked up in Florence a few years back, and he saw, a few minutes into this, that he was going to ruin them. But he pressed on. He looked up and caught a glimpse of Schultz, a distant ship on the horizon, her presence there still marked by the dress, but the fading light was making it more difficult to find her each time he looked up.

A few minutes later, he looked up again, but she was gone, whether into the woods or enshrouded by darkness or by enacting some more magical disappearance, he couldn't know. Perhaps she was lying down, he thought. He looked back toward the house to mark his progress. He was probably halfway between the woods and the house now, and he was beginning to think there was something metaphysical happening here, that he was some unwitting exemplar of Zeno's Arrow, and that each step took him forward only some infinitesimal increment, but not closer to his goal really. And it would go on this way forever.

—

Inside, Nicholas and Sharon watched for a while, and then retreated to the living room.

I hate it here, Sharon said finally. I thought I'd love it, but I don't. I hate it.

He nodded.

I don't know, she said. I just wanted to change. I wanted to grow up, find ourselves, start a family.

I know, he said.

They sat there above the factory and were quiet for a very long time. It was practically dark now, a beautiful fall dusk.

What do you want to do? he asked.

I don't know.

But what is it that you want, Sharon? Let's start there.

She looked up at him. I want, she started, and then changed tacks. I don't want weird guys from your office coming over here, for starters. I don't want to play shortstop. I don't want to receive *Travel & Leisure*. I never want another pesto chicken sandwich. I want to cast off this crap. I don't want to go to France ever again. The list of things I don't want goes on forever, Nicholas. But above all, I don't want to live above a factory. I don't want to think about where these parts end up and what they're actually used for. I don't want to think about the lives of the workers down there. I don't want to think about capital, about leveraging anything.

Nicholas nodded. He knew that she was right, that everything she was saying was giving voice to the inchoate thing floating around in his own mind these months.

I want to forget everything I've ever learned, she said.

He nodded again.

Everything has been for some stupid made-up idea, she said. I throw like a fucking girl. I don't like the bugs in the country. I don't like our old house. I just like the idea of it. I see now that those things are different.

What do we do? Nicholas wondered.

I don't know, she said. We start by getting rid of this place. I won't be part of it.

Me neither, he said.

And I want to go swimming. I want to go swimming now.

Now? It'll be cold.

It was Nicholas' cautiousness that was his worst enemy. He knew this. It had been the thing to almost cost him the relationship back when they were on-again off-again.

I don't give a goddamn, Sharon said. I want to go to that river that flows through town and take off my clothes and jump in.

Okay, Nicholas said, seeing that something was going to be won or lost here, today. And allowing that truth in, he felt a little giddiness. We'll start there.

They left the back door open for Nicholas and Meredith to gather their things, and then they drove the two miles into the ancient village and found a way down to the slow-moving river, which rose out of the farmland fifteen miles to the west and moved to the southeast, slow and snaking, into the hills. They picked their way through undergrowth—the trees and weeds and bushes thinned out now in late autumn—to the banks of the river and they both took off all their clothes and waded into the water.

Oh my God, Sharon said. It's cold.

I told you.

She waded out to where she was up to her waist, and then she dove beneath the water, and then Nicholas did the same. When he surfaced, he yelled.

Shhh, she said. The freaking constable or whatever will come down here to see what the problem is.

Oh there's no problem, he said. Except this water is two goddamn degrees.

It's not so bad, she chided.

Do you remember CPR for when I lose consciousness?

I know CPR, she said.

Thank God, he said.

Sharon moved to a deep spot in the middle and swam in circles. Nicholas followed her out and treaded water. Soon she swam over to him and they embraced, their legs kicking in unison beneath the water's surface. Nicholas held her, really held her, as they were suspended, their heads bobbing up and down with each movement of their legs. I'm sorry, Nicholas, Sharon said.

What are you sorry for?

She was quiet except for the repetitions of her breath. For wanting.

We can't help what we want.

We can, she said. We absolutely can.

They stayed in the water until their bodies grew numb from the cold, and when they couldn't take it anymore they climbed out of the river and onto the bank where they'd left their clothes and dressed without drying off. Nicholas was thinking that they stood on the edge of a precipice, the kind he'd not known in years. He'd forgotten what it was like to have so much at stake.

Back at the car, they sat with the heater blowing over them.

I wish we could just leave that house and go right now, drive out of this place and never come back, he told her.

That would be really great, she said. I was going to suggest burning it down, but your plan is better.

They sat there in the warmth of the car as the stars wheeled above them, the Earth spinning to make it seem so. For a while, they tracked Cassiopeia through the moonroof and, eventually, they fell asleep. When they woke, it was nearly dawn, the murky, ashen color the world is at that hour. The car was out of gas and it was very cold. Nicholas woke first and looked over at his wife. Sharon Keller, he thought—surprised that in that moment her maiden name came to him—this girl he'd met a decade ago on a backpacking trip in the desert with a phys ed. class. He was thinking of that girl, that other girl, from those years before. He watched her inhale and exhale. It was strange what happened to you in life, he was thinking. People always said life was strange— there were even songs about it—but it wasn't until that moment that he quite understood the idea. And in that instant, while she slept there next to him in the passenger seat, a small wave of hope flooded through him and he wept quietly—for no real reason, but because life was long and though he'd made a mess of it over and over again, he would get another chance to get it right. Or had good reason to think he would.

Dishonor

AFTER THE LONG TREK TO TALLIL, the president called the whole thing off, and Desert Storm became Desert Calm for those with the stomach to say it. They returned by aircraft to Saudi to await further orders. It was in camp there that Phillip beat a boy to within an inch of his life, a PFC named Francis China; he'd cut in front of Phillip at chow, possibly unwittingly. The kid probably wasn't even nineteen. He was nothing to Phillip Dante. Just some kid who'd ended up on the wrong end of his infinite anger.

But it wasn't the China incident that did Phillip in. Later that evening, drunk on some contraband hooch, he accosted a Saudi woman in the street, fiddled with her burqa. He didn't even know what he was doing exactly. The street was crowded and the keeper of a small electronics shop called the police. American MPs were on hand within minutes and the onlookers dispersed. Things happened quickly. The woman was whisked away by two marines and Phillip found himself in the back of a sedan. He lost some time in there to the booze, but later woke on a cot in a makeshift lockup, still feeling the alcohol sludging through his blood. He lay on his back and closed his eyes, tried to look into himself, wanted to find some thing there, a piece of good. He sensed that it was there, believed it. But just then it was not available to him. His dad had once told him that this thing was missing. His dad had told him many things, though, most of them bullshit.

His commanding officer, Second Lieutenant Robert Hedge, showed up late the next morning, a Styrofoam cup of coffee in his hand. Hedge was a Buckeye like Phillip, from Defiance, in the north of the state.

Dante, he bellowed. Goddamn you to hell.

Phillip stared back at him from his cot, placid.

The boy's in the infirmary, for starters, Hedge told him. Busted up bad.

The empty room smelled of sweat and something burnt, probably a microwave meal.

Critical condition, Hedge went on. You get me? Critical goddamn condition. For what?

When Phillip didn't respond, Hedge said, Party's over. You're outta here, Dante. Homeward bound.

What home? Phillip said.

He meant to clarify if Hedge meant back to Bragg or to his actual home, which did not exist as such.

I don't know what home, Dante. Home is not my problem.

You can't just discharge me. There are procedures.

Procedures, Hedge said. Those aren't my problem either. You messed with a local woman last night. That's a potential international incident. They'll get rid of you. You'll see how quick they do it, too. I can't help you.

Phillip looked at Hedge for a long moment, though he wasn't

sure why. Perhaps he wanted to be reassured that, after all, Hedge still had some respect for him—that this was essentially bureaucratic.

But Hedge said nothing and did not return his gaze.

I hope this rattles something loose, Hedge said, and then he was gone. Phillip stood in the dim room now and his head, his back, his entire body, burned with humiliation and anger.

He was wheels-up by lunch, in an Air Force Hercules on its daily route to Frankfurt, where he was under arrest for three days while someone in some office somewhere filed some paperwork, and then an airman first class named Scott Brigham got the unlucky assignment of escorting him back to Bragg.

I already heard you're a case, Brigham told him. Don't give me a reason to use force on you.

Phillip did little more than look in the direction of the man.

I do appreciate the ride home, though, Brigham said. I have not seen my son since August. And for that I am going to keep you comfortable.

On the long flight across the water, Phillip was distracted, though not particularly circumspect. His mind was blank, really, not filled with Private China or the Saudi woman or Hedge or the dry desert or anything that had happened there. He gave not a thought to his next move, or what would happen at Fort Bragg, if he would be court martialed or what. He'd been in for three years, and he had no skills to speak of, which, come to think of it, was what had landed him in the army in the first place. He did not think, either, of Tara Sanders, whom he had once given an engagement ring to but who was now apparently married to a boy named Kerry.

At Bragg, Brigham, to whom he'd not said a single word over the last day, handed him over to two MPs, who used respectful voices with him—whatever he had done, he had been in it, and they had been here Stateside. They escorted him to a barracks—not his own—where a sergeant was given the lowdown, and from that moment on he was cleaning every crevice of every building within walking distance. He slept at night and ate his meals, but was otherwise scrubbing something.

Hey Serg, he said, some days into this. Am I in purgatory or some shit? Is something going to happen here or what?

Don't 'Hey Serg' me, the sergeant told him. I don't know anything about it except that you are to be busy until I am otherwise notified.

After two weeks, some MPs came and got him and took him to some administrative offices on a part of the base he'd never been to. There he spent the better part of a day in an empty room, waiting. Finally, two officers entered. One of them had some paperwork in his hand.

They didn't bother working him over, but simply told him the two ways it could go. If he didn't sign, it would be bad. That was all he needed to know. If he signed, he could walk, discharged. Other Than Honorable.

He gathered his things at his old barracks and loaded them into his aging Chevy half-ton, which his MP escorts had to jump with their own truck. He collected his last paycheck, just over a grand. He wanted to stop off at the PX to get some cheap snacks for the road and some CDs, but the MPs said their orders were specific. And so, like that, he was out, escorted to the gate.

In Fayetteville, he drove along the drag, hungry for something. He decided on Denny's. Only inside Denny's, looking around the room at the sleepy-eyed people eating their breakfasts, did it dawn on him what had happened and that he was back in the United States of America.

He thought about the strange turn of events, and about his unit still whiling away their days in Saudi, playing basketball in the heat, cards. They would probably be home soon, too, in any case. War, he thought. He'd had nightmares about it beforehand—they all had, whether they admitted it or not. But it hadn't been like that. At least not for them. It was another thing entirely for the Iraqis getting disemboweled by GPS-directed smart bombs. Mostly Phillip's battalion had encountered dead Iraqis along the road, their bodies already rotting in the winter sun. He had not fired a shot himself.

He bisected the Appalachians on his way north, stopping at the Hoot Owl Motel in Carnot, Virginia. The girl who served him his fish sandwich and fries in the tavern couldn't have been more than seventeen. She was pretty but had a slight lisp. He couldn't stop thinking about her that night, alone in his room, about the meannesses the world would unleash on her for the imperfection.

The next afternoon he went fifty miles out of his way to cross the Ohio at Ironton, where he'd had one of the best games of his high school career, picking off a pass for a touchdown in the third quarter against the top-ranked Tigers. Though Atlas had lost, Phillip had matched up tight against a second-team all-state flanker all game and had been lauded in the paper the next day.

He resisted the urge to go to the ancient stadium on Seventh Street—the remnant of the semipro Tanks, who had played their last game there in 1930. He had hated all of the saps from his team who wanted to talk about their senior season every time he was home on leave. He wasn't interested in the past, exactly; it was more that he was looking for clues forward, as if he could find the spot, the actual location, where things went wrong, so he could go back to that place and start again.

He went to a restaurant nearby and sat nursing a coffee. It had already been over five years since the night of that game. He was surprised to discover that he couldn't remember much more than the play in which he'd dropped into zone coverage and gotten a jump on a down-and-out and had only the quarterback to beat in a thirty-yard sprint to the end zone.

Photos of Ironton football stars adorned the walls, including several of Coy Bacon and Kenny Fritz, two boys who'd gone pro many years back. One of the Bacon photos was a blurry enlargement of his '70s-era Washington Redskins trading card. Phillip had never cared for pro-football. He couldn't remember the last time he'd even watched a game of any kind. His attraction to the game had been purely to the physicality of it, to its violence. It had been the running into people at a full sprint that he had liked.

He paid his check and headed north. A few hours later he came to Atlas, where he pulled over at the Jolly Rogers on Houston Drive and sat thinking for a while. Finally he dug out a pack of mail he'd received while overseas. Eventually he found the letter he was looking for. It was from his cousin Nate, who'd offered him a place to stay when he left the army—"a place to crash" had been how Nate phrased it. As he was putting the mail back, he saw the one letter he'd gotten from Tara during his time away, telling him, after over a year of no contact, that she had gotten married.

At the payphone in front of Jolly Rogers, he called the number, watching the stream of traffic along Houston while he waited. An answering machine clicked on after three rings—it could've been Nate's voice or someone else's; it had been many years since he'd actually talked to Nate. He decided not to leave a message.

Now there was just the decision of whether or not to try to see his mother before his dad returned from the ramshackle golf course where he apparently spent most of his days now. A year or so back, his dad had retired from Atlas Bolt after forty-five years, collected his inscribed gold watch and his last paycheck and he and Phillip's mom, his wife of those same forty-five years, bought a squat block cottage in the desert town of Ajo, Arizona, where they intended to spend the worst part of the winter from here on out. Spring, summer, and fall they were back in the tiny postwar Cape Cod in Atlas.

The last time Phillip had seen or even heard from his dad was three or four months before he'd left for Benning. They'd had countless squabbles—over the mess Phillip made, over his not paying for anything, over how his father treated his mother—all of which culminated in Phillip getting thrown out of the house and moving in with his maternal grandmother while he waited for his army paperwork to be processed. He hated his dad with a feeling so deep and pure it bore some resemblance to love. He'd lie awake at night sometimes in the Iraqi desert thinking about the old man, imagining the hurtful things he'd like to say and do to him.

Before he'd really made a decision one way or another, he was in the old neighborhood, aimlessly driving from street to familiar street. Finally he parked his truck a few blocks from the house, just in case his dad had stayed home from golfing for some reason. He wore his Desert Storm shorts and a T-shirt with the Eiffel Tower on it underneath a navy blue hoodie. He couldn't remember where the shirt had come from—certainly not from a trip to Paris.

He walked across the driveway, noting the presence of two cars—his mom's old Nova and a much newer Buick Regal—which was a bad sign. He entered the backyard through the rust-hinged gate that kept in his mother's toy poodle. He picked his way through the many piles of dog shit littering the yard and made it to the back porch, and then gingerly opened the door an inch or two. His mom stood in the kitchen, at the sink cleaning some silverware. Seeing him, she nearly screamed in delight. Before she did, though, Phillip raised his index finger to his lips. The television was on, and the announcer was talking about UFO abductions. Donald Dante was definitely here. Cable television had been made for Phillip's father, a garden of infinite pleasures for his simple mind.

You bring me another one of those goddamn yellow pills? his father said. Phillip motioned for his mom to come outside. She took the pill into the living room and then returned to the kitchen.

I'm going to let Cherub out, she called out over her shoulder. I'll be back in a minute.

I don't give a rat's ass, he heard his father say from his couch.

Phillip walked to the farthest corner of the yard, not twenty-five feet from the door. She followed him. When she reached him, she took him in her arms and squeezed him tight.

You've made it home, she said. Praise Jesus. It's so good to see you, Phillip. How did you ever get leave?

I was discharged.

She was perhaps the only person in the world he wasn't capable of lying to.

She looked at him for a long moment. Oh, she said. And then, You're home. That's all that matters. We've been seeing the pictures of over there. It's just awful.

He shrugged. How are you doing?

I'm fine, she said. We had a nice time-out to Arizona this winter. I sent you some postcards. I don't know if you got them.

I got them, he said. I'm sorry I haven't been so good with a pen and paper.

She didn't respond. Your dad is having a flare-up of his gout today. Why don't you come in and speak to him? He'd really like to see you.

Not right now, Phillip said.

She watched him, seeming to be aware that something wasn't quite right in all of this. What happened, Phillip?

Nothing. I got into a fight, he admitted. It was nothing.

They gave you a dishonorable discharge after all you've done for this country?

Not dishonorable, he said. Some other kind. He couldn't bring himself to call it Other Than Honorable.

He reached into his pocket and pulled out a hundred. Here, he said. I didn't want to send you cash through the mail. Phillip had long offered his mother these kinds of gifts because he knew his father, who was stoic enough to sleep out in the rain himself, had never allowed his mom anything frivolous—wouldn't even let her have a window unit in the bedroom for the heat of August.

Don't give me your money, Phillip. You're going to need this.

I'm fine. I'll stop back sometime and talk to Dad. Just not today, okay? I'll give you a call.

Where are you staying?

With a friend. I'm looking for work in Columbus.

What friend?

A guy I know from the army. He didn't want to tell her that it was Nate because she would have been able to find him. Nate's mom was her sister.

I love you, Phillip said.

I love you, too, Phillip. She watched him let himself out of the gate, holding the money he'd left her.

—

Campus was the one place in Columbus Phillip knew how to get to and from that first year after high school, when he'd spent many nights carousing in the bars that lined High Street in a perfectly straight mile-long alcoholic wonderland. He made his way there and then groped toward the address, stopping at a convenience store to ask for directions.

Nate Holland, laconic and affable, was three years younger than Phillip. Phillip had always liked Nate, mostly because he felt unjudged by him, but he figured the four or five years since he'd last seen him, during which Nate's father had died, had probably changed Nate.

He lived in a run-down turn-of-the-century house not far from High Street with a slew of other boys. He wasn't in when Phillip knocked, but a roommate, a kid named Jared, invited Phillip in anyway. By now, Phillip was looking a little ragged. Before disappearing back into his room, Jared told Phillip to help himself to anything he could find of value in the fridge, which Phillip took him up on. He found some sausage and some cheese and some potatoes, some frozen peas. He mixed all of it together in a pan and fried it, threw in a little bit of the three spices he could find—thyme, basil and pepper. He was sitting on the couch watching syndicated comedies from the '60s and '70s—*Gilligan's Island* and *Three's Company*—and eating his concoction when Nate came through the door some time later, carrying a backpack just like all the kids wore in the movies about college. Nate had a girl with him, a good-looking, short redhead.

Nathan Holland, Phillip said.

Holy shit. Specialist Phillip Dante?

In the flesh, Phillip said.

Nate came around the couch and shook Phillip's hand and then introduced the girl. This is Georgia. Georgia, this is Specialist Phillip Dante.

Ma'am, Phillip said, realizing only afterward that his Southern military manners were going to be weird here. Georgia looked young, maybe just eighteen. Phillip will do, he said.

Phillip told Nate very little about his situation other than that he'd left the army. He made it sound as if the dissolution were somehow a mutual agreement. Nate and Georgia had some subs they were carrying in their backpacks, and they ate those at the coffee table while the three of them talked and the show switched to *Magnum P.I.* When they were done, Nate and Georgia left again for some late-afternoon classes. Before leaving, Nate showed Phillip an empty room with a single mattress on the floor. There's five of us here, he said. Which leaves two empty bedrooms. I'll talk to the other guys, but I doubt anyone will care if you sleep here for a while.

After they left, Phillip walked around the small room, inspecting it. The place was falling apart, the paint chipping; several layers of blue showed through on the windowsill. The wood of the doorframe was cracked from someone trying to force their way in with the door locked. A single milky shade in the form of two swans covered a bulb—probably sixty watts—hanging from the center of the ceiling. Phillip went outside and retrieved his bag from the truck, threw it on the bed. He found a corner in the closet where some ancient wallpaper was peeled back, and he took the balance of his cash, just over $1,100, and carefully hid it behind the paper.

That afternoon he slept on the mattress, with no sheets or covers. It was chilly, and he pulled out his coat and covered himself. In his sleep, he felt the earth sweeping past him, as if he were on a platform with it spinning at an exaggerated speed below, now the Great Lakes, now the Big Horns, now Hawaii. He was exhausted and slept for nearly five hours. When he woke it was evening, and he walked to the closet, found the light in there and checked his money. Three years in the army had made him cautious of theft. The money was where he'd left it, though, and he pulled it out and decided instead to put it in a hole he'd noticed in the side of the mattress. He smiled: hiding money in a mattress.

Out in the living room, Nate and four other boys sat around the TV on which the Chicago Bulls were playing Cleveland. Nate introduced Phillip to the boys and told them he was going to stay there for a few days. This was the first they'd heard of the arrangement, apparently, but they seemed to take it in stride. A few days was a downgrade of Nate's promise in the letter, but he figured it was just the way something like this was negotiated.

A little later, Nate and Georgia and Phillip went to a cheap spaghetti place for dinner.

Georgia wanted to know about Iraq. Was it scary?

It wasn't nothing special, he told her evasively. He wasn't ready to talk about any of it, didn't want to be reminded of anything about the army, which they picked up on, and the conversation moved on. Georgia was talking about how a professor of hers was sleeping with a TA and had gotten caught by his wife and was getting sued for divorce.

Phillip watched Georgia as she spoke. He recognized some familiar thing in her—a quality of self-preservation or arrogance or selfishness—a thing, whatever it was, that he knew he had too. He watched her as she spoke and thought about this thing, wondered if it would lead her down dark alleys similar to the ones the thing inside Phillip had guided him to.

They ate their dinner and talked about meaningless business. Nate complained about a twentieth century Russian history class.

I thought you could just drop a class you didn't like, Phillip said. His knowledge of college was based mostly on movies and anecdotes a guy in his unit occasionally told.

You can drop whatever you like, Nate said, but if a course is required, you have to take it sooner or later.

Phillip nodded. When he asked Georgia what she studied, she told him textiles.

Clothes?

Sort of. Fashion merchandising. Cultural history. But, yeah, apparel design is part of it.

She wore clothes Phillip assumed were stylish: a miniskirt and a blousy white thing on top with a low-cut neckline that left few questions about the shape and size of her breasts.

Back at the house, the roommates were on the porch yelling at passersby, drinking heavily, judging by the cans of Keystone lined on the banister. It was warm for March, but still it *was* March, and Phillip felt the chill through his thin shirt. The three of them joined the party, which went well past midnight. Sometime late, Phillip stumbled upon Georgia in the hallway outside the bathroom smoking a one-hitter. Oh my God, she said when she realized he was there, you scared the shit out of me.

Sorry. You should find a more private place for your doings.

Yeah, probably. She laughed.

Don't let me interrupt you. I'm just looking for a spare case of Old Mil that the tall guy said he kept in his room. What's his name again?

Wait. You can't tell Nate about this. He thinks I quit smoking.

I know nothing, he said—not too ridiculously, he hoped. Then, What does he care?

He cares, Specialist Dante. It's complicated.

Whatever. Doesn't matter.

Jared.

Jared?

The tall kid's name. I'd be careful what I touched under his bed if that's where he said to look.

Duly noted.

Remember what I said.

Don't worry yourself, Miss Georgia.

It's just Georgia.

Right.

—

After four or five days lounging around the apartment during the day and drinking with Nate and his friends in the evening, Phillip began to look for work, knowing very well that he had it in him to burn through his cash with no backup plan and had already started down that path.

The economy had gone from bad to worse in the years since he'd last been looking for work. But after a week of asking around and driving out to the suburbs to look into the jobs listed in the classifieds, he finally found some work at a nearby country club, grunt work on a landscaping crew. It was physically hard and boring. The other workers were almost all in school, and this fact or some other thing about them annoyed Phillip for reasons he didn't fully comprehend. He kept to himself on the job, did not joke with these kids or go swimming with them in a reservoir near the course when they invited him on his third day. One night not much more than a couple weeks into the country club job, he went to a string of bars with a couple of Nate's housemates and didn't get home until three. He woke the next day at nine, somehow lying on his own mattress in his own room, his head throbbing in that familiar way.

He thought to call the country club—his shift had started at seven—but then decided not to, and went back to sleep. He would, he knew, have to go out there eventually and get his paycheck. When he finally did get up at eleven, there was a note on the kitchen table from one of the guys that the golf course had called.

In this way he found himself again loitering around the apartment during the day. He watched a lot of TV, and eventually one of the guys got him hooked on Nintendo golf, which he got pretty good at. The irony of this was not lost on him.

Late that week, Georgia asked if he was still looking for work. They were eating chicken noodle soup that Phillip had made for all the housemates and Georgia and one other girlfriend, Sarah—a vast pot of the stuff.

Are you hiring? Phillip joked.

You wouldn't want to work for me.

No. I don't imagine so.

It's bouncing. Friends of mine are looking for someone.

Bouncing. He laughed.

May not be your thing. It's at El Río.

Uh-huh, he said. Go on.

They're looking for a couple of burly guys.

Philip flexed both arms.

Maybe not burly, but you *have* been in the army.

I've been in the army all right, Phillip said, something distasteful in the very sound of the word now. But what he was thinking was about Georgia's awareness of him, of his body.

Phillip met the friends first, an interview to see if there would be an interview. The manager called him the next day and asked him to come in.

The bar in daylight, its doors open to the sunshine and the spring warmth, felt naked. Phillip had been coming to the location of this bar since he was sixteen. During that span it had been called three different things besides El Río: The Brickyard, Fourth and One, and Sinbad's. There had been no appreciable difference between the four places, slight variations in décor was all.

We serve about six-hundred kids a night, the manager, Cal, told him. It gets messy out there. Kids get drunk, say and do shit they shouldn't. We ask them to leave. If they don't, we make them. Can you do that?

I can do that.

Cal gave Phillip three T-shirts that said *El Río* in black over yellow.

Dominick told me you were over to Saudi. To Iraq.

Phillip nodded. He had begun to understand better why men who'd been in Vietnam or Korea or even World War II never wanted to talk about it, because people were vampires about that shit. People who had seen those things, if they had even an ounce of human inside them, just didn't want to think about it. Except his old man. He'd talked about the war so much that Phillip never wanted to hear the words "Nip" or "Guadalcanal" ever again.

Cal, in any case, was sharp enough to see that Phillip didn't want to discuss it. He stood up and offered Phillip a hand to shake.

Shift starts at five, he told Phillip.

The first night was great. He checked IDs. He chatted with a ton of girls, almost all of them drunk, which was new enough not to be annoying. He helped the other three guys, Georgia's friends, escort a guy out. He wasn't resisting, but in case, the four of them walked behind him all the way to the door. Get some fucking manners, the one named Pete told the kid when he was outside on the sidewalk, a final insult to injury.

The next Thursday, a kid threw an empty bottle high into the air. It hit a girl in the head, and she dropped. Phillip saw the whole thing from his perch on a small rise of stairs. Pete and Garcia, the two working down below, saw the commotion and descended into the crowd and cleared the area to get to the girl. Phillip could see Pete mouthing the words to the crowd: What happened? One of the girl's friends was trying to explain.

Phillip watched the boy who'd thrown the bottle slinking off toward the bathroom, and he followed him and yelled at him to stop, but the boy kept going. Phillip caught up with him on the landing near the bathroom. He grabbed his shoulder, and the boy turned and swung at him hard, catching Phillip on the ear. For just an instant, Phillip was surprised by this; it had been a long time since someone had actually hit him, and he'd forgotten what it felt like. In the next instant, though, some chemical thing ran through his body. He wouldn't have fought it if he could've—a rush flashing through. And from some core crook of his being disassociated from thought, Phillip's hands and body went to work. He grabbed the boy's left arm and pulled him. Using the boy's own weight against him, Phillip applied the flat part of his forearm to the boy's head as he rushed toward him. Like that, the boy lay unconscious in a pile.

Garcia, seeing this new commotion, was at his side. Jesus, bro, he said. Holy fuck. Garcia leaned over and smacked the boy's face lightly, and the kid came to, his bewildered eyes opening slowly. You just had your first encounter with the 82nd Airborne, Garcia said to the boy.

Phillip left and went outside, where it was dark and the noise was deafening—the sub-woofer's boom-boom-boom and the screaming alcohol euphoria, the frenzy of Thursday night. It was fucking deafening, Phillip thought. Soon Garcia appeared at the front door of El Río. He had the boy, clearly a frat boy—a fact recognizable by a certain smugness in his demeanor—by the arm. He was being gentle. On his way back into the bar, Phillip made eye contact with the kid, as if there was something that could be communicated between the two of them. If there was, it was simple and crude.

—

Later in the week, Phillip drove out to the country club and sat in his truck in the parking lot watching the wealthy ladies of Upper Arlington and Bexley unload clubs from the trunks of their Saabs and BMWs. Women's league morning.

He didn't know how much the check would be for, but he'd worked nine days. And he had been getting $6.50 an hour. He did the math on the side of a Wendy's bag he found on the floor of the truck. It should be around four or five hundred before tax, but you never knew how much would be taken out.

He found the grounds manager in the large building where the equipment was stored, looking over some boxes of seed that had arrived by UPS.

The man, who Phillip thought was probably in his thirties, looked up and saw Phillip.

Well, well, well, he said. Look what the cat dragged in.

Phillip had heard something like this from so many people since he was twelve that the words and tone barely registered.

I just would like to pick up my check.

The manager stopped what he was doing and stood up and looked hard at Phillip.

You know, Phillip Dante, there's a little something called decency in the world. As in, when you have a job you don't want anymore, you call them up and tell them. Because, you see, there's people counting on you for whatever they hired you for.

Phillip breathed softly.

Instead of just going AWOL and leaving them high and dry, the manager said.

I apologize, Phillip said. It was everything he could muster to say these words.

You apologize, he said. Then, at the very least, you pick up the phone when they take time out of their busy day to call you to see if everything is all right. And then tell them. These things are what decent people do. What people with honor do. Did they not teach you about honor in the army?

They taught me so much about honor I nearly puked.

The man scoffed. Your check's with the girl at the pro shop.

Phillip turned without saying another word, knowing that the man, his name already gone from Phillip's mind, was watching him in disgust the whole time. It was easy, Phillip had found, to be the guy who was looked at in disgust.

—

Two days after the incident at the country club, Georgia and a gaggle of her girlfriends closed down El Río, dancing and drinking from the large plastic cups of Sex on the Beach the bar sold, replete with little umbrellas. That they were all underage was a fact they compensated for with their hips and the cut of their clothes and the way they now knew every employee, including Cal.

Georgia had already been lit up when she came in that night. Phillip had been working the door, had been the one to pretend to look at the fake IDs the girls dutifully produced, and then he'd wrapped the plastic armbands around their thin, late-adolescent wrists.

He looked for a long moment at Georgia as she crossed the threshold. You doing okay? he asked her.

Oh, baby, she said. You're a cute one. And then she disappeared inside to the dance floor, where he knew she and her friends would be as provocative as possible.

For a few weeks, Phillip had been avoiding her. He sensed a tension between them, and he feared it would boil. He knew he'd have to tread lightly tonight, and he lay low insofar as that was possible, studiously doing his job, watching the bathrooms closer than usual for drug use, because they were out of the way. After cleanup, he planned to slip out the back, but Pete spotted him moving in that direction at 2:30 and yelled after him. Dante, he said, come have a beer with us.

Weekend nights after closing, Cal would let the staff stick around as long as they didn't drink any of his liquor. Instead, he sold them a couple cases of Budweiser at cost. These after-parties were usually open to a few outsiders, friends of the employees, as long as the majority of the guests were girls. Usually someone put on *Physical Graffiti*, and they all sat around the tiki bar cove, joking, replaying the night.

I should get, Phillip told Pete.

One beer. Don't be a huge pussy.

One beer.

But after that beer, there was another one waiting for him. These guys were relentless. After three, it was done. Georgia and her friends danced around and did air guitar to Queen and the Cult and Motörhead. There were some shenanigans, some darts. At six, as everyone was starting to drift home, Georgia somehow found Phillip at the door.

Walk me home, she said. It was neither a question nor a command but some ambiguous thing between the two.

Sure, he said.

They were quiet along the way. The early morning city was cold and fresh. The noises of street cleaners and garbage trucks carried to them from distant neighborhoods. Phillip was buzzed. Georgia was saner than she had been six hours before, but she'd had enough to drink to stay afloat for some time.

You're a funny duck, Dante, she said after a few blocks.

I know, he told her, which made her laugh.

He didn't touch her, tried to think about how he would deal with this—if he was going to go inside with her, going to follow her to her room with its inevitable futon and Ansel Adams prints. She leaned into him on the walk. It was cold, and neither of them was dressed for it. A street cleaner turned the corner up the block and came toward them.

It's the red one, she told him, looking up the block.

Okay, he said. He could feel the electricity in her. Now was the time to say, Well, here you are. But he didn't.

As they approached the steps, his mind was still spinning, looking for the key to the situation. And then it no longer mattered because he caught a glimpse of Nate's Renault parked on the street. In the next instant, he saw Nate himself rousing from the couch on the porch. Fuck, he heard Georgia whisper to herself.

Hey, guys, Nate said, rubbing his eyes. Late night.

Some guys stuck around the bar, Phillip said.

Nate nodded, looked at Georgia.

I'm heading on up the road, Phillip said. You guys get some sleep.

Neither of them said anything, but it didn't matter. Phillip turned and walked the way he'd come, as nonchalant as if this had been his plan all along. It had not, of course. He knew it hadn't.

—

Back in the Syrian Desert, heading first east out of Saudi Arabia and then southeast toward the Euphrates, his unit had encountered scores of dead Iraqis, victims of the Thunderbolts and Apaches from the week past. The bodies lay in the sand, hung out of personnel carriers, sat against the tires of trucks, as if just to rest.

When they encountered the bodies left behind as the Iraqis retreated toward the capital, they already had flies blowing around them, larvae in some cases coming out of their eyes. At first, no one could quite believe it. They had expected something gruesome of a different sort. They had expected stiff resistance, a Battle of the Bulge. Instead they found no enemy to speak of. Just these dead men and boys, one after another. They didn't have time to deal with the bodies—that was for some less lucky unit farther back—but they stopped and looked at them, and a few took snapshots. Eventually the count grew so high that there was no time to even slow down. In some stretches, dead littered the road like fallen leaves.

On the fifth day of the ground war, as the press had been calling it, they came across an encampment devoid of human life southeast of Al-Salman. There were eight dead young men, each in his late teens or early twenties, just like most of the boys in his company. While Hedge radioed back about the bodies, one of the younger kids in the outfit, a boy named Hernandez, from Texas, went a little crazy. Not long out of Airborne School—not to mention high school—he lost it and started kicking one of the dead bodies. First he kicked it in the side. You want some of this? he said. A few of the other guys egged him on: He was saying shit about Mrs. Hernandez.

Don't do that, Ruckers said. But it didn't matter. He kept at it, until he stepped back a few yards and took a whopping kick at the dead man's head and it came loose. It did not fly into the air, as he had probably intended, because of the sinewy tendons and the spinal column still connecting it. But it was dislodged from his body nonetheless and lay off to the side of the boy in the dust.

Phillip laughed at this, along with three or four other guys nearby. He kicked his goddamn head off, one of them said. Just then Hedge came around the side of a truck and saw the scene. Someone please say that I am not seeing what I'm seeing? he said.

Everyone was quiet.

Hedge looked down at the ground. He seemed to be saying a prayer or something, talking himself through this or asking God how to deal with the venality of these young, godless men. A radio squawked.

You think it's funny to kick a dead man's head off, Hernandez?

No, sir.

Higgins? You?

No, sir.

Dante.

No, sir.

Where is your sense of right? he asked them all. He looked at Ruckers, who was smoking, as if for some help.

Are you human? he asked Hernandez.

Hernandez looked taken aback.

Sir.

You heard the question.

Am I human?

That's what I asked.

Yes, sir. I'm human. Hernandez laughed a little, but no one else did.

Because I'm not sure. I'm not sure about any of you. Can you imagine how your family would feel if we had to ship your body back to Texas and when it got there the head was disconnected?

Hernandez watched him, seemed to be considering this horror.

And your family, your dad, is looking down at his dead son and asking the marines delivering the body, Why is his head not connected, when he was shot in the gut?

The specter of a gut shot seemed to register for all of them.

And what will the marine tell your dad? Hedge went on.

Hernandez looked at him and then at the ground.

Dante? What will he have to tell him?

That some Iraqi kicked his head off for a joke.

What do you think of that, Private Hernandez?

It's not good, he said.

It's not good.

Higgins, he said. Dante.

Sir.

Is this what you call leadership? Is that what you call helping Hernandez to grow?

No, sir, they said.

If this is the type of behavior I'm out here defending, he started, but then trailed off, looked around the great wide desert full of billowing smoke. Above, the occasional scream of a jet. The men were silent as Hedge turned and disappeared to the other side of a Sheridan, and they could hear him say to the guys over there, Let's get these rigs moving down the road.

Phillip and the others stood there for a long moment. Before he went to retrieve his pack, Phillip looked at the dead body, and for reasons that didn't make sense to him, he smirked.

Ruckers, who stood nearby, saw this. What's wrong with you?

Fuck off, Phillip said.

—

Phillip found the number for Alba's by calling information and asking for the town of Talbridge. He called the store then. If she answered, he would hang up. He didn't want to talk to her on the phone; he wanted to see her. If she didn't answer, he would ask for her—it wasn't so likely that there would be more than one Tara working there—and he would go out there.

The phone rang. Twice, three times. Then he heard someone pick up. It was her. He meant to hang up, but he stayed on, wanting to hear her voice as she asked who was there again, and then again.

Finally she grew frustrated and hung up the phone. He sat for a minute and thought about this and then went to his truck. It was ten after ten. He could be there by eleven.

—

A hundred-year-old statue of a Civil War general sat in the heart of the village of Talbridge. The general rode a rearing horse as he commanded a charge into enemy lines, perhaps at Antietam or Gettysburg. It sat in the middle of a traffic circle—the only traffic circle Phillip had ever seen until he left Ohio. In his GMC, he looped around the circle and parked just off the square in front of a hardware store and popped inside and wandered the aisles for a while, getting up his nerve. A man behind the paint counter yelled over to him, above the noise of the loudly jiggling paint mixer, did he need something in particular? Just looking around, he told the man.

He scuffed along the ragged hardwood floors and found a water fountain at the back of the store and took a drink and then sat on a small bench next to the fountain. The store was old, like the other buildings in Talbridge, and had probably looked and smelled this way at least since his own father's boyhood. In addition to the two men behind the counter, there were four or five others roaming the store, farmers all, by the looks of them.

He decided to buy some gum and go. He paid in change and thanked the man, who eyed him suspiciously, as people eye all strangers who enter any kind of store in a small town.

Down the street, he passed a dilapidated restaurant called Der Hirsch.

He'd been in there once with his parents. "Hirsch" must have meant "deer" because there was a giant head of one above the door, and he remembered dozens of paintings of deer inside. The food had been German and not very good, though his dad loved it, which was why they'd gone there in the first place.

He slowed as he came to Alba's. It was a small store with an all-glass front. He paused there for some time before finally closing the distance to the door and going inside. He looked around and saw two or three women, none of them Tara. He worked his way toward the back, thinking maybe she was there doing stock or something. But she wasn't. Soon a woman approached him. Can I help you find something?

Phillip hated store clerks. They were always hounding you. I'm just browsing, he said.

After fifteen minutes of looking at various items, Phillip finally said, I guess I'm just not sure yet.

Well, hon, the lady said, you think about it and stop back.

I will.

He was too embarrassed at this point to mention Tara, so he stepped back out into the cold afternoon. He drove aimlessly through the hills afterward, feeling frustrated and stupid and angry.

He knew he could not look Nate in the eye—something that made him sick inside because Nate of all people had been so openhanded toward him. He thought about sleeping in his truck, but the thought made his back hurt, so he found a dirty motel outside Atlas—mostly it housed long-termers, immigrants who were doing some sort of early-season agricultural stuff out in the country.

The next morning he returned to Talbridge, parking again off the main square, a block down from the store. He sat there and sipped from a cup of weak coffee he'd bought at a convenience store. He had the remainder of his money in his thin jacket, and his bag was in the back of the truck, under a tarp in case of rain. Anything was possible. He might go back to Columbus; he might drop down into the hills to the southeast, where he figured he could probably squat in an empty cottage. He might do something else entirely.

He sat drinking his coffee, watching the store as the first of the employees arrived to open it. Soon there was a ringed-fingered tap on the driver's-side window.

Phillip? He heard her voice from the other side of the glass.

Oh shit, he said, and rolled it down.

She looked along the block both ways and then toward the store. What in God's name are you doing?

I'm not doing anything. I'm sitting here drinking coffee, waiting for you.

I guess I meant, *why* are you waiting for me?

I want to talk to you.

You want to talk to me? Now?

Yeah. Can you talk?

No, I can't talk. I've got to work.

She started to walk away from him.

Wait a second, Tara. Come on. Just five minutes.

I'll meet you in the parking lot at the reservoir at twelve-forty, she said. I'm married, you know.

Yeah, I know.

I don't think you do.

He waited.

Bye, she said.

Okay, he said.

Now, git.

Okay, he said for a second time. He started the truck and headed off in a westward direction. That road led out of town and became the main artery between the hamlet and Atlas. He followed it for a while. It was a brilliant morning now. He followed a sign to a picnic area at the reservoir. They'd gone there a few times, during the year and a half they'd gone out. He couldn't remember why, because she wasn't from this part of the county; they used to just drive around a lot.

He found a very old pack of cigarettes in the glove box and smoked a few. They were stale, and after the third one he got out and threw the rest of the pack into the large dumpster near the boat put-in. He'd never cared much for the habit. His dad, who'd rarely done anything without one in his mouth, had likely put him off. His father had a cigarette dangling from his lips in every picture Phillip had ever seen of him, here assembling a tricycle, there playing third base for Atlas Bolt's C-League softball team.

He found a book under the seat that someone in his outfit had given him a year or two before. It was a true-crime story about a series of bank heists out West. He was just hitting a good part when, for the second time that day, someone tapped on his window. It was a deputy sheriff.

Morning, the man said.

Good morning, Phillip told him.

Everything okay here?

Phillip was confused by what might not be okay. Yeah, I'm fine. Is there a problem of some sort?

No problem, the man said firmly. I just like to be thorough.

Phillip was still confused, but he figured the fewer questions he asked, the better.

You just hanging out here reading?

Killing some time.

What you got there? That a good book?

It's okay. Friend of mine gave it to me. True crime.

I read some, the deputy told him. On my off days. I've actually been working on a book myself.

Is that right?

The deputy seemed embarrassed now and looked out at the lake, possibly toward the ducks, before looking back at Phillip.

I see you got an Airborne decal there on your window.

Yeah, Phillip said. That's a historical sticker. I am no longer in Uncle Sam's employ.

Roger that. I was in the Tenth Mountain back in the day.

Yeah. I know some guys from up there.

The deputy seemed satisfied with things, though it wasn't clear to Phillip if the deputy was sussing out if he was a serial killer or if he was just lonely.

Sorry to bother you, the deputy said. I just like to keep close tabs on things. I didn't recognize your car. Enjoy your book.

Thanks, Phillip said.

He watched in his rearview as the deputy pulled away. He didn't know how the man had crept up on him in the first place. He must've been pretty engrossed in the book.

He read until just before noon, and then he went back to Talbridge and found a diner and bought two BLTs and a salad, then returned to the reservoir.

He watched the park entrance intently, as if just watching would produce Tara. At 12:39, she did appear, driving a new Cavalier. She pulled up beside him and rolled her window down.

I got you a sandwich, he told her, pointing to the bag on the floor of his truck. But you have to come sit in my truck to eat it.

She got out and opened his passenger door and sat down. She pulled out the sandwich and started eating. Thanks, she said. I didn't eat breakfast.

There's some salad in there, too. And some plastic forks.

She ate, and they were otherwise silent. Phillip left his sandwich for later.

Out on the reservoir, the ducks—they were mallards—floated around aimlessly, or so it seemed.

So, Tara said. Phillip Dante.

So, he responded.

What brings you back to boring old Ohio?

Nothing special, he said.

The army everything you hoped it would be?

The army was many things.

She nodded, chewed.

So how did you get married? he asked. He'd not wanted to get into a fight about that, though he wasn't sure why else he was here.

It's an old story, Phillip. Girl meets boy, falls in love with boy, marries boy. They live happily ever after.

Happily ever after, he said.

She shrugged.

He looked over at her. Seeing her now, he literally couldn't believe she had done it. It wasn't so long ago that they'd been sitting in some similar place, talking about a future together.

What about all of your school plans? he asked.

Come on, Phillip. You left here and joined the goddamn army. Three years ago. You said you were going crazy here and you just left. So don't talk to me about my plans and decisions.

He sat quietly.

You've got no claims on me. You've got no right to talk about my mistakes or to make wild suggestions, like I've not followed my dreams. That's rotten, Phillip.

I wasn't doing that, he protested. I wasn't even doing that. But he saw that that was exactly what he had been doing.

Why are you here, Phillip? You come here to win me back?

You're the one who stopped talking to me, Tara. You're the one who got mysterious and started doing things without consulting anyone else. And then you marry this fucking kid and I get a clipping from the paper in the mail about it from my mom?

I wrote to you and told you, she said.

This was stupid, he thought. I got thrown out of the army, he told her.

I wish I could say I was surprised, she said. She looked at him coldly. And now what? she said.

Nothing. I don't know.

You're such a dumbass, she said. You think you can just destroy yourself to get back at everyone.

Get back at them for what?

I never understood why you joined the stupid army. Didn't you think there was some chance you'd have to go to war?

I didn't think about it. I figured I'd just be painting Quonset huts in Guam or some shit.

That's some ambition. Anyway. I don't fucking care what you do.

I never said it was my ambition. It just seemed better than sitting around here getting old.

With me, she said.

With myself.

They were quiet for a time.

You're not the only one that's frustrated, Tara.

Yeah.

I came here because I didn't know if it was real. I didn't come here to make trouble for you. I just kind of couldn't believe it. I know we haven't talked in a while. I mean, I didn't really expect you to leave your husband or something. Kerry.

She was quiet. It just happened, Phillip. I can't explain it. It just happened. One day I came home and I got fed up. I quit school and I came out here to see him at his parents' farm. You met him once at the racetrack.

I know who he is.

I guess I just decided to do it.

What. You just came out here and asked him to marry you?

I mean, it wasn't all in one day. But that's about how it happened.

And then what?

And then this. That was fourteen months ago. His family bought us a house. It's out on their land. It's back in the woods a ways.

Uh-huh. And Kerry and you?

Look. Honestly? I'd leave here with you today and go to Guam if I thought it would make me feel any better, but it wouldn't. I know that. It's all the same.

He looked at her, trying to see what was behind her words.

I'm going to go, she said.

Okay.

Phillip, she said.

Uh-huh.

I'm sorry things worked out the way they did.

Things haven't worked out in any way, he said.

She touched his hand. Take care of yourself. I mean it.

I'll be fine, Tara.

You talk to someone about what happened while you were over there.

He looked at her and nodded, but he didn't care about any of that. He'd known Tara to be right about many things, but his problems were not with what had happened in Iraq. His dreams were not haunted by any of those things, by PFC China or by the dead Iraqi boy without a head or any of it. It was something much deeper that was the matter, something so far down inside him, he was starting to see he might never quite be able to get an angle on it. Whatever this thing was, it was in there, like an abscess beneath his skin, growing, somehow still unchecked.

As he watched her slide into the seat of her car, he realized that someday he would look back on this moment and feel his guts turning, and there was not a goddamn thing he could do in the intervening years to prevent it from happening. Out on the reservoir, the ducks—there were about six of them—all took off to the southeast, their wings flapping violently as they skimmed along the water's surface. They hovered there, issuing raucous quacks, the water splashing all around them, for what seemed too long, as if they were not going to be able to gain altitude. And then, finally, there was separation between them and the water, and they pulled up their feet and were in the air, rising now with seeming ease. He watched them as they eventually turned toward the west and continued to rise and finally disappeared into the hills.

.

We're in Danger, All of Us

WELL AFTER BASKETBALL SEASON, in early May, a man showed up at the door in a red sweat suit with blue and white stripes running down the sleeves and legs. I knew a lot of men who wore such apparel—most of them were coaches of some sort—so I was not troubled by it. I'd been in my room trying to memorize Ohio's counties for an exam, but it was hard to concentrate because the twins were giggling in their own room down the hall, talking to each other in their new language, which they'd made up that winter, sometime after Mom kicked Dad out—once and for all, it appeared—and he'd moved across town to a room in a boarding house.

This boarding house where Dad now lived was an old blue Victorian next to an empty lot, which butted up against the foreboding woods on the north side of town. It was not in a great neighborhood and not in great shape, but there weren't a lot of houses around in great shape, including ours, which wasn't really ours anyway. Dad's was managed by a guy named Holt, who everybody knew had done time for armed robbery. He wasn't the owner; he was just supposed to fix leaky toilets and collect rent and so forth. The robbery business had been in the paper when he'd been released from jail a year or so back. I didn't catch it at the time, though I sometimes did inadvertently read the news after scanning the sports section, but Mom remembered and went back and found the paper, which sat among great piles in our basement, awaiting the 4-H drives in the spring. It was a front-page piece, bottom-right corner. It recounted the details of the crime, which involved the theft of some stereo equipment. He'd been carrying a snubnose Smith & Wesson, the paper had said, which was something not easy to forget. He'd done seven years for the crime.

Dad said Holt wasn't so bad, and maybe he wasn't, but it was weird being around him. I knew a lot of people I figured were criminals of some sort, but Holt had been convicted, and that was different. Typically, he sat over there on the porch and listened to music on a tiny portable cassette player. He had a slew of tapes in an old tangerine crate, not one of which had a plastic cassette case. They all were apparently warbly recordings of heavy metal bands, not that I knew much about it. That spring, I was fourteen and paid very little attention to music or school or politics or really anything that wasn't basketball.

Hey buddy, Holt would always say when I went over there. You studying hard?

Yeah, I'd say.

You should study hard, he'd tell me. Because you don't want to go down certain paths. We had this conversation a number of times.

Get yourself a basketball scholarship is what you should do. I hear you're a damn good player.

I don't know.

Still gotta have the grades, though. That's the thing now. It's not like it used to be.

I wondered what he knew about how it used to be.

I wasn't, in fact, studying hard. I almost never studied anything. But if I didn't pass this Ohio history exam, I was in danger of being held back, which had already happened once, in fifth grade, which, in addition to being embarrassing, was really boring, going over the same stuff a second time. I couldn't stand the idea of another year of Mrs. LaSalle pacing the room, going on about Thomas Worthington and Tecumseh and General Morgan's Raid.

The day the guy in the sweat suit showed up, my mom was at the motel, where she now did the books in the afternoons and early evenings—she'd learned to do that at a business college after high school, I guess—and I was supposed to be watching the twins, but there was nothing to that, because they just stayed in their room and were weird together. Not long before this, I'd heard them squealing in there and when I cracked the door, I saw them chasing each other around, both completely naked. They would be eleven in October, so this was not particularly normal. I quietly shut the door and walked back down the hall to my own room. I didn't tell Mom, either, because I figured she had enough to worry about.

The guy at the door looked familiar, though I couldn't immediately say from where.

Hi Chris, he said. I preferred C. R. Everyone called me C. R. Only my dad called me Chris, which also annoyed me.

I had the screen door locked.

Hey, I said.

I'm Coach Buford from up to Billings.

I know, I said. I recognized you.

You got a good memory, he said. Hey, listen. I'd like to talk to you about something. You got a minute? Your folks home?

I didn't have folks, I wanted to tell him. I had a mom. My dad was a nutcase that made his living doing drug studies at a pharmacy college up to Columbus.

I can't actually let you in, I said. My mom's away for a while.

I get it, he said, looking at his watch. Maybe I can come back a little later? When you expect her?

She'll be here at six.

I'll come back then, he said. And we can have a little chat?

I didn't ask about what, because I figured he wanted me to play for some basketball team or another. Coaches were always asking me to be on their teams.

Where can I grab a sandwich around here?

At first, I thought he might have wanted me to make him one. I guess I looked at him too long and he caught on.

There a restaurant that's any good in town?

Pizza subs at Pizza Barn, I told him.

What's that? A submarine sandwich with pizza toppings?

I nodded.

That sounds all right. I'll go try one of those.

Back inside, I turned the TV on and caught the end of a *Get Smart* rerun before the news came on. Another successful space shuttle launch was the first story. Soon Mom was home and I helped her make some spaghetti, and then I told the twins to come down to eat. Mom asked all of us questions about school, which the twins ignored as they giggled to themselves in their new language. Uga uga ooga, Teri would say. Keri would laugh. Ooga erga. They had both been A students in the past, but lately they were getting Ds, which was more my department.

Mom huffed in frustration, but just poured herself some more milk and ate her spaghetti. She'd told me recently that we were probably going to have to go to family counseling—I think this was related to everyone's poor performance in school—but we hadn't yet, and I was thankful for that, because it had been a colossal pain when we'd had to do that before, when I was about eight or nine, when Mom and Dad were first having a lot of problems.

Buford returned at about seven o'clock. Keri and Teri were already back up in their bedroom. I think they were playing Risk, but with rules of their own devising that involved some stuffed penguins and a small green ceramic frog as participants. Mom gave Buford some coffee, which she made in an old pot on the stove that eventually boiled over. Buford was overweight and limped as if he'd been in some war or another, which I suppose was possible, but I think it was just because of his weight. He sat at the kitchen table, his apparent bad leg stretched out an angle, and told us that his youth basketball team from up to Billings had been invited to play in an international goodwill tournament in Romania.

Romania? my mom said.

Romania, he agreed. Bucharest. It's the capital. We'd like C. R. to come along with us, to play with us.

He's not from Billings, Mom said, ignoring for now the obvious and more pressing concern of travel all the way to Romania.

I know, he agreed. But it's more of a traveling team. And we want to make a good showing. We'll sort of be representing America, see. And everyone knows C. R. is one of the most promising talents around this part of the state.

Uh-huh. Well, she said. That's very nice to say. And it's kind of you to think of him. But I don't think C. R. can go to wherever it is.

Romania. Bucharest, Romania. I can appreciate that, Mrs. Conner.

My name is Tara.

Pardon me. Tara. But you might consider what a great learning experience it would be for the boy. That's the way we've been thinking about it with our own boys up to Billings.

Bucharest, Romania, Mom said. I don't mind saying I'm not even sure where that is.

I wasn't either until I looked it up, Buford said. I sat across from my mom, pretending to scan the newspaper.

That's why I brought this along, he said. He pulled a book out of a yellow duffel bag I hadn't noticed. It was thick, textbook-sized. I watched, curious where all this was going. What I was thinking was that if this happened soon enough, it might get me out of some school.

Lookee here, he said, pointing to a map in the middle of his book. This is Romania, which is one of these Eastern Bloc countries. It's right here connected to Bulgaria and Serbia. Pretty close to Czechoslovakia.

Communist? my mom asked.

Well, yeah. Sure. That's why we're having this goodwill tour in the first place. I've got about nine boys—mostly from my own team up to Billings—and some boys from Weston and from Atlas.

Who? I asked.

He rattled off the names. I knew a couple and knew that none of them were especially good.

Anyway, the government is sponsoring the whole thing. The boys will stay with families over there. Won't cost anyone a penny.

Why did they ask Billings to go instead of some other team? Mom asked. C.R.'s team must've beaten you all by fifty points last season.

She was close. It was forty-two.

That's a fair question, he said. Honestly, it wasn't random. My wife's got a brother-in-law works in the State Department over in Washington. It was his idea.

Well, Mom said. Doesn't matter, really. C. R. can't afford to miss any more school. He already got the chicken pox back in January.

That's the best part. It'll happen in June, after school is out.

I wanna go, I heard myself say. I don't know why I said it.

I don't think so, my mom said, getting up in order to indicate that the meeting was over.

Come on, Mom. It'll be a chance to learn about other people, I thought to say.

Communists, she said.

They're still people.

See, that's the point of all of this, Buford interjected. To get their kids to see our kids as people and vice versa. So we don't have so many missiles pointed at each other down the road.

What makes you think those families the boys stay with aren't just going to try to convert them?

They've given our government their word there will be no funny business, he said. The trust has to start someplace.

My mom looked at Buford and then at me and then back to Buford.

You can ask your dad, she said, which was her throwing her hands up in the air. Of course my dad would let me go.

—

Dad had been gone for a few weeks. He'd been at the pharmacy school where they gave him small amounts of this or that drug and then watched him for a few weeks to see how his body responded. It was the main way he'd been earning his living lately. By his account, he made okay money at it, and all he had to do was stay in the hospital for a while. Meanwhile, he could watch TV or read or play chess with the other subjects. He said he spent a lot of time down in the cafeteria, talking to people, which I knew was true, because he was a talker. It was what he did best.

The only real downside was that he wasn't able to run, which he was sort of fanatical about. He'd tried running the halls of the pharmacy school in a big loop, but he'd gotten in trouble a number of times—so many times that they'd threatened to ban him from the studies—so then he just walked the halls fast and for longer. It wasn't the same, but it held him over until he got out.

When I went over to ask him about the Romania thing the next day after school, he was grilling sausages on his hibachi out back. He'd just been running, I could see; his shoes were sitting on the back stoop, airing out. Holt was also back there with him and he had a guitar in his hands, which he was trying to form chords on with his left hand and then hacking away at with the pick in his right hand. It sounded like no kind of music I could recognize. I guess the two of them hung out quite a bit since neither of them had a proper job.

Hey junior, Holt said, stopping his assault on the guitar for a minute.

I nearly told him not to call me that, but I didn't figure it would do any good.

Chris, my dad said.

I have something to ask you, Dad.

This sounds serious, he said. It was a nice spring afternoon, some bluebirds were singing in the trees that bordered the yard of the place. Dad drank from a bottle of spring water that I knew he went out to Hammond Hill and procured himself once a week in five big plastic vats. He was a bit of a health nut, I guess. The sausages were actually not sausages at all. His, anyway, were made of tofu. He had to go all the way to Columbus for them. There did seem to be some real sausage on there, though, which must've belonged to Holt.

There's a group of kids going to play in a tournament over in Romania this summer. The coach from up to Billings asked me if I want to go and play with them. It'd be for ten days in June.

Romania? he said, looking up from the grill. That's the Bloc.

The what?

The Eastern Bloc. The Soviet Bloc. The Communist Bloc. Call it what you will. The Russians control all of that, he said. He looked down again to turn his fake sausages. No way, he said. And then again, No way. You have no idea what can go down over there.

It's a goodwill thing, I said. I thought of Buford's words. They're having this so there won't be any more missiles pointed at each other down the road. No more wars.

More wars, Dad said, as if he'd entirely missed the word *no* at the beginning. He'd done a tour in Vietnam, the year I was born. I knew almost nothing about it except that my Uncle Larry, Dad's brother, had told me once, when he was drunk at a picnic, that that war—that that country, that the rice paddies and the mountains, the soil of the place—had altered my dad. It bent his goddamn keel, he said to me. I must've been eight at the time and had no idea what a keel was, but I got the gist just the same and I was pretty sure I knew what he meant about my dad.

Let the boy go, Holt said. He'll learn all kinds of shit over there. Jesus Christ. It's like a thousand trips to the Center of Science and Industry. Getting to see those stupid shits pulling carts around with dogs and eating their gruel.

Dad thought for a long minute. He was wearing a T-shirt that said *Waterville Turkey Run, 1980.* He was in his bare feet in the high, uncut grass. It was probably Holt's job to cut the grass.

Yeah. That's true, Dad said. You could really learn something on a trip like that. An educational eye-opener. There's more than one way to skin a cat, if all of these books aren't sticking.

I ignored the comment about my performance in school. He seemed to be thinking about it.

So it's okay?

Ah, hell. The Eastern Bloc, he said. He looked up to the sky, and then back down to the grill.

You want one of these sausages? he asked me.

Those aren't real, Holt said. You can have a real one there if you like.

No thanks, I said. But what about the trip?

Yeah, okay. Holt's right. You might really learn something about the world over there.

Sweet, I said. Thanks, Dad.

Sure you don't want one?

No. I gotta go.

When does practice start? he wondered.

Next week, I lied. The first practice was actually Friday.

Maybe I can drive you up there.

That'd be great.

—

The twins apparently called in a bomb threat to their school the next morning. There'd been a spate of bomb threats in the last few months, though this was the first to an elementary school. I don't know why, all of a sudden, everyone thought it was a good idea to call in bomb threats to schools. Nobody had ever found any bombs, but of course they had to take each threat seriously.

The police didn't have to work too hard to figure out who had made the call; a simple look at the General Telephone & Electronics records of where the call came from revealed our account, at 259 Second Street. Two officers showed up at our house just before I was leaving for the junior high, which was running normally. The twins' school had been canceled, which we already knew about from the radio. This had presumably been the point of the threat in the first place.

I answered the door; I almost always answered the door now. The men asked to speak to my parents and I called to my mom, who was at the kitchen table paying bills.

She came into the living room and they explained to her that the call for the bomb threat had come from our house, and they said they wanted to talk to us all. We assembled in the living room, and Sergeant Tacoma asked us questions. He was focusing on me at first. I guess maybe because my voice was still high and reedy. But he quickly redirected things toward Keri and Teri when he discovered that I was in junior high. The other sign that it was the girls he was after was that they didn't respond to any of his questions in English.

What were you two doing this morning before school? At 5:49? He read the time from a slip of paper.

Chur chur, Keri said.

I wondered absently if that meant sleeping.

He sighed and explained to the girls how serious this was.

What I think most disturbed Mom was that they had apparently used English to make the call, which we hadn't heard out of them in weeks.

They took the two of them downtown in the cruiser to question them further and, I guess, book them. There would be no getting out of family counseling now, I knew. The juvie system would get its claws into them and would pull in me and Mom and maybe even Dad, too.

That night, when I got home from school, the girls were home again, up in their room acting like nothing had happened. Apparently, since neither of them would say anything intelligible, they were both being charged with the crime, and it was a serious offense and would involve all manner of court appearances and someday community service. In the meantime, they were suspended from school, which I believe may have been the first time in many years that fifth-graders had been suspended. They were basically not allowed out of Mom's sight, which meant that, during the ten-day suspension, they had to go to the motel with

Mom. This was a problem because her boss, Jim Shemp, who not a nice guy to start with, was not at all happy about the idea of their being there. There was a stretch of time that I used to go with her to the motel, when I was nine, and I spent her shift out in the courtyard, sitting around on the one coil-spring caterpillar they had there. There was no basketball court anywhere near the place.

Things got stressful around the house then, so I started avoiding it as much as possible. I played more basketball, and rode my bike around town. I even went past Dad's a few times, though I didn't go close enough to be seen. I stopped once and talked to some girls who hung out on their bikes up the block from his place. A few of them were in my grade, and one, Marcia Moll, was on the seventh-grade girls' basketball team.

Hey C. R., she said. What are you doing around here?

I shrugged. What are you guys doing?

We're keeping an eye on that creeper down there.

What creeper? I asked, though I knew very well what creeper.

That old dude that was in jail. We heard he was a child molester.

I was relieved that they hadn't figured out that my dad lived there too.

Oh, I said. That sounds made-up.

Says you, she said. What happens if he drives past here and jumps out and chases one of us down and takes us off to the woods and dismembers us?

You're out in the open right here, Marcia. I think you're safe.

If you're so confident, why don't you ride down there in front of his place.

I gotta get home, I said.

That's what I thought, she said.

—

On Thursday afternoon, Dad called me. I'd been playing pickup at the courts down the street after school, and when I got home, there was a note from my mom about the call on the chalkboard that hung by the phone. I could hear her upstairs, cleaning.

Dad hadn't called our house since he'd left, which was coming up on eight months, so that was the first thing on my mind, that it must've been weird for her to talk to him.

I found a package of cookies sitting on the counter and opened it and had a few, and then I went down the hall and, reading the number Mom had written down on the board, called him.

Dad? I said when a man's voice answered.

This Chris? the voice said. It was Holt, I knew. They only had one phone in that house. I remembered it now, sitting on a bureau in the dark hallway at the bottom of the stairs.

My dad there? I asked him.

Let me see if I can rouse him.

I waited. Outside some young kids, maybe six or seven of them, were making quite a racket as they tried to organize themselves into two teams for a game of three-on-three on a rusty hoop the Argots had bolted to the side of their house. The kids—it was the Argot boys and some other voices I didn't immediately recognize— seemed to be making very little headway, screams for order rising and then dying down and then starting again. I heard someone say that he was going to come see if I wanted to play, and then there were several loud protests to this.

Chris? Dad said. Chris? He seemed startled, like he'd just been woken up or caught on the toilet.

Everything okay? I asked.

Chris? he said for a third time. Is that you?

Yes, Dad.

Good. He seemed to regroup. You got time for some pizza tomorrow or the next night?

I didn't want to go over there for dinner tomorrow or the next day or any other time.

I can ask Mom, I said.

Okay.

You want me to call you back? She's vacuuming upstairs.

It's okay. I'll wait.

I went upstairs to where she was working on the twins' room. I didn't know where they were, possibly gymnastics. They'd been doing gymnastics lately, against their will as far as I could tell. Their room, I noticed, looked like burglars had ransacked it.

Mom, I yelled.

She didn't hear me or pretended not to.

Mom!

She turned and in the same motion flipped off the vacuum cleaner. What, C. R.? What?

Dad wants me to come over for dinner one of these nights.

Is he cooking something? She seemed to not quite believe he was capable of that, though in fact Dad had frequently cooked meals at our house.

I don't know. No. He's getting pizza, I think.

I don't care. Whatever. That's fine. You have homework?

No.

I don't want you over there past nine, she said, flipping the vacuum back on and attacking an apparently stubborn patch of the carpet.

Dad, I said, back at the phone.

Yep? He was breathing heavily. I think he was doing crunches.

She said okay.

Great. Okay. Let's say nineteen-hundred tomorrow?

I'd long ago learned to tell military time. Yeah, okay.

Dad didn't mention anything about the twins, so I didn't either. I guess Mom had decided not to tell him.

—

That evening was my first practice with the Billings team. I didn't tell Dad about it because I wanted to go in alone and not have him hanging around talking to people. I knew that eventually he would do that, but I didn't want it to be the first night. I wanted to speak for myself.

So Mom took me and dropped me off. She and the twins and I all crowded into the Datsun and made the forty-five minute drive north and they dropped me off at the elementary school and then they went into the nearest town of any size, Atlas, to do some grocery shopping.

At practice, I met the rest of the kids on the team as we shot around beforehand. I recognized many of them from the previous season. The boys on the Billings team were terrible. Their best player was a kid named Sam Watson, though he wouldn't even have started on my team. There were some better recruits from Atlas and Weston, which made me feel like the Romanian thing wouldn't be a complete humiliation.

Coach Buford swaggered up and down from foul line to foul line, calling out plays we were supposed to be learning. The rest of the new kids and I were struggling to grasp the offense, which was antiquated, some holdover from a forgotten epoch, and involved a million picks. It wasn't hard to imagine a bunch of guys out there running this thing a hundred years ago, flinging a large ball at a peach basket.

During the first break, the Watson kid held forth at the water fountain.

You know what I'm going to do when I land in Romania? he asked me specifically. I shrugged.

I'm going straight to the nearest McDonald's, and then I'm gonna go find myself some Romanian ass.

I doubt they got McDonald's, I said. You have to pay like a hundred dollars for jeans over there.

I sure as fuck ain't eating Hungarian goulash for two weeks.

I shrugged again.

He eyed me closely then. So you're C. R. Conner, he said. How come everyone goes on about you? Nothing to you but arms and legs.

That was true. Watson had fifteen pounds on me and had already developed muscle definition in his triceps and lats and pecs. I had my dad's body, long and thin, almost no muscle definition.

I thought about ignoring him entirely, but I could see that that wouldn't be possible. So I shrugged for a third time.

Coach said, We're gonna get C. R. Conner from down to Moraine. He was all jazzed up about it. But I was thinking, Who cares?

I just watched Watson now. The other kids seemed to be steering clear of him, and I could see he was a danger, the type of kid to smack you in the back of the head on the bus and then look away when you turned to see who had done it. I could see, too, that I was going to have to reckon with him.

I'm just saying, You don't seem like much to me. Shit—you've not scored all morning.

That was true. I hadn't even taken a shot.

I scored thirty-three points against you guys last winter, I said.

I can't do everything for these scrubs. He gestured toward the gym.

Bite yourself, Watson, one of the boys from Billings said.

He very briefly shot a look at the boy and then returned his gaze to me. What I'm saying is that it seems like a lot of fuss for a hillbilly from Bumfuck, Egypt.

There were just two boys left in line in front of us. He may have had size on me, but I'd dealt with plenty of older kids, bigger kids. I didn't know about Billings, but Moraine was boiling over with mean kids who harassed you after school. I was not afraid of Sam Watson, however big a deal he was here.

When the last of his audience had gone back into the gym, I said, You got a problem with me?

He seemed to think for a minute. It was his turn at the water fountain and he bent down and took a long, confident drink.

Nah, he said, lifting his head and turning back toward me. I was just messing around. You should come out to my farm some night after practice and ride some fucking ATVs in the dark. It's sweet.

I nodded, as if that idea wasn't totally ridiculous, trying to figure out where the trap was.

Seriously, he said. We got four. My brother'll come. It's awesome.

I'll have to ask my mom, I said. I live in Moraine, so I have to get a ride to practice.

I know where you live, douchebag. My dad can take you home. Up here we don't have to rely on oxen. We have something called cars. Shit, if you had a damn airstrip in that coal-mining town of yours, he could fly you there.

—

On Friday after school, I was playing basketball with some high school kids at Hilltop Elementary, which had the best outdoor courts of all the schools in town, when someone actually bombed the school. There was no threat, just a real bomb exploding. It went off in a toilet stall of the second-floor bathroom and we heard it from the courts. It was about six p.m. and no one was inside the school. The glass windows of the bathroom shattered and fell in small bits near the court.

What was that? one of the kids said.

Probably a bomb, I said.

They all looked at me like I was a nut.

A bomb, a kid said, scoffing. What is this, Ireland?

What do you think it was? I said.

It wasn't the school that Keri and Teri went to, but of course the police were at the house later that night asking questions. Mom sat in the tattered armchair that had belonged to the neighbors at our old house.

You're telling me that yesterday, you two call in a bomb threat and today there is actually a bomb that goes off at a school in the same district and you don't know anything about it?

Broosh, Keri said. Teri nodded emphatically.

Oh my God, the detective said. You people. He looked at Mom and then at me.

You know anything about this?

No, I told him. I didn't want to mention that I was there when it went off.

Later, I was peeking in the keyhole of the twins' room, trying to figure out what they were doing. Mom caught me and whispered for me to get away from there. I went downstairs and she followed me. In the kitchen, she said, What were you doing?

Nothing.

What were you looking for?

I think she thought I was doing something weird, like watching them undress.

I don't know, I told her. I don't know.

She watched me for a while, poured herself some water and drank it.

What did you see? she asked at last.

I couldn't see anything, I told her.

This wasn't really true. Keri and Teri were kneeling. They looked like they were doing some kind of prayer.

You don't think they bombed that school, do you?

No way.

She shook her head.

Why no way?

I don't know. They wouldn't know how to build a bomb.

No, she agreed. They wouldn't.

Later still, Dad called.

What's going on over there? he wanted to know. I got a call from a friend at the police station who said the girls were maybe involved in this bombing at the school.

I don't know, Dad. All I can say is that things are not okay with them.

He sighed, probably looked out the small window next to the phone at the boarding house.

What should we do?

I don't know.

He was silent.

What should we do? he said again.

I don't know, I said again.

—

I ran into Holt out on the front porch on my way to my dad's for pizza the next night.

Hey, I said. His cassette player squelched, its volume too high to enunciate all of the guitars.

Hola amigo, he said. *Qué pasa?*

Huh?

I knew what *qué pasa* meant from TV, but it was annoying to have Holt use it with me.

Means "what's up?" in Spanish, he said.

Nothing. Just visiting my dad. I opened the door.

You know where to find him, he said.

Upstairs, I saw that he'd already ordered a pepperoni pizza for me; he never touched pizza or anything else that was high in fat or made from animals. He'd read something that said that eating meat causes cancer. He'd told me all about it, and I might've been inclined to believe it, except that he was frequently citing this or that research that said not to do something or another.

He was eating a small salad he'd made from some early season garden vegetables. He was also drinking some of that pure hillside water.

As I started to eat, he plopped down a city map of Bucharest on the small kitchen table. I couldn't imagine where he'd gotten it. There couldn't have been more than two or three maps of that city in all of Ohio.

Why are we looking at this?

It's Bucharesti, Romania.

I think it's called Bucharest, I told him.

That's what we call it. They call it Bucharesti.

Why should I care? I'm not going there to learn their language.

You care, he said. You should. You have to know your enemy.

I watched him and could see that obsessive thing settling in. He used to get into it with the garden and yard, everything just so.

You're aware that our nation is at war? he asked. He was scanning the map, as if he was looking for a train station or park.

War?

I was pretty sure I knew what he meant, but I didn't want to make any assumptions.

The Cold War. With the Communists.

He grabbed another map, this one of all Europe, and slapped it down on top of the first.

I know about the Cold War, I said.

Let me explain something to you. There are missiles here and here and here. Those are Russian missiles. We have our own, American missiles—NATO missiles, officially, but you better believe that they're American—here, here, here. All along here. It's like a big tinder keg over there.

Yeah, I know. It's on the news every day, Dad. That and they don't have any food and also Levis cost like a hundred dollars.

A knock came at the door. I knew it was Holt, and he probably did too.

Who's there? Dad said.

I smell pizza with meat on it, Holt said from behind the door.

Come in, Dad told him.

Holt opened the door partway. You sure?

Get in here, Dad said, as if he were worried that someone might see what we were doing.

I was pretty hungry and didn't really want to share my pizza.

Just one piece there, okay, junior? he said to me, perhaps seeing my proprietary posture. I got a real weakness for the stuff. In lockup, the pizza was inedible. You shoulda seen it.

I did my best to ignore Holt as I ate.

So, you're going to be right there in one of their capitals, Dad was saying. Pretty much in the heart of the godless empire.

Am I in danger or something?

Well yes, Chris. We all are. When I was your age, the Russians almost blew us up right where we sat eating our lunches. President Kennedy stopped that one at the eleventh hour.

Holt nodded profoundly. Holy shit that was a close one, he said.

The question, my dad went on, isn't if all of us are in danger. It's are we going to be in danger down the road? It's: What can we do to make it so that *your* children aren't in danger?

It's a basketball tournament, I said. I don't really understand why we're taking about all of this.

He sighed. I've got to hit the head. I'll be right back and I will explain to you why we are talking about this.

The bathroom was tiny, just off the room—a converted closet, it must've been. You could hear everything he did, the undoing of the belt buckle, the stream of his piss hitting the water in the toilet.

Holt and I sat there in silence. He ate slice after slice of pizza, looking at me several times with raised eyebrows to suggest either how much he liked the pizza or how sorry he was that he couldn't stop himself from eating more of it.

Soon, the toilet flushed and Dad washed his hands and was back in the room.

I talked to a friend of mine who works intelligence, he said. You know what that is?

I looked at Holt and then at Dad.

I don't know. Intelligence is like smarts.

Yes, that's one definition. It's also what we call it when we try to understand the way our enemies operate. Governments use intelligence to know what's going on in other countries.

Like spies.

Exactly, like spies.

I know what spies are. Why didn't you just say spies?

He drank from his glass of water. He looked too thin. Holt was nodding to everything Dad said. I wanted to smack him across the face.

I told my friend—he and I were in-country together—Dad never said the word *Vietnam*, it was always "in-country"—I told him about your situation, how you are going over there for this tournament, and he told me that he thought they could use you. He thought—he's checking on this with his superiors—that they might ask you to collect some information for them while you're there. Small stuff, but stuff that could help them ultimately. Because of your age, you'll have unfettered access to everyone and everything.

What are you talking about? I said.

I'm talking about you doing some reconnaissance for your country during your stay in Bucharesti.

I felt sick.

It's a great opportunity to help your country, bub, Holt said.

I thought I *was* helping my country. I thought that's what the goodwill was about.

Now, listen, Dad said. Don't get razzed about this. Give it a night. Sleep on it.

I shoved another piece of pizza in my mouth. I'm tired, Dad. I've got to go home.

I'll be hearing from my friend in the morning. We'll talk about it again later. Let me take you home.

I can walk.

You sure?

I'm fine, I said.

Okay.

You're not going to finish this? Holt wondered.

It's all yours, I told him.

Outside, I walked fast. It was a cool evening. Peepers were singing from the nearby woods, I guess from swampy puddles. What an odd turn my dad's life had taken, I thought. He seemed, at moments like this, barely pegged to reality.

—

On Wednesday, I took the history test I'd been studying for. It was over Section Five in our book, *An Illustrated History of Ohio*. Mrs. LaSalle sat up there on the desk, her legs crossed, a smugness about her. The questions on the page swam in my head. Was President McKinley from Ohio? President Truman? What happened at Buffington Island? I'd spent too much time on the counties, I saw;

the county section was relatively small. I just had to pick ten out of a list of twenty names. Easy. But there were these other questions, about battles and politicians, trappers and the Ohio and Erie Canal. I turned my test in with a good third of it blank. Mrs. LaSalle glanced at it and then back at me, cocking an eye. It made her day to see that, I was sure.

The bell rang and I was out in the hall, feeling like I'd escaped some battle myself. It was the last period and I breathed deeply as the noise of lockers clanging and students yelling enveloped me.

I went home and sat in the silence of the house and stared out the window. Noises from the neighborhood drifted in through the screen door. I heard one of the Argot boys bouncing his Kmart basketball and shooting a bunch of bricks at their crooked rim. I did not think once about my dad or Romania or, really, anything else.

Mom brought the twins by at four-fifteen and dropped them off. She came in the house and told me that Jim Shemp told her the girls couldn't be there anymore—they must've done something— and that she needed me to watch them until she got back from her shift.

You're not to let them out of your sight, she said.

I was going to play basketball, I told her.

I'm sorry, C. R., she told me and turned around and went out the door.

The twins were already at the top of the stairs by this point, on their way toward their room.

What is the matter with you two? I yelled at them.

They looked back down at me and kept going. Mooga, Teri said to Keri.

Arsh, mooga, Keri said back.

I went up the stairs after them and they scurried down the hall and ducked into their room and locked their door.

You think this is helpful to Mom? I said to the door.

There was silence. I grabbed the door handle and shook it, tried to force it. I stepped back. You're acting like goddamn four-year-olds.

I went back downstairs. I looked at the two books I'd brought home sitting on the top of the buffet, math and literature, and considered doing my math problems for a short moment, but then decided to copy the problems from someone in homeroom and take a chance on not being called on to discuss whatever story it was we were supposed to read. Instead I went over to the Argots and played some pig with Billy Argot. I kept an eye on the front door in case the twins tried to sneak off, but they didn't have any intention of sneaking off. I let Billy win a few games by trying ridiculous hook shots that I missed. After he beat me once, Billy wanted to play one-on-one, but I didn't feel like it. Sometimes it just wasn't any fun to beat someone 10–0.

—

There was no practice that night, because we were having an organizational meeting for the trip instead. We were going over the details, filling out paperwork, and learning about the customs of Romanians. Someone from the American government was apparently going to teach us some things.

But Mom called at five-thirty and told me that there'd been a problem with the accounts from the day and that she was going to have to stay until it was sorted out. I could hear Shemp's whiny voice in the background saying things like, Well that doesn't make any sense at all. Mom was obviously very frustrated.

I have this meeting for the trip, I reminded her.

Well, she said.

Well?

I don't know, C. R. I can't make everything okay just now. Maybe your dad can take you.

Great, I said.

And you'll have to take the twins with you, she said.

I know.

I'll see you later.

Goodbye, I said.

I dialed the boarding house and waited as the phone rang. This is so stupid, I thought. I assumed I would have to talk to Holt first, but then Dad answered.

Dad, I said. It's C. R.

Chris, he said. What a surprise. I was just thinking about you. What's happening?

Can you take me to an organizational meeting in Billings tonight?

Tonight? he asked.

Yeah. Mom wanted to take me, but then something went wrong today at the motel and she's got to stay there.

I'm supposed to have this thing, he said. But let me call you right back.

I waited by the phone. The girls may have been asleep or something; it was that quiet. Possibly they were planning their next caper.

The phone rang. Let's do it, Dad said. I'll come over and pick you up?

Sure. The other thing is that the girls have to come along.

Oh, he said. Okay. Sure.

I went up to their room after I hung up and told them to get ready, we were going to the store. I made no mention of Dad, because I knew then they wouldn't come out. I got them out on the curb, so we could get going, and when he pulled his truck up front, Keri said, Shup shup to Teri. And then Teri said, Shup shup *shup*. I think they were about to turn and run, but I grabbed them both by the shirt. We crammed ourselves into the cab of the truck. I knew that the girls were a monkey wrench that Dad was not going to be prepared to deal with.

It's good to see you all, Dad said, easing back onto the street. It may have been the first time the three of us were alone with Dad in over a year. Many things had happened since then. I sat by the door, to prevent them from bolting at a stoplight.

They were whispering to each other. I couldn't tell in which language, though I assumed the new one.

They're not going to talk to you, I told him. I don't know if you know that they speak a different language now.

Is that right?

I shrugged.

What language are you speaking? Dad wondered.

They were silent.

Keri, he said. What's this language? Can I hear it? Maybe I speak a bit.

Ors, Keri said.

Ors, Dad repeated.

Ors, she confirmed.

What's that mean? he asked.

Froop, ors, Teri said.

Froop, ors, Dad said. Okay.

It didn't go any further than that.

We listened to the radio—mostly the news, but then, as we pulled within range of Columbus, a rock station Dad liked that played CCR and The Doors and The Animals. When we got close to Billings, I read directions that Coach Buford had passed out at our last practice, which I realized as I read through them were to Sam Watson's house. His parents were apparently hosting the event.

At seven-thirty, there was still plenty of light to get a good look at the farm Sam had been boasting to me about. It was obviously massive. The house itself sat on a hill maybe a mile from the road and looked out on a plain of horse paddocks. There were manicured trees lining the long lane from the state route we'd turned off. It was, I saw, more of a plantation than a farm. Horses littered the paddocks—dozens of them—double white fences running up and down the undulations in the land.

We passed a sign at the head of the lane that said, *Watson Farms.*

Watson Farms, my dad said. Watson Farms?

Watson Farms, I repeated.

You never heard of Watson Farms? he asked.

No. Why would I have heard of Watson Farms?

A kid on your team lives here?

Yeah.

You never heard of Watson Farms? he asked me again.

No, Dad, I said, impatient. I haven't.

This friend of yours, his dad is Ben Watson. He's a damn bigwig. This is no ordinary horse farm. It's a big damn deal. He sells horses to these rich ladies from the clothing company up to Columbus. Breeds, boards. The whole works. Big-time operation. He's also got a wild boar hunting preserve. Some of my buddies have come up here hunting big game.

He's not my friend, I said.

Sam's dad came out to meet us wearing an old leather bomber jacket. He guided us toward the house, pointing out some nearby flowering dogwoods. He talked to all of us, and tried, also, to get the girls to respond, and when they wouldn't, Dad said that they were very shy.

This sucks, is what I was thinking. Dad was quite impressed by it all, though, and made mention of several of the tree and shrub and flower species that were along the path to the house.

You're a gardener? Sam's dad wondered.

I dabble, Dad said.

Dabble was an understatement. He had planted dozens of things in the backyard of the boarding house already, many of which I knew he pulled from the national forest out near where he got his drinking water. It's good to reinvigorate the native flora, he liked to say. There was barely anywhere to step in the tiny backyard of the place.

I like to see things come alive, Dad told Sam's dad. I've done it since I was younger than the kids here.

It's a great pastime, Sam's dad agreed, though it wasn't clear if he himself participated in it.

The inside of the house was ornate and immaculate. A woman who appeared to be a maid was cleaning up dishes in a sprawling country kitchen. The parents of some of the other boys from the team were chatting in a living room that bordered the kitchen. Sam's dad said Sam and some other boys were up in Sam's room. He said to follow the music, which I could already hear was "Another One Bites the Dust" from the bass line drifting down the stairs.

Upstairs, several boys from the team were playing a game of spastic Nerf basketball in a wide section of the enormous bedroom. Another kid—I didn't really know everyone's name yet—was playing a video game on a color TV.

C. R. Conner, one of the boys yelled.

Hey, I said.

C. R., Come 'ere, Sam yelled. He was on a balcony; it looked like he was throwing old cookies at some yaks in a nearby fenced-in field.

I got something for you, he told me. When I stepped out there, he picked up a Los Angeles Lakers jersey that was draped over a chair and handed it to me.

What's that?

It's 33, he said. Kareem.

He was already wearing 42. James Worthy's number.

We're going to be the twin towers over there, he said.

I would never wear Kareem Abdul-Jabbar's jersey, especially not with Sam wearing Worthy's. If one of us was James Worthy, it was me, but I couldn't think of any way to turn down the gift.

Thanks, I said.

During the meeting, Buford and the government guy went over in excruciating detail what would happen on the trip. We all had to get passports if we didn't already have them. And he told us about how we would be staying with families who spoke English and that we would be paired with another player for the homestays, and then he told us who our partners were. I was paired with Sam, which I knew immediately had been no coincidence. I looked around the room and saw that Sam was giving me a thumbs-up.

Keri and Teri sat quietly during this time in a corner, looking at a book and talking to each other in whispers. Dad sat on a couch across the room and drank from the army canteen he almost always had with him.

Out in the driveway afterward, some of the kids got a game of three-on-three going, which I joined, even though it was more or less dark. Sam had a full-length court in the driveway with baskets at both ends. The whole thing was painted onto the driveway, though one end was filled with cars. Many of the parents were standing around talking, nursing drinks in heavy glasses.

When the light finally faded, the game died and I went to find my dad to go home. He was standing over near a little Asian pond, talking to a few other men. When I came up on them, Sam's dad addressed me directly.

Sam says you're going to come out for a visit, C. R., to maybe do some off-roading.

Yeah, I said, looking at my dad. Sam mentioned it at practice.

You should come out this weekend, he said. You ever shoot?

I looked at him, confused.

He held his arms up as if holding a shotgun. We've got a skeet-shoot set-up, he said.

I didn't know what that was.

You shoot what they call clay pigeons, Dad said. This machine flings them into the air—they're like Frisbees. When you hit them, they explode.

It's a lot of fun, Sam's dad said.

We'll be there, Dad told him.

Everyone was quiet then. Dad looked to me and asked if I'd seen the girls. I hadn't. We found them out in the yak pen, head to toe in mud and presumably yak crap. I knew that Dad was going to get in trouble for this, but that was his problem, not mine.

On our way down the long drive back to the road, the cab of the truck smelled terrible, and I was thinking that there were too many things about all of this that I didn't like.

You and Sam's dad are new best friends, I said to Dad.

He's a pretty good guy for a rich fella, Dad said. I remembered that "pretty good guy" was exactly how he'd also described Holt.

I might do some work for him, he added.

What kind of work?

Some gardening.

Doesn't he already have a gardener?

His guy is good, but he's spread a little thin, I think.

I didn't figure I needed to tell him that I prefer he not do that.

———

During practice on Saturday morning, Sam was acting strange, demanding a ridiculous number of high-fives from everyone, but especially from me. The kids from Billings seemed inured to Sam, or resigned to his manic hectoring. The horse-farm business explained a lot, now that I knew about it. I could see the way he held it over them. Billings was otherwise a farming town, a feed store, a mill, a hardware store, a plastic-cup factory. Now that I knew what I was looking for, I saw signs of it everywhere. One of the kids practiced in a Watson Farms T-shirt. Another wore a hat with the logo on it. Sam apparently passed out gifts on a regular basis. I also gathered that he and his dad frequently took kids to events, like Columbus Clipper games and big-time wrestling. And then there was the entertainment on the farm, the horses, the ATVs, the video games.

Buford had decided, probably wisely, that the team had gotten out of shape since just about everyone had been playing baseball for the last month, which was a joke when it came to staying in shape; all you did was stand around and say, Hey batter, and then every once in a while sprint for fifteen yards to catch a pop-up. He had us on the line running sprints all night. Kids were dropping all around, though disproportionately the ones from Billings.

At the first water break, everyone dragged themselves out into the hall, holding their hands on top of their heads or bending at the waist.

What the fuck? a boy named Kent said. I didn't even want to go to Romania.

Suck it up, Susan, said Sam, who was obviously straining against the workout himself.

Screw you, Sam.

Drink your water and get out of my face, Sam said to him. He pushed Kent, and Kent hit the wall and spun around as if to do something about it. But he didn't. Screw you, he said again and then walked back toward the gym.

In the gym, Buford had heated up a hotdog in one of the

cafeteria microwaves and sat on the small stage that adjoined the cafeteria/gym and ate it and drank from a Big Gulp he'd been nursing all along. Okay, he said. Let's get back to it.

The onslaught continued. Suicides, laps, defensive shuffles up and down the court. This stuff was a normal practice on my team, so I wasn't particularly bothered, though I would've thought twice about signing up for more of it if I'd thought this was what Billings practices would be like. Toward the end of practice, a bunch of parents started filing in the open doors at one end of the gym and they all sat on the small set of bleachers or milled around along the baseline. After we'd run our last suicide, we all put on sweats and street shoes. There were no showers, which was fine with me. I wanted to get out of there.

We hadn't actually touched a basketball during the entire practice. I heard Buford explaining to one of the Billings moms that he couldn't take a bunch of out-of-shape Americans over to Romania and give the impression that Americans were soft. He apparently didn't pause to consider that he himself was no great specimen of Americanness.

I was on my way across the fields adjacent to the elementary's playground to where my mom told me she'd pick me up when Sam came running up behind me. I hadn't had to deal with anyone quite like Sam before and I'd pretty much had enough.

C. R., he called.

Yo, I said, turning, but continuing to walk.

Hey man. Where you going?

Home. My mom's over here somewhere.

That's cool, he said.

I was still walking.

Hey, he said. Guess what.

What?

I'm in this thing with you. My dad told me about it.

What thing? In some remote corner of myself, I knew exactly what thing.

Dude. Are you fucking with me?

No, Sam. What thing?

The taking-down-the-Commies thing, he said. The spying-on-the-Romanians thing.

We hit the sidewalk and turned the corner then and I could see Mom's car and was thankful.

Oh, I said. Right. That's cool.

I felt some stray and out-of-control pulse running through my body. It was anger, I knew.

It's badass is what it is. It's going to be fucking sweet.

Keep your voice down, I said. My mom's right there. I looked over to where she sat in the driver's seat and saw that Keri and Teri were in the back.

Sam eyed me like I was an alien. Why would he care if my mom heard him swearing? was what he was thinking, I could see. But he was trying. I didn't know why exactly, but he was trying. He'd obviously never tried before.

Oh, he said. I just wanted to let you know I'm in. I didn't know if you talked to your dad much.

Why wouldn't I talk to my dad?

I don't know, Sam said.

What do you mean, Sam? I said. I just wanted him to say it.

Man, he said. I don't know. Your dad's kind of off, I guess.

Off?

He's just a fucking nut is all. I didn't make him. It's no big deal. I got an uncle like that.

Something inside me snapped—something that had been lying dormant for a while.

You're a little prick, Sam, I said, turning and shoving him. I let my Marauders duffel bag drop and shoved him again.

168

It's not my fault if you're old man's a nutjob.

And Ben Watson is just a genius because he tends the horses of rich people.

He is rich people, you peasant, he said, and shoved me back.

The sky was low and felt suffocating. I'd never noticed it before, but I hated when the sky was like that, gray and close and unchanging. I didn't really sort out on what grounds I hated Sam Watson, but I did, and he probably didn't really deserve it.

Mom, who'd seen us shoving each other, had gotten out of the car and run down the sidewalk to where we were.

What in God's name is going on? she wanted to know.

Your peasant son started it, he spat. You're a peasant, he said to me.

That's enough, Mom said again.

Sam was feeling his throat, which I guess my shove had caught.

You fucking people, he said.

Don't talk like that, Mom said. Where are your parents?

That's not your business, he said.

C. R., she said. What's this about?

Let's just go, Mom. I walked over and picked up my bag and started walking toward the car.

Sam picked up his own bag. I don't know why my dad wastes his time trying to help people like your dad. He's a peasant. You all are.

Sam, Mom said. Please stop talking like that. Come back here C. R., she said.

I stopped, but did not make any movements back toward them. I was wondering where my mom had learned Sam's name.

You can't tell me what I can say, he said.

I looked around myself and out of the corner of my eye, I saw the twins getting into the front seat of the car. Teri was making goggles out of her hands and watching us through them. Keri was settling into the driver's seat and had one hand on the steering wheel.

Mom grabbed Sam by the arm. You'll not talk to me that way, she said. I could see that she was squeezing his arm hard. Sam tried to swing at her, but she held him at bay.

Mom, I said. Let him go.

And then a loud crash came from behind us, and we all turned and saw that Keri had driven the Rabbit into the International Scout that was parked in front of it.

Mom turned and saw this and instinctively let go of Sam's arm.

Sam started laughing. He grabbed his bag and jogged away from her a little, then made a bigger show of laughing. You fucking people, he said.

—

Later that afternoon, I walked over to the boarding house. Of course Holt was sitting out front listening to his music, only today he had on some old headphones. What a weirdo. I almost told him as much, but then decided I wasn't even going to speak to him. I was just going to go inside and climb the stairs to Dad's room, but he called out to me, his voice too loud because of the headphones.

Not here, he yelled.

Where's he at?

He took off the headphones. Let's see, he said. He looked at his watch, holding his headphones in one hand. I could now see that they were ancient; he'd probably bought them at the Salvation Army.

Imagine he's running, he said.

I nodded and turned around.

Tell him I stopped by, I demanded over my shoulder.

Will do, he said.

I was halfway back to the street when I heard him call from behind me.

You know what, he said. I think he's down to the AMVETS, now that I think about it. You should check down there.

Okay.

You know where that is?

Yeah.

Okay. He's probably down to the AMVETS. He goes down there on Saturdays sometimes.

I thought it strange that he would know such things about my dad's comings and goings, but I guess he didn't have a lot else on his plate.

I was on my way again when he said, You know you ain't gotta be scared of old Reynolds Holt?

I turned around. I know, I said. I'm not scared of you.

I ain't never hurt a flea, no matter what anyone tells you. And you can tell those girls up the street that I'm no danger too. They skitter off into their backyards when they see me coming. It makes a guy feel bad.

What girls? I asked, but I knew he meant Marcia Moll and her crew.

Some girls up the road, look about your age. I bet you know 'em at school.

Oh, I said. Up by the intersection.

Exacto, he said. I'd be much obliged. Also—he was still yelling, because I was twenty yards away from him—on a different note, if you know anyone needs pelts, you send 'em my way. I've got some really nice mink and muskrat right now. But you name it, I got it. Even beaver and otter.

Otters?

River otters, he said.

Okay, I told him.

I know you're just a kid, he said. I know you don't need pelts. But you run into people that might. Maybe teachers at school or something. Or maybe for a gift for your mom.

Okay, I told him.

Your dad's probably up to the AMVETS. He's got some war buddies and whatnot that go up there on Saturdays. Reliving the good old days, you know.

I walked down along Mulberry to Main and then down the alley to the AMVETS. It was in the back of a small, low-slung building whose front housed a dental office and a small branch of the Highland Valley Bank. Inside it was smoky and quiet at three p.m. There was one group of men sitting at a table in a dark corner. A bar ran alongside one wall and was empty and also dark. Two maroon taps, both apparently serving Genessee, poked up behind the counter.

The men stopped their conversation when one of them spotted me.

Can I help you, son? he said.

All of them looked then, across the dark room.

That's Joe's boy, one of them said.

I'm looking for my dad, I said.

So you are, another said.

I think he's in the can.

Just then, Dad came through a doorway and toward the table.

I could see that the table was crowded with glasses of beer. A mostly empty pitcher sat in the center of it. In front of Dad's empty chair was his canteen.

Chris, Dad said. What's the matter?

I need to talk to you.

He looked at the men. Sure, he said. And then he said, Excuse me fellas. I guess deal me out.

You lose your ante, one of them said.

Fuck that, another said. He needs to talk to his goddamn kid.

I'll deal with you when I get back, he told the first man.

Come on, he said, walking past me toward the door.

Outside, we stood on the handicap ramp to the alley below.

What is it?

I wanted to tell you that I'm not going to go to Romania.

He eyed me for a long moment.

What?

I decided not to go, I said.

Why's that? He was calm.

Because, I said with finality. I didn't want to get into it with him. I didn't know why I'd come here to tell him this without giving him a reason, but now that I was here, I really didn't want to fight with him about it. I didn't want to talk anymore about spying with him or anyone else.

We've worked all of this out, he said. It's a lot of preparation that's gone into this.

I know.

Something happen with the team?

The twins wrecked Mom's car today, I said.

Some kids I knew from school went into the side door of the pizza place across the alley. Conner drives and scores, one of the kids said. Another of the three waved. I wasn't sure if the mock radio broadcast was laudatory or not.

Jesus, he said. Really?

He thought about that for a minute.

Are they okay? How did they do it?

They're fine. It was nothing. Mom got out of the car for twenty seconds and they got in the front and drove it into the truck in front of it.

She left the keys in the ignition?

I could see that he was missing the point.

It wasn't her fault, I said. It happened fast.

How could it not have been her fault?

Me and Sam were fighting.

You and Sam?

Yeah.

Okay. Why?

You know why.

I don't think I do.

Forget it.

What?

Why did you tell Sam's dad about it?

About what?

I didn't say anything for a minute.

Romania. Why did you tell him about the intelligence stuff? It sounded so dumb when I said it.

It's important, he said. I saw an opportunity to get some help.

You're insane.

Don't talk to me that way.

What is the matter with you?

I said not to talk to me like that, Chris.

You don't know anymore about spying than I do. Neither of us knows anything.

I walked down the ramp.

Chris, there's an awful lot you don't understand.

I know, I said.

Come back here for a minute.

Nah. I'll talk to you later, Dad.

I walked back down the alley the way I'd come. He called after me, but I kept going. He did not chase me as he threatened to do.

Out on Main, I walked west toward home. When I got there, the house was empty; Mom and the twins were probably getting an estimate on the car at the shop. I went to my room and closed the door and pulled off my clothes and crawled into bed. I hadn't showered after practice and I was sticky from the sweat, but I didn't care. I was very tired and I fell asleep immediately. I didn't dream at all, or wasn't aware of dreaming. And when I woke, it was morning. I saw that the sun was coming in from the other side of the house. I'd probably slept sixteen or seventeen hours. But I lay there for a long time and stared straight ahead, and after a moment, I realized that I didn't recognize anything. I calmly looked around, not registering any knowledge of any of it—a lamp, a globe, some books on a table. I couldn't place any of it.

There was some part of me that knew that I would eventually figure this out, and that was the part that said, don't panic, just lie here. In that long moment, I simply reveled in what I did not know. I did not know where I was. I did not know what I was doing there. I had been asleep for a very long time and I did not even know who I was. I felt an incredible relief at this absence of knowledge.

Then of course, it all came rushing back to me. I saw a statuette of myself—a photograph of me, cut out and posted on a cardboard backing, posing for the seventh-grade Marauders in my shiny maroon and gold uniform. There I was: C. R. Conner, starting forward, nineteen points a game, nine rebounds, five assists. I focused on this little idol of myself. If that's me, I thought, then all of the rest of this must be mine, too. This must be my life.

Long Story, No Map

THE DAY BEFORE CHOI FELL FROM THE ROOF at 283 Constable, a Thursday in late November, Martin asked Choi how he'd come to America. They were walking along Midland toward Prince's Subs.

Airplane, Choi said. Long ride.

I meant, why, Martin said, though he wouldn't have guessed that Choi had flown. He assumed that this had all happened long ago, when international travel was done by boat.

Choi smiled. America land of opportunity.

Right, he said.

I want to live in Columbus, Choi tried again, again smiling.

A block later Choi said, My wife want to come to America. She read magazines. She not like Communist. She—he paused to line up the word right in his head—bourgeoisie.

Bourgeoisie, Martin said. He didn't know the word, but its French sound got the gist across. You like the Commies, did you?

It seemed safe, all these years removed. Truth was, Martin

179

didn't know much about any of it. Until Choi had mentioned Communism, Martin had forgotten it was even involved.

My family poor, Mr. Professional Roofer. Communist feed us.

Martin was quiet.

It was the most Choi had talked about himself in the five days they'd been reroofing the old house where Martin sublet a room.

After Japanese go, more war, Choi continued.

Martin didn't ask what the Japanese had to do with it.

So you were still there for the war, were you?

Not just one war, Mr. Professional Roofer.

Martin looked over. My old man went to Korea, he said.

Ah, Choi said. Special Forces.

My dad? Hell no.

Marine probably, Choi said. Semper Fi motherfucker.

Martin had to laugh. Nah.

Choi lit a cigarette, shrugged. Look, he said, pointing out a flat, grassy area where two kids were throwing a football. The area appeared to be a park, but upon closer inspection, Martin could see it was really just an empty lot abutting a small cemetery.

This is grave, Choi said.

What? Where? Martin said.

Here, he said, pointing with his chin.

The kids were junior high-age and Martin wondered absently why they weren't in school. Maybe it was some kind of holiday.

Where those kids are playing? he asked.

Six hundred seven people, Choi said.

You're kidding, Martin said. Six hundred and seven bodies are buried below where those two kids are playing?

Choi nodded. Spanish Flu. 1918 bad year Columbus. Same in Pyongyang.

Martin looked at the field and then back to Choi. How do you know how many people are there?

We dig. Long time.

Why?

Why we dig?

Yeah. Why you dig.

Choi looked at Martin, obviously catching the jab at his English.

Science, he said.

Science. The word was starting to take on some dimension in his mind, something quite distant from the inanity of General Biology with Mr. Hemsley senior year, dissecting a cat with Sarah Lot.

You? Martin said, unable to hide his incredulity. You were a scientist.

Is, Mr. Roofer. Not dead yet. Retire, but still scientist.

Martin had to laugh at his mistake. Yeah, okay. You *are* a scientist. What kind of scientist are you, Joe? This girl I know studies mosquitoes. You study mosquitoes, too? Ones that live in old graves?

Epidemiologist. Choi was careful with the word, pronouncing each syllable slowly.

And what does one of them do? You looking for a cure to the flu or something?

He smiled. No cure for flu, Choi said. How spread.

Somebody paid you to do that?

American government. Ohio State University, Choi said. Branch of government, no? Word "State" right in name.

The story just kept getting better.

They turned onto Rolston and then into the shop. The girl at the counter was already familiar with them because they'd been in every day this week.

Outside the double-glass doors, a few cars drifted past.

Government pay enough to buy beautiful house, too, Choi added while the girl made their sandwiches. He pointed back out the doors behind them, in the general direction of the house some blocks distant, which he owned. I become capitalist.

Martin had to admit to himself he'd never met anyone like Joe Choi. He looked like a Korean hick, but he was full of surprises. He also looked like he should be in an old folks' home, but he was climbing ladders, putting down shingles at least as well as Martin.

Man, Martin said.

They were quiet for a while.

So how does the flu spread? Martin asked on their way back.

Snot, Choi said.

No kidding, Martin said. Snot. You had to dig up six hundred and seven people to figure that out.

We dig thousand and thousand bodies all over world.

I been thinking about this all wrong, Martin said. I'm starting to think I need to go to college after all.

You? Choi said and shook his head.

What? Martin said.

Probably not college material.

The fuck does that mean?

Choi shrugged. Backpack not look right. You know?

This hit a nerve, because Martin did carry a pack—mostly to fit in around campus—and he felt self-conscious about it.

Whatever, he said. I could go to college.

Yes, Choi said. Boy with one ear in house go. Why not Mr. Professional Roofer?

There *was* a boy missing an ear in the house. Martin was pretty sure he was majoring in engineering.

Funny, Martin said.

Choi smiled. College easy, he said. Keg party, naked girls.

I'm not sure where and when you went to college, Martin said. But if you want to graduate, I don't think it's quite like that.

Hard part later, Choi said.

What's later?

Next part.

Martin looked at him.

Medical school or something? he said. What?

No, Choi said. No. He thought for a minute—or pretended to.
I remember, he said. Life.

—

In the months before Choi fell, Martin had already been thinking about leaving town. Maybe to Chile or one of these former Soviet Bloc countries where you could be a prince with a couple hundred dollars in your bank account. Who knew. He'd been scanning the "Items for Sale" in the *Dispatch*, checking out what kind of cut-rate plane tickets people were getting rid of. So far, there'd been a one-way ticket to Reykjavik—that turned out to be in Iceland; no thanks—as well as tickets to Dallas and Amarillo. Why were there so many excess tickets to the state of Texas? And, he wondered, how did someplace called Amarillo even have an airport?

He'd been in Columbus for going on eight months, but the place was seriously wearing thin, the gunshots out his window at night and the ubiquitous circling police helicopters, the sitting around in traffic you had to do to get anywhere. But mostly it was the fact that, since losing his job at Penney's, he couldn't find another one. There didn't seem to be any decent jobs anywhere. He'd spent a day crushing hard plastic beams into tiny pieces with a sledge—for what purpose was anyone's guess—and another holding up a sign at the corner of Bethel and Sawmill for Little Cesar's Pizza, 39 degrees outside. Those were not good days. He'd stopped going to the temp agency that got him those gigs. It's a bit of a recession, the lady there had told him by way of an apology. Normally, she said, these jobs would go to other types of clients.

Here her eyes swept the room in both directions, like those lurking behind a painting. She meant Mexicans, Martin knew.

A mini-recession was what they'd called it on the news, whatever that meant. Martin didn't know or care if it was a recession or a Great Goddamn Depression. As far as he could tell, it was just a plain old shite market. That's what they would've called it in England—what they probably were calling it in England— where Martin had lived for a few months with a family when he was sixteen. He hadn't really retained many memories about the place itself, not Stonehenge or the Cliffs of Dover or Buckingham Palace—all of which the family had dutifully dragged him to. The town where he'd spent the summer was called Chester, not far from Liverpool—and it was not so different from his own crappy hometown in Ohio. The only saving grace was the way everyone talked. That was, all by itself, worth the trip. Shagging meant having sex. Mental meant crazy. Gobbling was slang for a blowjob. It was hilarious. When he got back to Washburn, Martin tried to bring some of it with him, but nobody got it. They thought he was being pretentious, which was infuriating.

The whole thing had been his dad's idea and he'd set it up with an old friend of his, a guy he'd known from when he was stationed in England forty-some years back. Martin had heard the boring stories many times, the nostalgia in his dad's voice as he talked about England, and, mostly, about its beer. The air force was over there keeping an eye on the Commies, according to his dad, never a particularly reliable storyteller, though that more or less checked out when Martin asked his tenth-grade history teacher about it.

But then everything went to hell when his dad's bomber group was transferred out of good old fish-and-chips-with-a-stout England and sent to stinking, corrupt, VD-infested Japan, in case they were needed there, which it turned out they weren't, because their old Second War bombers were too slow to deal with the

Russian-made MiGs the Chinese were flying for the North Koreans. Martin's dad had never really gotten past his hatred of Koreans for ruining the good time he was having up to Oxfordshire.

It had been through his dad's connections, though, that he'd also gotten the sweet job at JC Penney's mothership distribution center, driving a van around with tricycles and boxes of underwear to suburban malls. Obviously the idea was to get Martin on his feet after high school graduation and, more importantly, out of the house.

During the nearly four months at Penney's, he'd had his own place, a one-bedroom apartment in a brand new low-slung building just outside the city's outer belt, on the east side, not five minutes from work. The day he signed the lease—fronting over $1,200 in first and last month and security deposit, most of it graduation money—was a great day.

All the way out there at Martin's bachelor pad, there'd been no helicopters—at that point, he hadn't even known that there could be such a thing. The nightlife wasn't much, but he did have a car. A Chevette, but still. And also the job had been super easy, a no-brainer you could do high, which he sometimes did. Lots of guys did their jobs high. Even the forklift operators, who got piss-tested on a regular basis, mostly did their jobs high. They apparently had a number of systems in place to deal with the drug tests, though Martin wasn't around long enough to figure out what those were.

But when the market turned really shite—who knew where these things originated and how the results of that finally reached someone like Martin—he'd gotten called into the small office near Dock 16, really just a closet with a large window on one of the walls that looked out onto the loading area. He'd only been in there one other time, the day he got the job.

His foreman, Tom Barrett, said nothing, just made dispirited faces, contortions of his cheeks and lips, until Martin had said, So I'm fired then? Barrett made a noise, a clicking with his tongue, in order to confirm. Low guy on the fucking totem pole or what? Martin wanted to know. Barrett nodded, waited. Do I at least get a few weeks to look for something? Barrett held up his thumb and index finger, the way they do in Europe, which Martin thought odd. From beginning to end, Barrett never actually uttered a word. It was like being let go by a mime.

When he left the office, he walked past Clay Black, who was also a van driver, and Jerome Tully, who worked on the floor in the warehouse.

Oh shit, Black said when he saw Martin approaching. Whether he had picked up on something in Martin's posture or was in possession of some inside knowledge, Martin wasn't sure.

What? Tully wondered, looking up from where he was taping some boxes that had gotten eaten by the mechanical sorter.

Look at Young Martin, Jerome. I'd bet three dollars he's been made redundant.

Tully looked at Martin, squinting. What the fuck's that mean?

Laid off, Black said. He's become part of the Great Let Go. It's happening everywhere. You get the paper?

Shut up, Clay, Tully said. What's the deal, son?

I'm fucking toast, Martin said.

It's the economy, stupid, Clay said. It's killing us all by increments. It's capitalism is what it is.

Shut up, man, Tully said. You think this dude needs to hear your philosophies right now?

I'm off, Martin said, though just then he didn't know to where. He was still stunned.

The Great Let Go, Black repeated, apparently lost in his own world now.

Good luck, son, Tully said.

—

He rode things out for a month, mostly relying on his Sega Saturn for companionship, but his bank account, never robust, dwindled, and he'd had to give the place up. He lost his security deposit in the process because he was breaking his lease, and so he'd screamed at the cigarette-smoking blue-hair who managed the place, Edna something. Or maybe Ida.

I'm sorry, hon, she said. Reality is harsh. Believe me, I know. But yelling isn't going to get your deposit back.

He seethed. She went back to her accounting calculator, entering figures, a cigarette smoldering in a full and obviously ancient Baltimore Colts ashtray.

Goddamnit, he said and slammed the glass doors of the complex behind him, thankful afterward that the doors hadn't broken.

Next, there were two days of living back in his old basement bedroom at his parents' in Washburn, another bad couple of days, the culmination of which was his dad hitting him in the jaw late in the afternoon of the second day, both of them drunk. Afterward, he stood on the front stoop with his bag—he'd never unpacked, unsure of how things would play out there. Looking out across the old neighborhood, he could practically see into the dim light of his future, which he could feel was already, just months out of high school, veering toward catastrophe or some similar fate. He saw, or perhaps merely felt, that he'd misjudged things, starting some time back.

He spent the next night with Frank Stellar, a high school friend he hadn't talked to since May. Frank was in his first quarter at Ohio State, what Frank and his friends called the OSU. While Martin talked through his next move, they smoked some weed Martin had bought from a shady long-haul Penney's driver.

I could fucking do anything, he told Frank. I could go to Israel and work on a Kibbutz. I could join the army.

What's a Kibbutz? Frank wanted to know.

I don't know. It's like a commune. But it's supposed to be a pretty sweet time. Huge hook-up scenario. Some guy I met out at Penney's had done it and told me that it was just too many girls.

Israel? Frank said. Are you supposed to be Jewish?

I don't know the details, man.

Well, either way, Frank said. I wouldn't do that. People are blowing shit up over there all the time. And I especially wouldn't join the army, man. That's a real bad idea.

He shrugged. It'd get me out of here. Will Sennet joined and he's stationed in Germany, smoking himself some cheap PX cigarettes, probably hooking up with German girls like that kid in *European Vacation*. You remember that girl?

Nobody can forget that girl, Frank said. But you know that was a movie?

Whatever.

I'd go air force if I had to go military, Frank offered.

"Why walk when you can fly?" Martin scoffed. My dad always says that, but it's bullshit. The air force is just as much bullshit as the army.

Your call, Frank said. Not my life.

Man, Martin said. I wish I had my old job back. I wish we didn't live in such a crappy country where everything was going to hell all the time.

Dude, Frank said.

What?

Nothing. I gotta go to bed.

Go to bed, Martin said.

You know you can only stay here a night or two, he said. My RA's kind of a dick.

Yeah, okay. Thanks, man. I'll be out of your hair.

Martin drank the rest of the beer by himself—there were just two left from the twelve he'd bought with his fake ID and he looked out from the eleventh floor of the high-rise dorm toward campus, and beyond that, the city of Columbus glowing dimly out there in the ether. Close by was the stadium, placid at this hour, flood lights running along the upper deck casting an early dawn's worth of light on the field.

When he left Frank's dorm three days later, he didn't go far, sleeping on the couches of guys he knew less well, all of them from Washburn, mostly sophomores and juniors. They were all business majors, because that was apparently easy and didn't require a foreign language or anything too taxing except for some accounting that they all had failed a few times. There were a couple packs of these guys, loosely affiliated, in a series of sprawling apartment buildings on Wilcox. He passed most of that time without ever encountering anyone not from Washburn, except at bars. They were an island, these guys. Among them, Martin noticed there was a lot of talk about the girls they called The Unapproachable, the Mustang- and Fiero-driving girls who lived in the large sorority mansions down along 15th. Martin was annoyed with the whole scene and was immediately looking for a way off their couches.

The saving grace of it all was going out to bars, which were crawling with girls. A couple weeks into his couch rotation, he met Iris at a sit-down-and-have-a-European-beer kind of place just down the street from one of the Washburn complexes. She was a scientist, of all things—or training to be one. The two of them spent quite a bit of time drinking at a few different bars, sometimes even dancing to Al Greene and Hank Williams. The dancing was a new one for Martin, but he took to it just fine.

Martin quickly—too quickly, it turned out—began sleeping at Iris' place every night, assuming that this was his new address. But then Iris—she studied mosquitoes; he honestly hadn't known people did things like that, though once he thought about it, it made sense—called him on it. She told him that she'd made this mistake before and that he shouldn't see what was going on between them as anything more than what was going on between them. Which stung Martin a bit.

But then what did he have to complain about? He was shagging this twenty-four-year-old girl who was actually from another state and who took off to places like Borneo on a regular basis. She had all kinds of mementos on her walls of these travels. New Zealand. Easter Island. She was not beautiful, not in the way Kelli Hallis was; he'd spent a great deal of his senior year obsessing over Hallis' blonde bob and long, lithe legs. But still there was something about her, the bangs hanging in her eyes, which were dark brown and huge, and the gray skirts and woolen sweaters she wore. Most of all it was her feistiness. It wasn't mere confidence but a kind of certitude. It was refreshing, emboldening even.

A bit chastened, but still happy to be in the game, he checked his bank balance and figured he had enough for a cheap room for a few months, during which time he could hopefully find some work. The place he found was tiny—barely big enough for the single bed that was somehow stuffed into it. Good luck getting that thing out of there when the day came, he thought when he first saw it. It wouldn't be his problem, in any case.

The room was in a massive house about nine blocks south of the Washburn Boys. He hoped he'd never see any of those guys again, ever. There was a serious load of students in the new place, so many that there was no real way to count. Probably twenty or more. The building sagged at the junctions of its various built-on sections. In the whole house, he appeared to be the only one not going to college—this fact of his life was drawn in stark relief so close to campus, something never far from his mind now—though one of the guys was doing some kind of automotive diagnostic degree at DeVry, whose brochures Martin remembered looking at during the college fair senior year. He would never have gone to a college fair himself, but it was just after football practice, and he was walking home with Frank Stellar, actually, whose math-teacher father had made it clear that Frank was definitely going to college. So Martin had followed Frank around for a while that night and listened as he talked to some seriously bitchy girls from Miami University and representatives—nearly all of them good-looking girls, come to think of it—from a whole bunch of other schools. Bowling Green. Wright State. O.U.

From where Martin stood that night in Washburn senior year, college seemed like a nightmare, like more high school that was both harder and cost money. Now that he was here, though—at least living here, if not actually attending college—it didn't seem like such a big deal. Certainly a sizable chunk of the inhabitants of his building didn't have much on him in the intelligence department. One of the kids—an English major—had flooded a bathroom with a backed-up toilet because he didn't know that there was a valve at the base to turn off the water. Martin had come in, tiptoed through the water and turned the knob.

Oh Jesus, the kid had said. I didn't know about that.

Martin wanted to say, You've shat in a toilet your whole life and never bothered once to look down and see that there was a little knob on every bloody one of them.

But he shrugged.

Martin started seeing Joe Choi, the kooky old Asian dude, around the place almost immediately. He was at least seventy and was short and wore high-water pants and running shoes long past their expiration date. Martin hadn't figured him for the landlord, but he also hadn't known what to figure him for, because he sure as fuck didn't belong there.

Martin's dad's prejudice against Koreans had apparently rubbed off on him some, because the first few times he'd seen Choi, he'd almost yelled at him to quit lurking around. He almost said, Just because there's a lot of people living here, you're not going to get away with mixing in and stealing food. To be fair, this perception was aided by Choi's scruffiness, by the holes in his sweatshirts and the tape on his glasses. But for Martin's dad, all Asians were boat people, and this idea was pretty strong in Martin's mind, too, even if he didn't like to agree with his dad. There's something to the power of environment, Iris liked to say, which he figured meant that there was no escaping his dad's vision of the world; that some part of it was in him, no matter what he thought of his dad.

Ensconced in this mammoth house on Constable Street, Martin got a new job plan. He was trying to get a union card down at the United Steel Workers, because he had a cousin who worked on these high-rises going up downtown, and he made serious money. This cousin, who drove to Columbus from Washburn every day— just over an hour—already had his own place out in the country—a trailer house, but still—as well as three motocross bikes and a pretty nice '79 Chevelle, and he was just two years older than Martin. He'd vouched for Martin with the union folks, and so Martin was trying to break into this line of work. Eventually, he'd have to go to welding school, but the thing was to get in first, according to the cousin.

Problem was, the scene at the union hall was dismal. The place was worse than a locker room at halftime after the coach has gone outside—just incessant bitching. These guys did three things: they sat around and played cards, they smoked, and they complained. There was no work, they said. You could apply for a card, hang around if you wanted. Bide your time. Who knew what would come? Probably nothing in this market. Probably we'd all be on government assistance for the rest of our lives. Could be another government cheese scenario, one of them said. This got some uneasy laughs. But someday, another said, you might get a call. For instance, these folks came in from Atlanta a few weeks back looking for some good workers and off to Atlanta a slew of guys went to work on a new tower. The story sounded like the myth of hobos. Martin had no intention of going to Atlanta and he struggled to see how this story was supposed to be encouraging.

In three days he was back on the porch at the old house on Constable. Screw that, he said. I don't have time to sit around a union hall all day. He sat on the porch instead and smoked and drank coffee until his body couldn't take it anymore. He continued to plot his next move.

Gradually Martin was learning the faces of the house's inhabitants, if not their names. The Asian guy remained a bit of a mystery, though. And, what was more, this guy seemed to have noticed Martin hanging around; Martin caught the guy eyeing him in the long hallway off the kitchen one morning, which made him uncomfortable, so he'd kept moving. There were so many people milling around the house it was hard to imagine anyone knew who they all were, least of all an Asian; he assumed that Asians couldn't tell white people apart any better than white people could tell Asians apart. Martin was subletting the room, so he hadn't even met anyone when he took the room except for the girl who was leaving. Her name was Bridget and he was pretty sure she was a lesbian. Her hair was really short, anyway, and she wore men's jeans. He'd seen a fair amount of that around campus these weeks and months and was growing used to it.

Out there on the porch, he kept circling around to the army.

When he'd told Iris about this option at a bar one night, she spat out her rum and Coke on the floor.

Hijo, she said. You can't be serious.

Why wouldn't I be?

They'll love you in there, she said.

Har, he said. Don't be a dick.

She laughed. You've been watching too much TV. The army is an unmitigated nightmare.

I don't watch any TV, he said. It was more of a complaint than a statement of truth.

No me importa, she said. It's your life.

He ignored the Spanish, which she used a lot, especially around her biology friends; they all spoke it, though he was pretty sure none of them had been raised with it.

What is it that you think I should do, professor?

I don't know, Martin. I'm not your guidance counselor.

No you're not, he said. What are you again?

Nothing, she said. Just some girl.

Just some girl, he agreed, nodding.

They went home then and had drunken sex, during which she would start to moan, and then shush Martin, as if he were the one moaning.

—

After the initial confusion over what Martin's mailing address was, they did work out an arrangement, and he spent a few nights a week at her place. She, too, lived in an old converted house, which she shared with eight or nine other girls. She had her own bathroom, though, right off her bedroom, and she had walls and walls of books. Martin had never been a reader, but faced with the prospect of sitting around the sprawling house on Constable thinking about employment on one hand, or reading some of these books on the other, it was an easy choice.

He discovered that if he kept a sandwich in the pack he carried, he could stay in Iris' room after she left for the lab, where she spent a good twelve hours a day. He wouldn't need to come out of there all day if he didn't want to, but he had to be subtle about it. No smelly cheeses or she would've been on to him. Peanut butter was okay, but he had to double-bag it. Whenever they were going out, he would make himself a lunch for the next day.

In the morning, she usually got up early to get to the lab, and he would just lie there, facedown in his pillow as she showered.

You know how to let yourself out, she would say as she was leaving. I'll talk to you later.

Hmmm, he'd say. And then, Have a good day.

Then he'd sleep another hour or two. When he finally got up, he'd shower and set up shop in a cracked leather Barcalounger she kept near a small bay window, and open up a book. First, he went through *David Copperfield*. Then *Wuthering Heights*. Then *Crime and Punishment*, which he liked best of the three. Now he was working on *Tess of the d'Urbervilles*, which he thought strange and downright confusing. In particular, he wanted to know exactly what happened between Tess and Alex that night in the fog. Anyway, he found that he really liked imagining the faraway world in these books, even if most of them were set in boring old England.

He had to keep quiet in there, though, tiptoeing around. Her housemates, mostly graduate students, came and went to classes. They were mostly gone, in truth. It took him some time, but he eventually learned their schedules from their footfalls. And he knew that between three and four there was no one in the house, and that's when he would slip out the back door, into the greasy alley— there was a line of fast-food restaurants opposite her place—and through the cramped parking lot, which was patrolled ruthlessly by the rednecks at Lucky Brothers Towing, which incidentally made it impossible for him to ever drive to her house.

It was a fifteen-minute walk from there to Constable, and he did it happily most days, refreshed from his day of reading. But it wasn't every night that he stayed with Iris. Many nights she worked late and didn't have time to hang out. Those nights, he lay in his small room. He might read or jerk off, but it wasn't great, either way. He might go out for a drink by himself, or go sit in one of the coffee shops around and watch people. On occasion, he wandered the halls of the old house he shared with strangers, but they all seemed fixed in whatever lives they were living. He rarely got past a simple hello with any of them.

One early morning after a night like this, he was back on the porch—a pot of coffee resting on the banister in front of him, *Tess* in his hand, the employment ads on the floor (nothing doing there)—and the Asian guy approached him.

Live here? he wanted to know.

Yeah, Martin said, practically incredulous that the guy was talking to him.

The man nodded.

You? Martin asked.

He laughed. I own.

You own this place?

I own. This. He said the word like it was the first time he truly understood its meaning. He waved his arm toward the door. Martin nodded. That made some kind of sense, at least why he'd seen him lurking around. It didn't account for the man's ratty clothes, but Martin was willing to admit all manner of weirdness in the world at this point.

You scientist? the man said. Archeologist maybe?

Archeologist? Me? No. I don't do nothing.

Nothing? he said. Do something. Sell drugs. Study literature. He pointed to the book in Martin's hand, obviously a classic by its jacket design.

Look old man. I'm not a student. And I'm not a criminal. I pay my rent. I'm looking for work, but I pay my rent.

The man was quiet for a while, looked out onto the empty block of Constable. The buzz of a busier street carried to them from a few blocks away.

Martin was waiting for the man to move on; he didn't care for small talk with old Asian landlords.

You know way to put roof in? the man asked finally.

Martin looked at him. Do I know how to roof?

Yes. To roof. I just ask you this.

Martin had done some roofing, in fact, with his uncle a few summers back.

Yeah, he said, easing up a little. I know about roofing.

Okay, Choi said. See? We solve job problem. Solve problem for Joe also. You think so?

You offering me a job?

Yes. I hire to help me put in roof.

You've already got a roof.

This roof, Choi started.

Leaks?

Very old.

Yeah. I guess I did notice that.

Observant, Choi said. Maybe scientist after all. He smiled.

Martin watched Choi as he pulled a pack of Salems out of his breast pocket. Martin lit a cigarette of his own and the two of them smoked in silence.

Afterwards, Martin took his coffee cup and pot into the kitchen and threw them into the sink, which was already piled with dishes—nobody reliably did their dishes, which he knew was a problem in the house from the many notes about it on the fridge door—and he went outside to help the old man fish some tools out of his minivan, which was parked across the street. The van had all but the driver's seat removed and was filled with tools and parts and about nine packs of cement shingles from Wykoff Lumber.

There was also a wholesale-size box of Salems. The two of them dragged a ladder to the side of the house and Choi gave Martin a tool belt and a nail apron.

You have a nail gun? Martin wanted to know.

Gun?

Yeah. An air compressor. It makes this job a lot easier.

Need work, right?

Martin saw where this was going.

We fix roof North Korea style, Choi said.

Martin knew nothing about North Korea, but he knew this line of thinking.

Alright then, he said.

They worked through the rest of the morning setting some hooks at the apex of the roof through which they ran ropes to tie around their waists. Finally, they started putting down some shingles, working side by side. Just before noon, Choi carefully made his way to the ladder and disappeared down the side of the house. They had done three rows, which didn't feel like much, but, in addition to the prep, it had taken them some time to figure out how to fit the sheets on.

Choi hadn't said anything about where he was going and Martin had assumed he was using one of the downstairs bathrooms—there were three or four of them on the first floor of the place, each dirtier than the last—but then he was gone for a very long time. After a while, Martin stopped working and leaned back under the cloudless, cool day and lit a cigarette, the last in the pack. This, he thought, is the dumbest goddamn habit in the world. It was probably the hundredth cigarette of his life, all of them since he'd left home. It was only out of boredom and a need for something to do standing around the dock at Penney's that he'd ever had his first. I will not buy more, he thought. As he smoked it, he heard Choi down on the ground.

Mr. Professional Roofer, Choi said.

Name is Martin, Martin said, peering over the edge of the Victorian's roof.

Choi nodded but didn't say anything. He held up a bag for Martin to see. He had brought back sandwiches for them both from Prince's Subs; Martin recognized the orange and green bag. When Martin made it down, Choi pulled his own sandwich out and handed the bag to Martin. There were large containers of Coke on the ground. *The Everything,* read a sticker that held the paper around the sandwich.

Take from pay stub, Choi said.

Yeah. Okay. Thanks.

Coke okay? Everyone like Coke.

Coke's great, Martin said. Thanks.

They sat on the decrepit chairs on the front porch and started to eat. We didn't talk about pay actually, Martin said. How much are you paying me anyway?

Fair price, he said.

What's that mean?

Five dollars.

An hour?

Five dollar hour, yes.

This isn't 1970. Should be more like eight or nine.

Eight dollar per hour for roofer?

Yeah, eight. At least.

Ball-breaker, Mr. Professional Roofer.

That's right. Martin laughed.

Roof expert, however. Eight dollar for professional normal?

It's sort of a steal.

New fair price, Choi said and smiled.

—

Late that week, Iris told Martin that she was going to go on a research trip to Baja California at the beginning of December. He was upset, in part because she would be gone, but also because she hadn't bothered to tell him about the trip, though she'd obviously known for months.

Her research group—which Martin knew included a boy named Sydney who was clearly angling for her; he'd seen all of the signs during a night out at a bar with Iris' lab friends, the ribbing and touching of the elbow, the nervousness—was going to fly to New Orleans on the way and take a cab into the French Quarter during their layover so they could drink coffee at someplace called Café Du Monde before buzzing back to the airport and hopping on the second leg of their flight. Hearing the anticipated details made him furious, even without the kid Sydney in the picture.

What is it that you do that you can just leave for a month? He wanted to know. Aren't you in school?

Come on, hijo, she said. I told you. I'm a biologist. An ecologist. Scientists have to go work in the field sometimes, if they're the kind of scientist I am.

He knew all of that. Stop calling me hijo, he told her.

Don't get mad. I told you we were just having a good time. I thought we agreed on this.

Sydney's going along to California?

It's Mexico, Martin. Baja California is in Mexico. It means Lower California.

What does Sydney have to do with anything?

He's obviously in love with you.

No, she said, slowly. You think so? She genuinely seemed not to have considered this option, or else was a better liar than he'd thought.

Martin shook his head.

He's got a goddamn girl's name, he said.

He did not want to talk about Sydney; he wanted to punch something.

I know, she said. Isn't that funny?

When will you be back?

She sighed. We're not understanding each other, Martin.

Oh Christ, he thought, and then said, I get it. You want to break up.

We were never really going out, Martin. We were sleeping together. It's not the same thing. Don't make me out to be an evil witch here. We've had an agreement. For instance, I never hassled you about using my room as your reading lounge.

He felt blindsided. He knew there were a lot of things about being in the world he should've already learned, from TV or books or from listening to the warnings of adults. And this one was common sense, really. He wouldn't make a mistake like this again, he thought.

But as things with Iris appeared to be ending, this was the moment he most wanted it to be real. His sense of isolation took on dimension and heft inside him. He thought of his parents in their dinky house down in Washburn and felt some misguided nostalgia for his adolescence, or, anyway, for an earlier time, before the world started hacking away at him with its persistent indifference.

Hey, she said.

What?

I'm sorry, Martin. I guess I thought of this differently.

He needed to get out of there.

It doesn't matter, he said. He knew he sounded petulant.

You're a good-looking boy, she said. And a sweetheart. And pretty good in the hay. Shit, Martin. You're a catch. But you should be messing around with nineteen-year-old girls. I'm like a spinster already.

I'm gonna go, he told her.

Okay, she said. But don't be mad.

I'm not mad, Iris. Good luck in California, he said.

She smiled. Thanks, hijo.

—

A few days later, clouds moved in midmorning. At eight a.m., when the sun had been bright, Martin and Choi had stripped off an entire pitch, which now sat exposed. They were working quickly, hoping they could beat the weather, but then Martin felt a few sprinkles.

We need to cover this, he said. If it pours, this could be a catastrophe for the top floor.

Choi nodded. Catastrophe, he repeated slowly.

They went to the basement, a place Martin had been just once to do a load of laundry. The washer and dryer were in the corner closest to the stairs. Beyond that, an expansive series of rooms set off in all directions like catacombs, all of them filled with junk. There was more furniture stacked in the basement than all the rooms of the three floors above. Not only furniture, but lamps and cat carriers; there were maybe eight bikes, shoe racks, damaged kitchen cabinets, spice racks, and boxes and boxes of trashy books, what his mom called bodice-rippers.

You just let everyone leave all their shit down here?

No let, Choi said. Just do.

See, a tarp is the one thing we won't find, because it doesn't take up any space. This is stuff people didn't want to move. How long have you owned this place?

He was digging under some boxes. 1971.

That's a long time, he said.

They kept poking into piles, searching. They didn't find any tarps, though. What they did find was a roll of plastic that you might use as a drop cloth, probably too thin for the job, but it was all they had, so they took it upstairs.

Some of the residents were milling around the kitchen.

What's all the racket on the roof? one of them wanted to know.

We fix, Choi said.

They looked at Martin oddly, apparently unsure of who he was, even though he'd been living there for a month.

Back outside, rain was coming down steadily.

Be careful on the way up, Martin told Choi.

Choi nodded, looked into the sky.

Martin followed him up the ladder, and once there, the two of them coaxed the plastic into position. Choi cut it into three strips with a razor knife from his tool belt and they did the best they could to cover the exposed part of the roof. It wasn't quite enough plastic, so about two feet above the eave was going to get wet, but short of driving back out to Wykoff's and getting real tarps— something Choi did not seem inclined to spend the time or money on—this would have to do.

Afterward, they sat on the porch, drinking coffee. Choi smoked cigarette after cigarette.

Am I getting paid for this? Martin asked. He wasn't serious; he just wanted to hear what funny thing Choi would say.

Choi smiled. Sure. I also now pay when sleep.

Martin chuckled.

The rain was slacking off by lunchtime, and they walked down to Prince's together. On the way back, they ate their subs as they walked. They'd been quiet since the cemetery, since Choi's story about the Spanish Flu, but then Martin started, Your wife. He didn't know why he was asking Choi about his wife.

Choi, though, was silent.

The one who wanted to come to America, Martin went on.

Bourgeoisie, Choi said.

Yeah. What…he started. He regretted treading down this path, but here he was.

Dead, Choi said.

Oh, Martin said. I'm sorry.

Choi shrugged but said nothing, instead took a bite of his sandwich.

When they got back to the house, as if in response to the recent conversation, a woman stood on the porch holding a plate of something.

Cookie, Choi said under his breath as they approached the steps. And then, as if to clarify, No-bake cookie.

The woman holding a plate, Martin surmised, was, for lack of a better descriptor, Choi's girlfriend.

She introduced herself to Martin as Kathy, was maybe ten years younger than Choi, tall, blonde, dressed in business clothes. She was on her lunch break from an office on campus, where papers got shuffled and someone with the title of provost called the shots.

You're brave to climb a ladder with this one, she said to Martin.

It's not dangerous if you're careful, Martin said.

You've not done things with Joe before then. He's accident-prone.

Choi smiled. Safety Job One, he said.

I made you some cookies, she said to Choi. You share them with your partner, though. She put them on the banister.

Choi nodded.

I'm going to use the ladies, Kathy said, and she went inside, which struck Martin as brave for a woman in such nice clothes.

When she disappeared, Choi eyed the cookies and then looked at Martin.

No-bake cookie killing me, he said.

Don't eat them, man, Martin said.

She bring every week. I don't like.

Martin shrugged, taking one of the cookies and tossing the whole thing in his mouth.

What mean "no-bake"? Choi wanted to know.

Look, he said. Relax. For another dollar an hour, I'll eat them.

Choi smiled broadly. New fair price, he said.

—

On the other side of the hollow wall that his bed rested against—the bedroom had obviously been part of a much larger room until someone had divided it up with sheetrock into two or three separate rooms—a boy and girl were having sex. In addition to the repetitious banging against the wall, he could hear their moans.

Godamnit, he thought.

It was anyone's guess which two people were over there, but it didn't matter, because whoever it was, it made Martin think of Iris and Sydney sharing a tent down on the beach in Lower California. He could only imagine what nights were like on these scientific trips. He'd met Iris' advisor once at the bar, when most of the lab showed up after putting a big grant application in the mail. Professor Harris, a lighthearted guy, probably no more than forty or forty-five. Obviously anything went with that guy. He had no difficulty imagining the place at dusk, the moon pulling the water out to sea, and all of these educated kids running out onto the shelf left behind by the retreating water, the sandy goo, oyster shells and sea anemones and kelp. And later, they would probably sit around drinking Corona, and eventually, in the small hours, pair off. No doubt Professor Harris would hook up with one of the many attractive girls from the lab. Whatever professional relationships there were in Columbus probably disintegrated the moment they hit Mexican soil. It made sense. Martin was beginning to see that everything was about sex—not just for boys, but for girls, too. You were kidding yourself if you thought differently. And he was beginning to see—to really see—the way the world will push you out, will take what you want most, and push you out.

Ah, fuck it, he thought. He went downstairs and used the one phone in the house and called Iris. One of the nameless girls who lived with her answered. She told Martin she hadn't seen Iris all day.

Is this Martin? the girl asked.

Yeah, he said, surprised any of them would know his name.

She might still be at the lab. You have the number there?

No, he said.

Hold on, she said.

A minute later she was back with the number.

Haven't seen you around, the girl said. He was trying to imagine which of the girls he was talking to. She said her name was Jen, but that didn't help.

He didn't really know what to say to this. He certainly didn't feel like getting into it with her about the breakup.

We're sort of on hiatus, he heard himself say.

Oh, she said. Sorry. I didn't know that. I don't see Iris much.

He thanked her for the number.

At the lab, a male voice answered.

Iris, the voice said. Let me see.

He held the phone to his chest, Martin was sure, and said something. He could hear the muffled sound through the boy's body. Four syllables. Probably: Is Iris here?

There was some shuffling, the phone's receiver picking up the jostling as loud sweeps of air. And then, a few seconds later, Iris was there, and he knew—or was pretty sure—it had been Sydney. His head burned.

Hey, he said, trying to regain some composure. It's Martin.

Martin, she said, not altogether friendly. What's up?

He nodded to himself. Listen. I know you're busy. I know

you're leaving tomorrow night. But I wanted. I'd like to buy you lunch.

Oh, she said. Um.

Platonically, he said. Why did he say that? He corrected himself. I mean, as friends.

She laughed, though he didn't know at which thing, lunch or the word Platonically.

That may not be a great idea.

I want to start a new phase, a friend phase.

A friend phase, she said. He knew that everyone in the lab—Sydney, at the very least—was listening to their conversation and he was probably enjoying this business.

It's harmless, he said. It's lunch.

Okay, she said. As friends. What time?

Noon, he told her. The Blue Danube.

—

He lay awake for a long time imagining the meeting, trying to figure out what kinds of things they would talk about. A friend phase? What a dumbass.

Later, someone banged on his door.

You Martin?

Yeah.

Phone, they said.

Downstairs, he picked up the receiver for the second time tonight. Somewhere in the back of his mind, he assumed that it would be Iris, calling back to bail on the lunch. She was the only one who really even knew he lived here. Not even his parents knew where he was exactly. But when he picked up the receiver it was not Iris' voice, but Frank Stellar's.

Dude, Frank said.

Martin hadn't seen Frank in nearly two months, since the morning he'd left the tower Frank lived in with his surly suitemates.

Frank? he said.

You're like in the Witness Protection Program or something.

Something like that.

It's the night before the Michigan game.

Yeah? What's that? They're like a team that our team plays?

Har, he said. Me and these douchebags are gonna hit some parties. You wanna come?

The game's on Saturday, Martin said. Even I know that.

You knew what I meant. We can swing by and pick you up.

Martin was inclined to say no. It hadn't been a great day. It hadn't been a great week, really. Frank and his drunk friends were not likely to cheer him.

Yeah, okay, he told him. He gave him the address.

Frank, he said.

Yeah?

How did you find me here?

That's a funny story. Frank told him one of the boys up on Wilcox—he meant the Washburn Boys—knew which house Martin was in because he used to bang a girl that lived there. He still had the phone number in his little black book.

Wow, Martin said, but thought, I've got to get out of this town.

—

He waited awhile on the porch for Frank, but then got antsy and took off with no particular plan. He walked to a pizza place along High Street and ate two bready slices at a small table back by the bathroom. Afterwards, he crossed High and entered a university building, a library as it turned out. The place was crawling with the girls the Washburn Boys called The Unapproachable. He chastised himself for even remembering the term. But if you were looking for a model-quality college girl tonight, this was the place. He walked from room to room, checking out the ancient building. In each new room, there were tables, sometimes dozens, filled with kids studying, or trying to. Not just girls, but their male counterparts, too, most everybody in T-shirts promoting—more like bragging about—fundraisers their sorority or fraternity had put on for leukemia or arts in the schools. Martin was aware that he was conspicuous. He had dropped the backpack because of Choi's comment and he still wore the clothes he'd worked in all day. He had no fraternity T-shirt, and he hadn't had a haircut in months. He felt eyes on him as he passed through the study rooms.

On the third floor, he found a room devoid of tables. There were a few soft velvet chairs, and he sat in one of those for a bit. Close by was a globe, which he spun around once, finding first the United States and then the tiny state of Ohio. He spun it some more, and thought to look for Korea, whose location he had no idea about beyond the fact that it was somewhere in Asia. He was surprised at its strange location, the oddly shaped peninsula hanging off the bottom of China, across the sea from Japan. That made sense, given his dad's experience there. It was of course divided in two, North and South.

How strange, he thought, to have lived in a place that you couldn't go back to.

Outside again, he wandered further into campus. Other than those first few days sleeping on the plastic-cushioned couch in the anteroom of Frank Stellar's suite, he'd spent very little time there. In the distance, he could hear the pep band getting raucous, leading a snaking crowd of cheering, Busch-drinking students around. He'd read about this in the student newspaper, how the band would go from dorm to dorm collecting members and it would all culminate with the coach and a few players speaking at the stadium later.

He walked toward Iris' lab, the only other campus building he'd been in. He didn't know if he would go in or not, or what he would say if he did. The cold air reminded him that he needed a winter coat and that he would have to find one somewhere—perhaps in the basement—or else he would have to go back to Washburn to collect some winter clothes from his parents', which raised the specter of his father and their last encounter.

At the Biological Sciences Building, he circled the place once. He found a bench and sat for a while and patted his pants for cigarettes—it seemed the kind of place he should smoke—but remembered he'd run out and then decided to give them up. He watched a few people come and go from the building, the band's music distant now. After a while, he got up to wander among the shrubs to see if he could get a peek of Iris' lab. The first few windows he looked into were empty basement-level classrooms, dark, lit only by ambient hallway light. The third was a lab, but it was empty.

He peeked in on two more empty rooms and then, slipping past some holly shrubs growing close to the building, he was showered in bright light, not of a lab, but of a class in session. The professor stood closest to the window, her back to him, and the class sat in individual seats facing him. They were all shaken out of their bored trance by his movement and raised their heads as if one being. He stood before them for a very long moment, startled. He scanned the faces of the students, who looked very young to him, though none of them could've possibly been younger than he was; he wouldn't even be nineteen until April.

Recognizing that something was happening behind her, the teacher spun around to see what was going on.

He had forgotten that she led a discussion session of an introductory biology course every Thursday evening. Or perhaps it was more that he had never paid much attention when she told him about what she did; he really only remembered anything of the teaching because she wasn't available to go out until after 9:30 on Thursdays.

He looked at her for an instant, and saw that she saw him, felt the heat of her on him. Anger? Some other thing? He couldn't say.

He did not stick around to see what would happen next. He turned and fought his way through two bushes and back to the sidewalk, where he almost collided with a pair of girls walking along the path. They looked at him like he was a creeper, which, to be fair, he seemed to be, coming out of the bushes like a hedgehog. He brushed himself off and walked to Midwestern Donut, a place he knew only foreign students ever went—he had heard the Washburn Boys call it Third World Donut—to sit among the immigrants in anonymity. Drinking a tepid coffee among papers from Jerusalem and Bogotá, he felt more at ease than he had in some time.

He was looking down at a paper in Spanish, trying to piece together the headline from the two years of the language he took in high school, when someone smacked the window nearest him from the outside. When he looked up, he saw the smirk of Frank Stellar and a slew of other kids, most of whom he'd met briefly during his tower stay. Frank, obviously drunk, held up his middle finger. Martin got up and reluctantly went outside to join them on their way to wherever it was they were off to.

—

The day Choi fell, Martin woke with a start from a deep, drunken sleep. The house was already buzzing with activity. He was going to see Iris today was his first thought. His second: I've got my boots on.

He got up and took the longest piss of his life and then went downstairs and ate some generic Rice Crispies and then went out on the porch with some coffee, where it was very chilly. He felt ill and wasn't sure the cereal was going to stay down. The trail of parties from the night before was a fog, almost irretrievable, at least at this hour. There had been some cheering about Saturday's game, but mostly there had been reggae music and sweaty kids dancing, many of them wearing expensive jackets. For a while, he'd considered stealing one of these at the last place, where a great heap of them lay on a bed, but he wasn't ready yet to go down that path.

Choi showed up at the usual hour. The students in the house were dispersing toward campus for Friday classes, those that had them. Martin spoke to none of them as they descended the porch stairs and none of them even pretended that he was sitting out there in the cold.

Even a few blocks from High, the pregame electricity was in the air. Everything seemed louder. Out on the porch, he could see a few obviously well-tended houses in the area that were inhabited by non-students—businessmen, probably, who graduated but never wanted to leave the college life. They had neat Arts and Crafts houses and flew their Ohio State flags every weekend in the fall. From where he sat, he could see four such flags already this morning.

A front had arrived, bringing Ontario air into central Ohio and Martin wore two hoodies against it, one inside the other; it was really all the warm clothes he had. He owned no gloves, so he kept his hands inside his sleeves. Choi came better dressed, in a tan pair of Carhart coveralls. He also wore Carhart gloves and a Carhart ski cap.

Dr. Choi, Martin mustered. Are you getting endorsements from Carhart?

Yes, Choi said, catching on. Carhart call. Decide good to use skinny Korean smoke too much. Very good for business.

As absurd as it was, he felt closer to Choi than to his own father, or maybe than to anyone.

They made their way down the north slope of the roof through the morning's cold, which emboldened them somehow, and they worked rhythmically as the sun began to cut the cold some. From up there, they could see over the neighborhood better. Whenever Choi stopped for a smoke break, Martin would lean back and relieve the burden on his lower back. They'd gotten better each day and now worked at a quick clip and were closing in on finishing the roof of the behemoth structure, probably in the next day or two.

At eleven, they finished the pitch, each of them on a ladder for the last row. Down on the ground, Choi smoked and they discussed whether they should get set up for the east side of the house now or later. Martin was keenly aware that after the east side, he was out of a job again.

Early lunch, Choi seemed to decide. Okay?

Sure, Martin said. I've got to go meet someone anyway.

Oh, Choi said. Mosquito girl probably.

Probably, Martin said.

They both looked to the sky then as if for signs of the afternoon's weather. The city had clouded over and it seemed like it would be this way until May, such was the apparent density of the gray above the place.

No rain, I think, Choi said.

Yeah, maybe snow, Martin said.

Maybe snow, Choi agreed.

Martin went inside and took a shower—his first in some days. He thought about cutting his hair, but knew that that would be a bad idea; he'd done that once back in August, and the guys at Penney's had given him endless shit about it, calling him Ringo and Bowly. He found a sweater in the bottom of his bag that was more or less clean and he picked the least wrinkled of his three pairs of pants and then he drove his Chevette up High to the restaurant just north of campus.

Inside, the Blue Danube was violent with Michigan-week lunchtime noise, plates being tossed into sinks, waitresses yelling to cooks, children sitting in high chairs wailing. There was a soundtrack of crackly alternative radio barely audible beneath the din. Iris was sitting in a booth along a bank of windows.

Hey, he said. He sat across from her. Thanks for coming.

You're not going to get all emotional on me, right?

No, he said. I promise not to get emotional.

She squinted at him. I've got a string of old boyfriends around this city, she said. Enough to fill a dumpster with.

That's a weird thing to put them in, he said.

Yeah. But it's where they go in my mind.

Because you're done with them.

You know, because it doesn't work, this thing we're talking about, or this thing going on in your mind. People say it works. It works on TV. And it seems super mature. But it's the opposite of that. In the real world, people can't watch other people move on in their lives. It's why people are always killing their exes.

Martin watched her. A waiter came and took their order—smugly, Martin thought, in his neat and tight apron, the wine corker hanging out of one of the front pockets.

I called you up because I didn't want to be a baby about this. Was that dumb?

She looked out the window, took a sip of her iced tea. Listen, Martin, she said—this struck him, because she almost never used his name—it's going to seem cruel to you, but I'm going to go now. You'll see later that it was the right thing to do.

He watched her speak, filled with humiliation. He had never dealt well with being spoken to sharply, with being instructed—particularly about the way things were in the real world.

I like you, but I can't have you lurking in the bushes outside the windows of my classroom, she said.

I'm sorry about that.

That's what I'm talking about. But even calling my lab.

I'm sorry, he said again.

It doesn't matter, she said. It was weird, though. You see that, right? Peering in the window of my class was weird.

I know it was weird. I wasn't doing what you thought I was doing. I was trying to find your lab was all.

Then what?

I wanted to talk to you.

You were going to see me today.

I know. But it felt more pressing than that.

You want to know what I think?

Probably not, he said.

Okay. She reached down and grabbed her purse.

Fucking hell, he said. What?

She stood up.

Oh, it doesn't matter. She put ten bucks on the table.

Great, Martin said, and stood up too. Goodbye, I guess, he said.

Yep, she said. He watched her weave through the crowded restaurant and out to her car. He sat there for some time, long after she had pulled her Tercel out of the lot. When the waiter appeared with the food some minutes later, he looked at her empty seat and then looked at Martin and frowned.

Just put both of them here, he told the kid. And get lost.

The waiter raised his eyebrows, but then did what he was asked.

Sobered up by a morning in the cold, Martin's appetite had returned and he ate his burger and her Cesar salad both and then just sat there, the racket of the place washing over him. Well, he said under his breath. Goddamnit it all to hell. Which was what his dad said when he couldn't find his keys or a stool's leg broke.

Outside, it started to flurry. He paid for the food, pulling change out of his pocket to cover the bill to the penny. You get no tip when you're a dick, he thought; another wisdom from his father—and he drove back to Constable Street. After he parked, he circled the house, looking for Choi, and found him, on the east side, lying on the ground, his leg tangled in the bottom rung of the ladder. The neighborhood stood perfectly still, it seemed. Choi was wincing, the ladder a too-large appendage. Martin wondered how long he'd been there.

Jesus, Joe, he said. Are you okay? What the hell happened?

Choi opened his eyes and then closed them again.

Unraveling Choi's leg from the ladder, Martin could see blood at about calf level.

Choi looked up again, stared at him, tried to bring him into focus.

Martin tried to raise the cuff of Choi's Carharts, but they were too tight.

Cigarette, Choi said.

Martin found the pack in Choi's breast pocket and tapped one out for him, even put it in his mouth for him and lit it. Choi seemed relieved, and regained enough strength to lift his right hand up to his mouth in order to pull the cigarette from his lips between puffs. He also torqued himself around into a more comfortable spot.

Your back okay?

Leg is all, Choi said.

I'll call an ambulance.

No ambulance.

Nobody ever wants an ambulance, Martin said.

Use van, Choi said.

I've got to get a look at this, he told Choi. I'll be right back.

When Choi didn't respond, Martin said, You hear me?

He nodded, looking at the ground or his leg.

Inside the house, he couldn't find any scissors and started screaming for one of his housemates, but, incredibly, they all seemed to be gone.

He found a paring knife in the kitchen drawer; he knew for a fact it was dull because he'd tried to cut chicken with it once.

Outside Choi hadn't moved.

We're just going to have a quick look at this and then I'm going to take you to the hospital, he told him. It was the way the trainer from Martin's high school football team had talked to injured kids.

Quick look, Choi repeated, then winced as Martin moved the leg gingerly.

Lunch bad?

No.

Look bad.

It was fine.

Friend study mosquito not real, I think.

She's real.

Girlfriend?

Not really.

Have girlfriend study mosquito or don't, Choi said.

Don't, Martin said, trying to puncture the coveralls with the dulled point of the knife.

Martin was thinking that he didn't have a girlfriend who studied mosquitoes or anything else to speak of. He didn't have any money. He didn't have a plan.

Listen up, Joe. I'm going to cut your pants. This is going to hurt.

Choi blew smoke through his nose.

Martin sawed with the paring knife, trying to hold the cloth taut without putting pressure on the spot he assumed was a compound break. Choi lay mostly impassive, quickly running through his cigarette. Playing sports growing up, Martin had witnessed three separate compound breaks. In each case, the kid screamed like he'd been bludgeoned by a mace. By comparison, Choi appeared to be on painkillers.

After a few minutes, he was able to rip the fabric and get at the wound. There was bone there alright, through the skin like a spear.

Jesus, Martin said.

Jesus, Choi said dreamily. Jesus H Christ.

How you doing?

Hwan Choi tough like nail.

Hwan Choi?

Choi smiled. American friend say, Hwan must change name. American think sneeze when say name. Hwan Choi. Just pick new name, he say. Okay, I say. Joe. Like GI Joe.

I wondered about that, Martin said.

Just above where the tibia jutted through the skin, there was a terrible scar, a place where the skin had healed improperly.

Noticing his gaze, Choi said, Bullet.

This is a bullet wound?

Maybe your dad, Choi said.

I doubt that. This looks like it was done by someone who knew what they were doing.

Know what doing, shoot here. He pointed to his chest.

Okay, doc, Martin said. I guess I'm going to carry you to the van.

After he pulled the van into the yard, he returned to the house once more, to the basement, where he retrieved a couple slender boards that looked to have been pried from a skid. Upstairs, he picked through his dirty clothes until he found a thin T-shirt—*Virginia is For Lovers*, it said in front of a sunset—and ripped it into three long strips.

He didn't explain anything to Choi, just held the wood strips to either side of the leg with one hand and wrapped the strips around and tied them off, not with much attention to the pain. He didn't look to Choi's face during the procedure.

When he was satisfied that it was stabilized for the trip, he said, one, two, three, and hefted Choi over his shoulder. He was a slight man, probably just 140 pounds, and Martin was able to carry him like he was a bag of sod. Choi complained, but it couldn't be helped. He didn't have to take him far, and then he slid him onto the floor of the van, and got in himself.

We're on our way, Martin said. They drove down Constable, then Midland.

Your old cemetery, he narrated, because Choi couldn't see out.

Nineteen-eighteen, Choi said.

Yeah. The Mexican Flu.

Spanish, Choi said.

Same difference, right?

Choi laughed. When go to college, learn difference.

Martin laughed at that too.

In the emergency room, Choi leapfrogged a kid with a sports sprain and somebody who had no obvious signs of trauma. A nurse led them into an exam room and took Choi's vitals. She put in a Hep-Lock and then ran something for the pain through that. The doctor'll be in in a minute, she said.

After she was gone, they were quiet for a long time and Martin thought Choi was asleep, but then he spoke.

Not hurt so bad, he said.

No? Martin looked over at Choi's leg.

Sting, Choi said. Burn.

Martin realized he was talking about the gunshot wound.

I've heard that, Martin said.

Saved life.

How was that? Martin asked.

Long story with no map. Short way to say: UN take over hospital.

Wow, Martin said.

Lucky.

You a prisoner, then?

Until war end, yes. Not so bad. American good guys, right? Then what?

After, he said. Apply to go to America.

What about your wife? I thought America was her idea.

Choi's gaze was on the middle distance. He said nothing.

You had to leave her behind? Martin said.

Choi shook his head, smiled. No wife.

You were never married?

Maybe like mosquito girl, Choi said. Maybe different. I don't know. Girlfriend with magazine of other place.

She stayed?

Schoolteacher.

In North Korea? Martin said.

Pyongyang.

And you never talked to her again?

Did I talk to her? Choi said, more to himself than to Martin.

A doctor walked in then and started to read over the details the nurse had written down.

Have charmed life, Mr. Professional Roofer, Choi said.

It's Martin, Martin corrected.

Choi nodded, a hint of a smile. Martin, he said for the first time. It ain't over yet, Martin told him.

No, Choi agreed. Not dead yet.

Panic

MRS. NOI HAD TURNED DOWN A NUMBER OF SUBTLE ADVANCES.
Maybe a dozen. More like ignored them really. I'd touched her
hand provocatively on numerous occasions and tried to hug her at
the end of our conferences, and once offered to take her to Serpent
Mound, which was no euphemism—it was a real place, a mound in
the shape of a snake, that Native Americans around here had built
about a thousand years ago for some god or for their dead or to
keep their people busy so they wouldn't get bored and revolt. I
forget which. I don't think I ever knew, actually. My class went
there on a school field trip when I was eleven, but I remember
being pretty fixated on Tabitha Dilger then: her brunette curls;
those light-green terry cloth shorts she wore. I think I might've
missed a lot of the content of that trip and several others from the
same period. I remember nothing, for instance—not the
Washington Monument, not the White House, not even the Air
and Space Museum—of a trip to D.C. except for a sweaty slow

dance with Tabitha at the cheap motel in Breezewood, Pennsylvania, that our chaperons crammed us into on the way home. I'm pretty sure it was to "Open Arms," from Journey's *Escape*.

I would now guess that it was a sadness—a kind of loneliness—that drew me to Mrs. Noi, though, at the time, I assumed that it was some sort of a *joie de vivre* she possessed. I don't know. Obviously it's strange that those things could be confused in my mind. I can see that now. But she had lured me in somehow, without even wanting to.

One time early on in our sessions, I fell down the stairs—someone had left a tray of cups on the landing that I hadn't seen because I was trying to read a flyer on the wall advertising a poetry reading—and I cut my head on the rusty railing, a gash running from my hairline down my temple to my cheek bone. Mrs. Noi had taken me into the women's bathroom and pulled some Korean first-aid materials out of her purse and bandaged my head in three places with the little butterfly Band-Aids that you don't see very much anymore. While she did this, I felt very comfortable, very much in the hands of someone expert and in control. Perhaps this event was key to my longing.

The thing that is especially vexing about my desire is the fact that I was untroubled by her marriage. I hadn't been raised that way. I'd attended Methodist youth group and had gone door to door to get pledges for the annual Crop Walk, even though most other kids just got their aunts and uncles to sign on. Quite apart from the abstract right and wrong, I knew adultery was not cool, because when I was thirteen my best friend's mom had an affair with some guy at the mill where she worked in the office, and my friend told me his dad had to go on some sort of medication afterwards. His parents had stayed together—I guess because of my friend and his little sister, Becky—but I just remember his dad was always sitting around watching bowling when we were in high school. It was sad. That was obvious to me even then.

At least part of my problem, I think, was that I had too much time on my hands. Sometimes I wandered around the branch library looking for old jazz records to make cassette tapes of. Who, my housemate Seth asked me, has time for that? This was from a guy who had an addiction to crystal meth and no discernible means of income. Even so, it was a valid question.

I sometimes spent hours on the couch in the dilapidated apartment imagining Mrs. Noi's life. Not her life then so much as the one she'd left behind: the neighborhood in Busan where I imagined her to have grown up, the young Mrs. Noi—though she'd never told me her first name, I imagined that it was Cora for some reason, though that obviously doesn't make any sense— coming home after school, haughty interactions with her parents over the friends she was choosing, the scooter she rode around on at The University of Seoul, where I knew she'd studied economics—because we'd worked a lot on the vocabulary of school—and where I guessed she'd met her husband.

Mr. Noi—that's what she called him at first, until I explained that since he had a PhD., we used the title "doctor," which confused her for all the reasons it confuses everyone else—he was nothing more than a theoretical being for me, at least until the viburnum business. Part of the equation, for sure. I knew I had to contend with him in some way, because he had what I wanted. But to me, Dr. Noi—he was some sort of postdoc in the biological or earth and atmospheric sciences—he was not so much a person as an invisible force, like Neptune's pull on Pluto.

Mrs. Noi showed me a picture of him once, but I looked away. That's okay, I told her. You shouldn't show that to me. It's rude in our culture to go around showing pictures of your family. It's like saying, I wish I were with these people right now instead of you.

But I did in fact look at it, quickly, taking in the man's slim, handsome features. He could've been an actor in a movie about stem cell research, I thought, *The Good Scientist*, maybe. In it, Dr. Noi's character would overcome the insidious backroom data fixing of his rival, Dr. Zhao. Even this thought, I know, was weird. And was, as my sister later pointed out when I told her about it, reliant on hurtful stereotypes.

The afternoon of the photo incident, a confused Mrs. Noi watched me for a long minute, the picture still in her hand, as the strange content of my English, in its broken little shards, slipped clunkily through those unworn neural pathways. She was trying to figure out what was going on.

You joke me, she decided.

I nodded.

We had a pretty good relationship, me and Mrs. Noi, in spite of the tensions brought about by my pursuit of her. And her English was coming on. I think that had a lot more to do with her will to get along here than anything I was doing, but she believed it had to do with me, which I'm sure is why she continued to employ me, in spite of my odd behavior. So I was not about to explain to her how unimportant I was to her success, what the literature—it's true I'd done a little reading about language acquisition—had to say about how people learn languages and how unimportant to the process people like me are.

—

This café where I met with Mrs. Noi, La Caverna, was the kind of place that time had left behind. In there, you were not going to find freshly roasted, organic, fair-trade, shade-grown coffee prepared with Italian-style processes. You were going to find large, twenty-five pound bags of already ground coffee from someplace in

Upstate New York called San Souci. Its package was silver and orange and I'd watched the staff there dump countless bags of it into the industrial-sized filters used by the large coffee urns.

But La Caverna was cheap, and because I had only four students—three Koreans and one Salvadoran—cheap was a good fit. Realistically, I needed a public place to meet them, because people don't want to come to your sketchy neighborhood for their language lessons. They also don't want to be met by your long-haired, drug-addicted housemate at the door.

—

Problems I then had:

1. A drug-addicted housemate.
2. A sketchy neighborhood.
3. A sore tooth. For going on one month.
4. A G.I. imbalance due to an over-reliance on Spaghetteos (39 cents a can at Sam's Club).
5. A student loan officially beyond its second deferment period. Imagine the paperwork involved in even getting a second deferment.

But the mother of all problems: panic attacks. Debilitating. Panic. Attacks. Which had started during my very first quarter of college, when my exams and papers began coming home to roost with stapled attachments delineating my legion missteps, and usually with a red C or D at the top. Sometimes it simply said, "Do Over."

I was forced, right out of the gate, to see that not only was I nothing special, but that I might in fact not be cut out for college.

Maybe you should be a fireman, a friend of mine suggested when I showed him the D I received on my first World History midterm.

Don't even joke like that, I said.

No, seriously. It's a pretty good gig. Good food, lots of TV.

Fire scares me, I told him, and it does. A lot of things do.

Oh, and then Trish, my high school girlfriend, broke up with me not a month into that first term. She didn't even do it in person, but by phone after we'd spent a weekend together in Columbus. I suppose she had seen the wreckage unfolding and got smart. When she got back to Bowling Green, she called me up, told me the lines she'd been practicing on her drive north. We'll never get this time back. We need to embrace our new lives and our youth.

Our youth? Who was this person? I thought. But then who could argue with such a thing? I sat in my stinking dorm room, my roommate Clive over there scribbling away on his differential equations, and felt misery, or what then felt like misery, for the first time in my life.

And one more thing: my parents had abdicated Ohio pretty much the week I left for college; they'd bought a place down to Alabama. Several postcards arrived in my mail slot that fall, most of which were of sunsets.

The panic attacks found their purest expression a year later, coming by then on an almost daily basis. When I would wake in the morning, they were there. Actually, they weren't there at first. There would be a brief, blissful period as I came into consciousness, when I had in effect forgotten about the problem. But then, my mind—my idiotic, C-getting mind—would think, I wonder if my panic attacks are gone? Guess what showed up then.

The final straw came in, of all places—and I'm sure this is fitting, though I don't know how—a Shakespeare class. I'd been sitting there listening to Professor Rhodes explain the historical significance of the "This England" passage in *Richard III* when I noticed my heart beating and an acute pain along the left side of my ribcage that, for reasons still mysterious to me, I took to be an incipient heart attack. It was everything I could do to collect my things and leave the classroom, Rhodes eyeing me suspiciously as I went; he'd already had me in his office the previous week to sort out my dismal performance on a *Lear* and *Hamlet* midterm. In the Gill Hall snack room, I slunk into the ratty, nicotine-encrusted couch and awaited death. Twenty minutes later, classes let out and the students from Shakespeare filtered past, looking in at me like I was in the tamarin cage at the zoo.

When I finally dropped out—"Academic Leave," my advisor, a graying *Moby Dick* scholar, wrote on a form I had to fill out, but we both knew better—I left behind the prized single dorm room I'd wrenched from the bureaucrats in Administrative Tower Number One at the beginning of the year—and I moved off campus into that shabby apartment far, far to the east. To talk about it in relation to campus was a little like talking about New Zealand in relation to Missouri. It could be done with maps and explanations, but it would make much more sense to use Australia instead.

Several months later, the time by turns boring and terrifying—I spent it loitering in buildings around campus, not knowing what else to do—I found myself increasingly isolated. I had been drifting from my friends for a while, so it was no surprise that I woke one day to discover that no one knew where I was exactly, not my friends, not my parents, down there in the tropics with their margaritas, not even my sister, who inhabited the selfsame Columbus as I did, or at least a Columbus connected by roads and strings of McDonald's to mine.

Trolling one of the engineering buildings during this time— what I was looking for, even day to day, was rarely clear to me—I saw an advertisement for an English tutor in the basement, down there where the unwashed engineering majors were simultaneously doing strength-in-materials homework and playing RPGs with kids in Bangalore.

What about tutoring? I thought. I could do that.

Tutoring second-language speakers, I have to admit, was not as easy as I had imagined in the giddy moment in that basement, when I first saw a way of forestalling all of the uncertainty and hardship. I knew, of course, that I would not always be a tutor. But I thought that maybe it was something that could get me to the next thing. Wasn't that the way it worked? You did a thing and that led to another thing and so on.

The chief virtues of the job were the scheduling flexibility and the lack of necessary qualifications. All you really needed was to speak English. Talk about setting the bar low. You just posted a sign that said, *English Tutor, $15/hour.* You needed some other things, of course. You needed to have the immodesty to put down a fictional number of years of experience on the sign. You needed to have a phone that was not disconnected, which was, once or twice, an issue. You needed, probably, to have few other options. The recession we were in the middle of helped out, but so did my general low ambition and spare skill set. The panic attacks were essential, though, because as a tutor I could excuse myself at any time, which I found incredibly useful, even necessary. In general, I was trying to avoid social situations altogether, because of an increasing number of episodes, one more terrifying than the last, my mind, like Zeus, throwing lightning bolts down upon me. At any other job, I would be expected to sit there at my station and weather that. And at any other job, there were just too many people, too many variables. As a tutor, I could just say, Lesson over. And I could go home.

—

My sister Jill, with whom I had never been particularly close, lived somewhere way out in the suburbs She was seventeen years older than me and had been out of the house by the time I came into consciousness.

Growing up, I had been routinely referred to as a mistake by my parents, such was the space between me and Jill. The joke was that I had seriously delayed their retirement, which was funny to a point. Except that, as I say, pretty much the week I finally left for college, they'd sold about eighty percent of their possessions in our town's large Labor Day yard sale and moved down to the Alabama coast—the Redneck Riviera, I guess they call it. Probably another great joke if you've ever been there. I have not. They were done with the Ohio winters, they said. I myself could've used some time on the Gulf, or at least a light box. My therapist, back when I still had one, had mentioned this possibility, but my insurance, back when I still had some, didn't cover it.

My parents' joking did no real damage that I could discern. I don't blame them for any of my strange behavior nor for my strange ideas about the world. I always took the "mistake" stuff as good-natured ribbing, a sort of apology for there being a whole generation between us. But it did point out the fact that Jill and I shared little culturally. When we tried to talk, it was as if we were from two ends of some loosely confederated empire whose mores and languages had only the thinnest overlap. And then there were the differences between our material lives. All the way out there in the suburbs, it was all plastic-mold toys and signs for school levies. Nearer to home, it was shoes hanging on power lines and uneven sidewalks and, on occasion, the thin crack of nine-millimeter handguns not quite far enough away.

But we tried to communicate, or were starting to. Jill's husband, Stewart Hollister, a nice enough guy, was very busy, working in one of these buildings downtown with a view of everything. He was heavy, Stewart, because all he did was work—I think it was sixty-five, seventy hours, most weeks; it was all about billable hours for him—and then he would come home and drink beer and eat nachos or pizza or ribs, all of which appeared to give him heartburn. Not that I blamed him for his diet. I think he rightly felt like he deserved whatever small comforts the world could offer; the heartburn was just an unhappy side effect of those comforts.

But it was a hell of a life. I mean, my life: I could see the dead spots in it. I understood that, a certain charm notwithstanding, my life left quite a bit to be desired. For starters, who wanted these panic attacks? Who wanted a drug-addicted housemate? Who wanted to have no real income? No health insurance?

But something desirable I did have was *time*, and Stewart never failed to mention it. Stewart and I were sitting in front of the TV once when Jill was upstairs getting the kids ready for bed. They had three—Caleb, Siobhan, and Ryan were their names, despite there being not a single Irish gene on either side.

Time, Stewart said pensively. Holy shit. Enough time, now. That's a fucking idea.

He had the Cavs on their giant TV—he was from Cleveland and everything was decorated in Cavs and Indians and Browns colors—and he had a giant beer in front of him—in a stein specifically designed for this particular beer—a Belgian beer, he told me, from this little town near Bruges or some other place that starts with a B, where all they did was make really, really good beer. I didn't like beer, which was a bit of a sticking point for the two of us getting on, because Stewart was the kind of guy for whom beer was a bit of a religion; it was also his only means besides the Browns for communicating with other social classes.

But we managed, Stewart and I. We were family after all. I managed to get along with just about everyone, actually, even Seth. I could talk to him about his day as if it hadn't been one long craving, the culmination of which was the theft of a car stereo down around campus, which he then sold to a guy he knew at

Whalers Appliance in order to score. Afterwards, he would sit on the ratty couch the place came with and watch cable news, almost all of it about the war in Iraq. He was obsessed with the stuff and had pulled some books about the region from the city library. He had nightmares, I knew, of going there, of getting drafted or whatever. Seth was a real waste of space, but he was good-natured, if you didn't count all of the theft and the drugs.

Man, Stewart said that night at Jill's. I can't even imagine anymore what it's like to just dick around all day.

It's not as great as it sounds, I told him.

Someday you'll see what I mean, he said. I spent a year before law school that way, living out to Seattle, working at Pike Place. I would serve coffee or danishes or whatever three days a week and the rest of the time, I did nothing but smoke about a thousand pounds of weed and wander the city, sometimes take a ferry out to the islands. He smiled and laughed. I didn't have enough money for food, but I always had pot.

Yeah, I said. I'd never mentioned to him that I didn't like pot either. I was glad then that it had never come up.

Shit, he said. I loved that. I shoulda stayed there. He chugged the remainder in his stein and put the glass down on the table surprisingly gently. He looked at me. Shit, he said again.

—

Something I loved about Mrs. Noi was the way she breathed in just before she spoke. It was delicious. But I also liked the shape of her hips, which I know is conventional. I liked to watch her form beneath her sweaters as she went to the coffee urn or to the ladies' room. She had brought three sweaters with her from Korea, a black one, a red one, and a blue one. The blue was my favorite, a little tighter than the other two.

There is nothing to compare all of this to except a junior high crush, who is in your head as you drift to sleep at night: what she will look like tomorrow, what she will wear, what color her eyeliner will be, what you will talk about during seventh period study hall, but even before that, what sort of gesture will you make toward her between first and second periods, as you cross paths after English, and then again, if you leave biology on time—if Mr. Cox lets you out on time, that is—and you don't dally, and you're able to cross paths again between third and fourth, before she cuts off from the main building to the home ec. wing. And there is also the walk past her locker after eighth. It was like that for me, Mrs. Noi.

On occasion, I contrived reasons for her to walk across the room. I might say, Would you mind filling up my coffee cup, since you're sitting closer?

I always sat farther from the coffee just in case.

A few of the male staff members in La Caverna—I'd gotten to know them some because I spent a good bit of time there—caught me staring at her as she walked across the room. One would usually nod, gave me a thumbs-up. I felt weird about that, so I would raise my eyebrows in response, suggesting something ambiguous, I hoped. Yes, indeed, this look seemed to suggest, on the one hand. Or, alternatively, don't be a creep. I believe, though, that they always understood the gesture as signifying the former, and they wouldn't have been totally in the wrong to do so.

But in these meetings, I taught Mrs. Noi many things about American English. I like to think that my services were useful in some way, like a good coach getting the most out of his best player. One day, not long before the thing with Dr. Noi, we were meeting at our usual table at La Caverna, and she was asking me a whole slew of questions she had written in a tablet.

Movie star Tom Cruise is scientist also? she asked, holding up a news clipping.

No, I said. Look here at the word. He's a *scientologist*. It looks like "scientist," but is slightly different. It's really a religion.

Oh. Okay. She was obviously completely confused by this explanation, confused by the stupid ways in which English sometimes did not make sense. I myself did not speak another language, though I'd studied Spanish for seven years. But I did understand that frustration, even from my limited experience.

What else you got? I asked.

She looked at a list she had in front of her, which was written in Korean.

What do you call room where we pee?

The ladies' room, I said, if you're a lady. Or the bathroom. But the truth is, I went on, we have a lot of words for the place where we, um, pee, and some of them are polite and some of them are the opposite of polite. I searched for the word: Impolite.

Impolite? she said and then thought for a minute. Why not unpolite?

She was a sharp one, which was definitely part of her appeal. She was far from the geeky wife of the geeky Korean scientist I might've imagined her to be.

Yeah, I told her. That's weird, isn't it? These prefixes. They must be from Greek or Latin or Hebrew or, God, I don't know where they all come from. But they don't make a lick of sense. I mean, they probably do, if you're like a Biblical scholar. The prefix "im" I guess means "not," I told her, making this up on the spot.

You have good examples?

I hated when she pressed me like this.

Probably, I told her. We could come up with some good examples. But let's not get too focused on that. It's better to just push forward. Plow on through, I said. You can't learn a language by learning its rules, I told her. Look at robots. They know all the rules, and yet, they can't speak any language at all. *Any* language.

She nodded. This was my robot defense, and it wasn't the first time I'd had to deploy it with one of my students. I'd found it to be highly successful in fending off rule-based attacks. I myself had learned about this from a linguistics article, but honestly it was an intuitive idea that my students got easily. Everyone seemed to understand the limits of robots.

—

I was dealing with my non-financial problems—or trying to—mainly, at this point, by keeping a journal. It was a remnant of something Dr. Lowe had me doing when I was still in school and in therapy. I'd had to stop using the university counseling center when I dropped out, of course. Dr. Lowe pointed out that there was a sliding scale for some therapists near campus, but I figured that I could just use the journal she'd started me on to get myself through this rocky stretch. I was aware that she would not have condoned this practice. Your means of dealing with the issues you're facing are insufficient to the task, she would've said. I could actually hear her voice saying these words.

I wrote for hours some days, most of it circular and melodramatic. For instance, from October 30 of that year: "I feel crappy today. I wish…I could start over. What do I mean by that? Life? College?" Then a bunch of white space followed by, "Man, I don't know. Things would be different if I did, right?" Looking back on it, I feel like it was someone else entirely who wrote this stuff. I literally had no memory of some of what I wrote in the pages of that notebook.

Like this bit from late January, not long before the thing with Dr. Noi: "I can see now that I have to stop thinking about her, that I have other things in my life that I need to deal with. My toothache has gotten worse for one. I should go to the dental school to see if I can get one of the students there to look at it for free. But I did some research today—I called in a favor from a friend in the registrar's office, a former student from Bogotá. Javier, a nice kid, anthropology major, the son of a general, I believe—and discovered that Dr. Noi (and presumably Mrs. Noi) lives at 482 River View Terrace. I guess I probably shouldn't have done that."

A few days later, I caught myself driving around up there. It's anyone's guess what I thought I was I doing. River View Terrace, I saw, was one of the apartment complexes along the river north of campus. Up there, it was all foreign nationals. In the spring or summer, you could ride your bike on the path along the river and rarely hear an English word spoken. Tons and tons of Chinese and Koreans and Malaysians. And Indians. India Indians. I'd never had an Indian student, of course, because mostly they all spoke English already.

I was just driving and listening to some jazz on public radio and imagining the many things Mrs. Noi and I would do in her bedroom while Dr. Noi was off working hard on his clever global-warming experiments. After some hours of this, in the midafternoon, I got hungry and pulled over and dug around on the floorboards and found ninety cents, which I took to a nearby Wendy's and got a junior cheeseburger. I had to borrow three cents from the take-a-penny dish for the tax.

Eventually, nearly out of gas, I went home. When I got there, there was a message from my sister inviting me to dinner, and I thought, Okay. This is probably better than spending the evening with Seth or going to La Caverna or driving around Mrs. Noi's neighborhood some more. I ate some Spaghetteos to tide myself over until then and I found a few dollars at the bottom of my bag for some gas.

When I arrived at Jill's later that evening, her kids were at their indoor soccer league and then going on to a sleepover with various friends. Who knew how Jill kept track of all of that. You'd need a spreadsheet. She had the place cleaned and I guess Stewart was out with his workaholic buddies. It was just the two of us. Jill poured me a glass of rosé, which I did not care for. Briefly, I wondered (an ungenerous moment, I know): do these people have anything to drink not made to blot out your memory?

The whole thing was a setup, I saw almost immediately. Jill wasn't being big sisterly. She had a mandate, I guessed, delivered by phone from the coast of Alabama. My parents were worried and needed to know what I was doing and what my plan was. They knew only that I was on academic leave. They couldn't, I supposed, be bothered to come back from Alabama and check into the matter for themselves. To be fair, they couldn't really call, because they didn't have my phone number.

So, Marcus, Jill said. What happens now that you're done with school? Is this tutoring thing something you're looking at doing long-term?

I eyed her. I'm not actually done with school, I said.

Oh.

I'm on hiatus. Academic leave. I still have about four or five quarters left. At that moment, I was sure I would never go back.

Oh, she said again.

It's psychological issues, actually.

Psychological issues, she said. She sipped her wine. I could see that she knew nothing about any of this. Of course she didn't, because my parents didn't know anything about it, or not much.

Like what? she asked.

Panic attacks, I told her. I have these panic attacks and they've made it impossible to focus.

What's a panic attack? she asked, scooting forward on her wooden stool. The kitchen was massive and incredibly clean. A small TV had been built into the wall just above the refrigerator and it showed silent images of some devastated European city after World War II.

I guess you'd call it a state where you start worrying about something really intensely—for me it's usually that I'm dying; I think that's the case with most people who have it—and you just keep getting more and more ramped up, to the point that you can't really move. You start to worry and then you become hyperaware of your body and you feel every little twitch very profoundly, which is more evidence that something is wrong.

Oh my God, Marcus, she said. Really?

I nodded. It's terrifying.

I used to have something like that all the time. My doctor gave me something. This was years ago. Nobody ever called it a panic attack.

Wow, I said, feeling closer to her. Then you know what I'm talking about.

I really thought I was losing my mind, she said.

We were quiet for a very long time. She poured herself some more wine and I even took a sip of mine.

So Mom and Dad put you up to sussing out my situation?

Huh?

Mom and Dad, I said. They ask you to figure out what my plan was? Is that what?

God no, she said. I haven't talked to them in over a month. They're on a cruise to Antigua.

Oh.

I invited you out because I wanted to tell you that Stewart and I are getting a divorce, she said.

I was floored and felt miserable for my assumption about her motive. I'm sorry, I said.

I know. It's such a cliché. He's been sleeping with some paralegal. Christ.

He told you that?

Yeah. He told me he'd had enough of all of it.

I'm really sorry, Jill.

Thanks, hon. I think it will be better without him. I've had enough of all of it, too.

What are you going to do?

I'll go back to work. Stewart's moving into an apartment in that new building by the hockey arena in the city. I'll keep the house.

Will you get alimony or something?

I don't know why I asked that. I didn't really understand what it meant all that well.

I don't know yet how all of it will work. There will be a bunch of lawyers involved, obviously.

What kind of work will you do?

I'm a teacher, Marcus. Did you not know that? I taught fifth grade for like ten years.

Oh, I said. Ten years? That's a long time.

She nodded, but didn't seem offended, just surprised.

Do you mind going back to it?

I like teaching. It's just going to be tough juggling that with the kids.

We ate some chimichangas that had been warming in the oven, which were delicious. I think she had made them herself. Afterward, we moved to the living room, which was also spotless. They had white carpet in there for some reason, and through what must have been sheer force of will she had kept it immaculate. I did once see in the basement that they had their own carpet steamer, so that's probably how.

Because she'd been so forthcoming, I got up the nerve to tell her about my own love-life problems.

Can I ask your opinion about something, Jill?

She nodded, sipped.

I've got a bit of a situation going on with one of my students.

What's up?

I've sort of got a thing for this woman.

Oh. Yeah, it's not a very good idea to be involved with your students. That's really just Teaching 101.

I know. And it's not just that she's my student. She's also married.

Okay, she said. Where is the problem? This is cut-and-dried.

Yeah. I know.

Who is she?

She's Korean. Her name is Mrs. Noi. She's the wife of a visiting scientist at the university.

You don't know her first name?

She's pretty formal.

And this interest is reciprocal?

Not really. I don't know.

Oh sweetie, Jill said. You need to let that go. You need to stop being her tutor, too.

She was speaking as someone whose husband had just cheated on her, I figured.

I know. But it's harder than that. I was driving around in her neighborhood today, looking for her house.

Don't do that, she said.

I know.

She looked at me hard.

I can see that thing in your eye. You used to have it when you were little. Mom would say, Don't touch that outlet. But you never took your eye off it. And the minute she turned her back, you would be over there trying to stick your finger into it. The whole time you'd be saying, No, No, No.

Though I did not remember this, of course, the idea of it was familiar.

Maybe you need to get away for a while, Marcus.

I can't really afford anything like that. I don't have any money.

Where would you like to go?

I don't want to go to Alabama, I said.

Obviously, she said.

I want to go to the Navajo Reservation. I'm not sure where that had come from.

What is there on the Navajo Reservation? she wondered.

There are these old *National Geographics* in the basement of my apartment, I told her, from the sixties and seventies. I was down there looking for something and found them, and I sat and read an article about it. It sounds amazing. The pictures, I said. It's just this sun-drenched place, with sheep and shrubby pinions. Mountains in the background of everything.

Listen, Jill said, getting up. I'm going to give you some money to go to the Navajo Reservation. If I give you this, will you go out there? She pulled a false bottom from a drawer on a small decorative desk they kept in a corner of the living room. She lifted out a massive wad of cash.

That's okay, Jill. You're getting divorced. Money is going to be an issue for you guys.

Look, Jill said. I feel like I hardly know you. I've missed out on so much. On our relationship. On lots of things. You're young, Marcus. Yes, things are a mess. But you can always fix them. If going away from here will give you some start on that, then this is the best investment of my life, bar none.

I watched her as she pulled one thousand dollars out of the wad. I hadn't seen so much money at once since working the cash register at Sizzler during high school. I almost cried, because the gesture was so pure and full of love and a desire to help. I knew there wasn't anyone alive I loved like that but myself. But perhaps the admission of this truth was a step.

Of course I had no intention of going to the Navajo Reservation. What would I do on the Navajo Reservation? You probably couldn't even get onto the reservation without some sort of Indian passport.

I can't take this, Jill.

Marcus, she said. Please take it. Please. Take it and go to the Navajo Reservation. Or somewhere else like it.

I watched her. Okay, I said. Okay.

We went back to the kitchen and she wrapped up the leftovers for me to take home.

Thanks, Jill, I said at the door. I don't know quite what to say.

Go, she said. And leave the girl alone. Do not go to her house. Leave her to her life.

At home, I didn't put the chimichangas in the refrigerator; I kept them in a cooler in my car, because I knew otherwise Seth would find and eat them.

—

The next morning, I decided to put the money in the bank until I could figure out what to do with it. My bank account was a vestige of my former life, because, until this moment, it had been many months since I'd had more than the minimum five dollars in it. As the woman at the window counted the money, she glanced up and took a long look at me in the event, I figured, that she would have to identify me later.

I stood outside of the bank afterward—it was cold and windy, a contrast to three or four days of false spring—and went over things in my mind. I began walking, idly, toward, I figured, the river. I really had no plan. I wasn't really imagining the interaction with her. I wasn't really intending to go to her house again. I was calm inside, in fact—my mind, for the moment, a quiet, normal machine. At the river, I looked down at the muddy eddies, the paltry winter flow. It seemed sad, because everything did to me then. Because of where all this water was heading, it got me thinking about my parents down there in the Gulf of Mexico or the Caribbean—wherever they were—enjoying their retirement. Which in turn reminded me of me and my sister, up here in Columbus fighting for our lives. My sister's divorce, of course. And then finally—inevitably—I thought of Mrs. Noi.

I turned north. Of course I did. And it wasn't long—thirty, maybe forty-five minutes—before I found myself up in the neighborhoods of the Asiatic substation that included River View Terrace, as well as about a dozen other similarly named apartment complexes. When I finally admitted to myself that I was heading toward her apartment—when I thought about it as a concrete thing—I suppose I had it in my head that Mrs. Noi would invite me in. I was only dimly aware that this was a serious transgression, a very large step beyond grazing her hand or ogling her while she got me a cup of coffee.

As I stood at last on the small stoop outside her building, waiting for her to answer my ring, I felt the familiar creep of anxiety move through my limbs. And then my left leg went numb. I tried to move it, but couldn't. I looked down at it and then across the yard of the complex, past the children's area, the slide and monkey bars, to the woods enveloping the south-moving river. A jogger ran by on the concrete trail. Jesus, my leg. And now my left arm, too. I couldn't let Mrs. Noi find me like this, I thought, and I managed to jump off the stoop and hide behind the bushes, some viburnum that someone had let get too tall.

From my hiding spot, I heard the door open.

Yes? a voice said in Asian-accented English. It was male.

A beat passed, and then again, Yes?

I waited.

Soon, I heard the man descend the small rise of stairs and shuffle along in the grass. I saw his slippers first, then his khaki-clad knees, and then a buttoned-down dress shirt. J Crew or perhaps Izod. I recognized him immediately from his photo.

Mr. Marcus, he said.

I wasn't sure if I was going to pass out. I had this sharp pain in my neck that I thought might be an embolism.

Mr. Marcus, he said again.

On the oak tree just behind him, I noticed a few of those leaves that hang on through the winter, shriveled and limping along, mustering everything they had against the chill and winter winds. I recognized their plight immediately as my own.

It's just Marcus, I said.

I can ask what you do in the forest?

Nothing, I said. Lost my keys.

I don't think you find keys in this forest.

Probably not, I said, and stepped out of the shrubs.

The pale disc of a sun, I realized, was already high in the sky, overhead really. Dr. Noi must've been home from his lab for lunch, I thought, and then it dawned on me that it was Saturday. When you don't really have a job or school to structure your days, you make this mistake a lot.

Marcus, he said. We have problem.

I nodded. Maybe I was having a stroke, because I still couldn't feel anything on my left side, including, now, the left side of my face.

Jin-sook no longer student for you.

Jin-sook, I thought. What a lovely name. I wondered if maybe it didn't mean honey bee.

You must leave. You must not come back.

I looked at my shoes. I needed new ones.

Please tell Jin-sook that she was my best student, I said.

Maybe you seek for new job?

Maybe.

He stood there motionless for a long time.

I'm going, I said. And then, I'm sorry.

I could feel my left arm a little. Thank God. I knew of course it was a panic attack. I knew of course that my mind was running roughshod over me, that I had allowed it far too much latitude and that it had taken all that I had given and more, and what I most needed to do was get it under control, because it was undoing me.

I started toward the river and the path. At fifty yards, I turned back toward the strange higher-education tenement. Movies, I guess, had taught me to do this. I searched the upper windows for Jin-sook. I thought we could share this tender moment the way couples always do, when someone is going off to war. But she was not there. Dr. Noi, however, stood on the porch pointing at me menacingly. It was galling, but then, it was fair. They had their own lives to live, and I, I guess, had mine.

—

At home in the late-afternoon, the TV was on, but Seth had a chair pulled up to one of the large windows looking out on the pitiful little yard to the west side of the house; across the yard was a falling-down house out of which a guy named Herman sold crack. Seth sat there like you imagine the commander of a surrounded army doing, perhaps thinking or remembering.

Hey, I said.

Hey man. He didn't turn to look at me, but seemed fixated on something. He was sober, I could tell from his tone.

Whatcha doing?

Check it, he said. These plants here, I think they're forsythias, are starting to bud, because it was so warm the last few days.

You're watching plants bud?

No. I'm watching these birds fighting.

They're fighting over the buds?

I don't know. I think it might be a territory war. These two guys are both males. I looked it up in one of your books.

I asked you not to go into my room, I said, though this was obviously a rare harmless burglary.

I'm sorry, he said. Last time.

I stood there for a while, waiting for something to happen, but nothing did. I did see one of the cardinals flit into the bush and then fly away again.

Somebody called about tutoring, he said. I couldn't tell what she wanted except I did make out the word "tutor."

A new student? I wondered. I really needed some more students if I was going to stay afloat, even with the money sitting in the bank. Especially now that I had lost Mrs. Noi.

I don't know, he said. I got the number I think.

She spoke English?

Not really. I mean, a little.

Could it have been her, I wondered. Her English was intelligible, even on the phone, but when she was nervous things degraded.

I looked at the number on the table next to the phone.

And so you know, he said, I'm moving out.

What?

My first thought was, This is great news. My second thought was that I would have to find someone to take his place. And this would be a colossal hassle.

Don't freak out. I paid Arthur through the end of the lease so you didn't have to deal with finding someone. Arthur was our shady landlord. He owned a toilet supply shop, in addition to a couple rentals like this in shabby neighborhoods.

You did what?

Yeah, he said. I'm getting it together, Marcus. Going home.

I didn't have any idea where home was, and was about to ask, but realized I didn't care. I was just thankful that I had a thousand dollars in the bank and wouldn't have to go looking for someone down on their luck enough to be willing to live in this neighborhood.

That sounds like a good plan, I said.

Time for the joyride to end, you know?

The two cardinals did appear again, one chasing the other.

That makes sense, I said.

This was the most we'd talked in months.

Probably going to go to law school.

Really? I asked, not even trying to hide my incredulity. The idea of this annoyed me for some reason. You couldn't, I reasoned, just teeter on the edge of death from drug addiction and then poof, head off to law school.

Yeah. I've been putting it off for a while. But it's time.

I have to say I'm a little surprised.

Yeah, it's weird, right? Life. I'll probably do corporate, he said.

I'm sorry, Seth. I'm a little confused about all of this. You're moving out of here and going home and you're going to go to law school in order to become a corporate lawyer? I didn't know you'd been to college.

You need to go to college first? he said.

I just watched him.

I'm messing with you, man. Of course I went to college. I have a BA in American Studies from Kenyon.

Kenyon, I said. Okay. I'd seen him lie to me before about stolen stuff and I knew he wasn't any good at it. Kenyon, I said again. Okay. When are you heading out?

That's the best part. I'm leaving now, he said. Right now. He flicked a hand toward the corner where an apparently full internal-frame backpack sat. It was from REI. And now that I thought about it, all of his stuff was top-shelf, just dirty and torn.

He turned to me finally. I know, man. It doesn't make sense. Also, there's a check there on the table for a thousand dollars. It's from my father. He asked me what I owed you and I told him one thousand dollars. That seem fair?

You don't owe me one thousand dollars, I said. Just a bunch of tuna fish and some leftover pizza and milk.

I know. But the damage we've both incurred out here needs some kind of compensation. Some reparations.

I could only watch him. I wasn't even thinking of the money, which would double my holdings—or in that moment, about Mrs. Noi. I was thinking that my drug-addicted roommate thought we were more or less in the same boat. He left then without further fanfare. He gathered his pack, did a visual sweep of the room, as if to take in this last moment of his nadir. It would be all up from here and he would tell this story to his future wife, his kids, maybe even his grandkids. He might get profit from all of this as a life coach or motivational speaker. I don't know what all he was thinking about this apparently strange phase of his life.

Adios, bud, he told me, and then he walked through our ill-fitting front door and out into the empty street. I watched him closely because I wondered what he was going to do. It was as if he thought the rest of this life would begin right there. And then, perhaps, it did: out of the nowhere, a black SUV pulled up. It even had tinted windows. He got into the passenger seat and the vehicle quickly disappeared down the street and around the corner.

See ya, I said to myself.

Back at the window, I took up Seth's spot, watching the warring cardinals. Dusk was coming on and the forsythia became dark first in the fading light. I thought, Sure. That could happen. All of that could happen. Sitting there, I think I began to see what he had been watching then. At first, I had assumed it was just a voyeurism of violence—more fixation on base impulses. But then something else dawned on me. Those birds didn't have a thought in their heads about what they were doing. They hadn't reasoned it through. I understood, or thought I did, why he'd been sitting there then. I watched until darkness enveloped everything and then sat in the dark for some time just listening to the muted sounds of the world—a garbage truck, a car horn, the hum of traffic on the interstate. When I finally got up, the room was very dark, but I didn't turn on any lights. My eyes adjusted to this new state and I made my way through the apartment, feeling almost giddy at the thought that I didn't need the light. Not at all.

The Defense

TURNER HAD BEEN THINKING FOR THE MANY MONTHS of his recovery about visiting Brian up in Jackson Hole when he was well enough to travel again, but then, just a day before he had planned to go—he was actually mapping out his route in the too-large and too-empty house on Maxwell Avenue—he got a call from his little sister Maggie in Columbus. She had news. And a request.

Turner and Maggie talked by phone at least once a month, had somehow remained close through many years and much distance and, in the end, very different lives. And so it was a surprise to discover that she'd been keeping this from him.

While he'd been on his sabbatical, she said—he knew she couldn't bring herself to say dealing with your cancer or in treatment or even just sick—she'd made a decision to finish her PhD. For fifteen years, her dissertation, on limb regeneration in starfish—the product of three and a half years' hard work and countless trips to the Sea of Cortez—had sat on some hard drive, mostly complete, he guessed, possibly entirely complete; it had been a taboo topic after she'd gotten pregnant and withdrawn from graduate school. He'd brought it up just once, and she had exploded, making clear that she wasn't inviting his opinion about the next step in her life. She was twenty-four when that happened.

She was strong and stubborn, like their mother, who had raised the two of them and their little brother, Michael, almost entirely on her own after splitting with their father. It had been financial woes, Turner had figured, though their mother, stoic Midwesterner that she was, had never said, and Turner, the oldest, was only eight when it happened. Their father had literally disappeared from their lives one day—a thin cover story about the Alaska pipeline eventually emerged—and that was that. Whatever the truth was of that situation, she took it to her grave eighteen years later. Christ only knew what had become of the man who had given them their long torsos and hazel eyes. Turner, for his part, hadn't given him too much thought over the years, having known him better than his younger siblings. Even before the departure, he'd not had a high opinion of him.

After Maggie's kid was born—she named him Louis, after Louis Agassiz, though she'd pronounced it as in English—she had gotten on with her life much as their mother had, though the circumstances were different. She'd taught courses at a community college and did scientific editing for some companies and journals. She'd stayed in Columbus so Louis could have a relationship with his father—even though she'd had to force the guy to submit to a DNA test, despite assurances of her monogamy.

He had been Maggie's advisor—Charles Cinca. Though Turner had never met the man—and though Maggie never mentioned him—the name had never left Turner's consciousness in all those years; it was like a minor aggravating injury, an ingrown toenail, a boil, an inflamed joint: always, somehow, there. It was Turner's role—his right—as her older brother to harbor this resentment, to carry it around with him. And anyway, the frustrating part—the infuriating part, really—was that this business with Cinca was a tired story. Turner had been irate with Maggie for falling into such a clichéd trap when she'd finally admitted all of it to him, five months pregnant, finally no longer sick every day. He'd seen this happen—or something like it—more than once on his own trip through graduate school in Southern California.

I know, she'd said at the exasperation in his voice. I know. But, Turner, it's spilled milk. I'm having a little boy.

But now, on the phone from Columbus, she was telling him that she needed him. She thought she was just going to do this, finish it, and then call him and tell him, but she saw now that the anxiety over it was mounting and she needed him. They had relied on each other in this way from early on because of their father's absence and their mother's busy life; she had almost always held down two jobs after the split. Turner and Maggie had practically raised Michael themselves, though they had to admit they hadn't done such a great job of that. He was estranged from them both now, a high school English teacher back in Cape Girardeau.

Could you catch a flight? she asked. To be here as, you know, support? To help celebrate? I'll pay for it.

He knew she meant in the event of calamity. He knew she meant, If I don't pass. These were unspoken things he just knew in his core; there was so much about the world he did not know or understand, he had come to see, so much he had gotten wrong or, more accurately, fucked up—his marriage, for one, Jill now gone almost two years, somewhere in Taos or Sedona if her Facebook status was to be believed, though he had promised himself not to check it anymore and had managed that for a couple months now—but Margaret, he knew. Margaret, he understood.

Of course, Maggie, he said. Jesus. Of course.

I'm sorry to spring this on you, Turn. And you have to let me pay for the ticket. You can't pull your normal crap about this.

An old point of contention, the difference in their incomes, her community college money versus his biotech money.

Enough of the groveling, he said. When is the exam?

Tuesday afternoon at three, she said. Seriously, I can't have you pay for the ticket.

There won't be a ticket, he said. If there were, I would pay for it. But there won't be one because I'm going to drive.

You're impossible. Why would you drive? You can hardly get here in that amount of time.

I like to drive, he said. I don't want to zip over this country again at thirty-thousand feet, for the hundred-thousandth time. I want to see the goddamn place in case I don't get another chance.

She chose not to challenge him on this point of mortality.

It's so far, she said simply.

As a young man, Turner had crossed the expanse between San Diego and Cape Girardeau all in one go three or four times a year. He had loved the sense of exhaustion you got from pushing yourself through such a distance.

Please, Margaret. You have a son to play mom to. My mom has been dead for seventeen years.

It's always a contest with you, she said. Everything.

I know, he said. I like to win. Even at noon basketball at the university. It's why I hate swimming. There's no one to beat but yesterday's time and these old ladies.

Turner?

Yeah?

Thank you.

You're really doing me a favor, he said.

Whatever. And Turner?

What?

I need your support. Nothing more. Entiendes?

Entiendo, he agreed.

He knew, too, what this was code for. She meant that he was not there, should the occasion arise, to have open conflict with Louis's father, something he'd never hidden his desire to have. They'd been over this on past visits, and each time he'd agreed, though the occasion had never arisen.

—

An hour outside of Boulder, somewhere just east of Fort Collins, Turner called Brian on his headset to tell him about the change of plans, about Maggie's defense. Brian, he knew, was familiar with his aunt's backstory and would understand.

Your doctor says it's a go? Brian wondered. That's a long fucking drive, sitting there on your nuts.

Ever since he'd gone off to college, Brian had seen fit to talk to Turner as if they were friends and not father and son. Turner had repeatedly—and embarrassedly—told Brian not to do this, but Brian felt like it was a matter of authenticity. I'm not going to fuck around and pretend to be someone I'm not with you, Dad, he'd said. I just won't do it.

So Turner gave up. He even came to appreciate it in a way, especially after Jill left and Brian, flawed though he was—stalled out in his pot-smoking, mountain-bike-riding life up in Jackson Hole—became Turner's main contact with the world outside of work.

You do know that the prostate is different from the testicles?

Yeah. No one sits on their testicles. It's just an expression. You actually sit on your fucking prostate.

The doctor said I'm in better shape now than I was year ago, Turner said.

His doctor hadn't said exactly this, but he'd said something along the lines that he had a good feeling this time, Turner's second go with the disease in three years. The doctor had a lot of experience with the comings and goings of prostate cancer, and there was something about Turner's case that made him optimistic—more intuition than anything about the prostate-specific antigen.

The chemo and the change in diet had made the last year pretty rough for Turner. There were months when his state of mind and energy level didn't allow for much more than watching DVDs of old World War II movies; he'd seen *The Bridge on the River Kwai* five or six times. He'd been on medical leave from Bioluminescent for coming up on six months now, which they had been really great about. The amazing part was that he had done it all by himself, Brian off in Wyoming and Jill, well, gone.

Turner was a survivor now. That's how he felt, like he'd come out the other side of it. And he believed he had it beat. His take—based on a few of the books Jill had gotten for him the first time around, which he'd not read then because they were extremely woo-woo—was that believing he was in the clear was at least half the battle. As a result of these books, he did daily meditation; he did yoga; he did visualization exercises. He was just superstitious enough now not to miss any part of these rituals.

All right, Brian told him. That's good news, Turner. You can come up here another time. Give Louis a wedgie. What is he, twelve?

I think he's like seventeen.

Holy fuck. Really?

In the background Turner could hear reggae. These kids, Turner thought—they were caricatures of well-off twenty-somethings, apparently unaware of how they were portrayed in movies and on television. Though to be fair, Turner hadn't given Brian a penny since he had dropped out of his engineering program at the Colorado School of Mines, and Brian had never asked for one.

We'll do some monster fucking hikes when you make it up here, Dad, Brian told him in a moment of touching earnestness. For all his self-involvement, Brian had come home often during the past year—eight hours when there was no snow—to make sure Turner was doing okay. He had cooked for Turner, cleaned the gutter, mowed the lawn, even scrubbed the toilets. Turner had been very thankful for Brian always, but this appreciation had grown inordinately over the past year, and he had anticipated Brian's visits with hope: the games of gin rummy they'd play at the kitchen table. When his own mother had been dying, Turner had sent money and called regularly but had only gone home when she was on her last legs. He knew that the circumstances were different in the two situations—that he'd had a family and a demanding job were two big differences—but he also knew better now that you could hide behind your responsibilities.

Talk to you next week, Brian.

No, no, no. You call me when you get there. And get out of the car and walk around every few hours. Also, none of those nasty truck-stop prostitutes.

Har, Turner said, and hung up, but then laughed for real. This is my son, he thought. He had never imagined his life being what it was just now.

Just as he was coming up on the I-76 interchange, he called Jim Hucks at Bioluminescent. He'd been putting off the call for at least two weeks.

Hucks was harried.

Turner told him that he was dealing with some family business, but he was doing better—he told him about the new PSA numbers—and that he really hoped to be back at his desk by the end of the month. Last time around, he'd pretty much worked right through the whole treatment, and that was one of many variables he'd decided to change when the symptoms returned.

Take your time, Turner, Hucks said. Jesus. Take your goddamn time. We miss you, but be sure you're where you wanna be.

Thanks, Jim. Things okay there? Turner asked out of courtesy.

Oh, this fucking bee syndrome, whatever it is. We're running the material of these dead ones. Looking for what? Who knows? Bugs, viruses. Parasites. Honestly, I don't think they have a clue what they're looking for. I think they're seriously considering aliens as an explanation.

Turner knew only the crudest outlines of what was going on with the bees or any of the other projects, and he intended to keep it that way until he couldn't anymore.

It's important stuff, he said, vaguely aware that, if nothing else, the almond industry would falter without the bees.

Apparently, Hucks said. That's why I got somebody from the Department of Agriculture calling me at home at ten o'clock at night. So yeah, I guess so.

Get some rest, Turner said. I'm going to take this little trip to see my sister, and then I'll be back and I can talk to the guy from the ag department.

Turner, he said. Take your time. Seriously. But—you know? That would be fucking awesome. I guess Reagan scored a goal the other day, but Turner, honestly. Between only you and me? I didn't even know she was playing soccer.

—

When Louis answered the front door of Turner's sister's place Tuesday afternoon, he was sweating and dressed in some deserty army camo shorts, a white T-shirt that gripped his underarms and, Turner surmised, almost certainly no underwear. The clothes had all obviously been thrown on in a hurry. There was a girl here somewhere. Turner had been sixteen himself once.

Louis, he said. How are you? Jesus, you're like six-three.

Uncle Turner, Louis said, completely unable to hide his surprise. Apparently Maggie hadn't told him that his uncle would be coming in from Colorado.

Turner stepped inside the small Cape Cod, a rental, he knew, not much bigger than a one-bedroom apartment.

Well, he said, not unkindly. You might as well introduce us, since there's probably not a back door.

It had been some years since Turner had seen the boy— perhaps three, as he thought about it, the equivalent of a decade in teenage time—and in that period, Louis had grown into a young man. He now had all the trappings of High Adolescence—baggy clothes and hair in his eyes and a colossal awkwardness in the world, as if as recently as last night he'd lived in an entirely different body. Now, however, he had this new, bigger one, and he didn't yet know quite what to do with it, except to press it against girls whenever possible and however awkwardly.

Louis seemed to consider the possibility of feigning ignorance about the girl but then went to retrieve her from his bedroom.

Ten minutes later, holding an iced tea Louis had gotten him from the fridge, Turner sat across from the two of them in a ratty loveseat on the small sun porch out back. There was a postage-stamp yard, but he could see that Maggie had a nice garden with clematis and phlox, some other stuff he didn't know so well.

So what's the status here? Turner wondered. Any word?

Not yet, Louis said.

Turner checked his watch. The defense had started at 3:00. It was 4:15 now.

How was she when she went in?

Okay. Nervous, I guess. You never know with her, you know?

Yeah, Turner agreed. That's true.

It wasn't really; Turner could read his sister's nerves in a cool second. But he had an unfair advantage in this.

The girlfriend's name was Beth, and she was sharper than Turner had imagined she'd be based on a quick first impression. Now she sat trading insults with Louis and complaining about the idiocy of political figures in the headlines of the paper on the table between them. Turner's misevaluation was based mostly on fading memories of Brian's teenaged girlfriends four or five years back. Brian had apparently been particularly attracted to the vapid.

Beth's legs, Turner could not help but notice, glistened in the humidity. They were muscular, an athlete's legs. She could easily pass for twenty-one, he thought, with her blonde locks and full chest and throaty college-girl laugh. But she was not a college girl; she was a year ahead of Louis at Whetstone High, he learned, a rising senior, not a cheerleader or athlete of any kind, but the daughter of a plumber—he guessed, from reference to some work her dad had done on the bathroom—and on her way into the air force come this time next year. Or so she said and hoped. The vicissitudes of life, Turner thought. She had no idea. Neither of them did.

What about you, Louis? Turner asked, sipping his iced tea. What's in store for you?

I don't know, Louis said. I'm only going to be a junior.

This idea was pretty simple: Beth might have to get her shit together, but he still had time to dick around.

You've got time, Turner agreed.

I wouldn't mind heading out West, Louis said.

You should talk to Brian, Turner told him. You know he's in Jackson Hole.

Jackson Hole had at first been a point of contention. Not Jackson Hole so much as Brian's general trajectory, of which

Jackson Hole was merely a symptom. Whatever had driven Brian's college grades—he'd had a 3.9 in mechanical engineering through his junior year, before chucking the whole business—seemed to have vanished completely over the last few years. He sometimes talked about corporate sponsorship for his mountain bike riding, of some companies Turner had never heard of. This was the long and short of it, in terms of ambition markers. But a lot of the tension over Brian's decisions had dissipated within the past year.

Jackson Hole, Louis said.

Turner sometimes forgot that these youthful Western enclaves—Jackson Hole, Bend, Moab—weren't the same kind of shorthand outside the West that they were in it.

I guess you're too young for the beer commercials. It's in Wyoming. It's a cool town in the Tetons. Hiking, biking, skiing. That sort of stuff.

Turner knew that cool on his lips sounded dumb to them, old—a sad attempt to speak their language. It couldn't be helped. Cool had been a word of his generation, too.

As the three of them made small talk, Turner could see that Beth was taking out some anger on Louis for getting her trapped here with an uncle who was, by definition, creepy. Get it yourself, she told him, when he asked her to grab the bag of pretzels while she was up refilling her iced tea.

In the midst of this carping, Turner excused himself to use the bathroom. After noting his shabby face in the mirror, he relieved himself into the small toilet, his stream itself shabby. Because of this, he thought for the first time since Sunday about the cancer— he'd been distracted by the drive, the landscape, the quick sweep through Cape Girardeau and a few slices of the pizza he'd eaten every Friday night for years—and about the fact that, en route, he had neglected his routines. He gave himself a pass but also made himself a promise to do those things later tonight.

Back in the sunroom, the kids had made up, based on the new geography of their bodies. But he remembered that there was little difference at that age between making up and calling a truce for the sake of messing around.

A phone on the coffee table buzzed. Louis picked it up and glanced at the screen and then slowly read what was there: It's over. They're deliberating and I'm waiting in the lobby with the coffee cart in it. Did Turner make it?

Tell her I'll find her there in—what—ten minutes? Fifteen?

Louis typed something into the device.

Turner looked around for his keys. Can you tell me how to find the building? he asked Louis.

I'll just go with you, Louis said.

Are you sure?

Yeah. We'll both come, Louis said. He looked at Beth. She shrugged.

They readied themselves and then went outside and piled into Turner's Explorer.

What is this stuff? Beth asked, holding up a bottle of High Gamma Tocopherol she'd found on the backseat. She took three stabs at Tocopherol before giving up.

It's old-guy stuff, Turner said. He really didn't want to get into cancer with her.

You shouldn't take anything you can't pronounce, she said.

I know how to pronounce it, he said. You're the one who was struggling.

That, at least, got a smile.

—

Maggie sat, meditatively, on a cushioned bench under a painting of a stodgy-looking guy in a gray suit, presumably a biologist of some sort based on the presence of an ancient and far too large microscope on the table in front of him. Apparently he was someone who had once graced these halls or, more likely, halls that were in a much older building; this one was new and shiny, with massive public spaces and Gehry-esque curves.

Hey, stranger, Maggie said as they approached. She hugged Turner first and then both of the kids.

You're done! Louis said.

Well, yeah, she said. Maybe.

How you feeling?

Not great, she said. But the worst is over.

Turner knew how this all went; it was the same for nearly everyone, the grinding of a rusty screw into the one spot where it hurt most.

Do you think you passed? Beth asked.

I don't know, sweetie, she said. It's really hard to know. It was like a tough job interview. They wanted something particular, but I didn't know what it was.

So maybe not?

Well there's 'passed' and then there's 'passed.'

The difference being?

Turner liked Beth, he decided. She was not cowed by what she didn't understand. Louis he wasn't so sure of so far.

I may have to rework the entire dissertation if they decide it's too deeply flawed.

That sounds like bullshit, Beth said.

Maggie nodded, looking a little beleaguered.

So we just wait? Louis said. Where are they?

There. She looked at a door just off the lobby.

Do you want a coffee? Louis asked.

No, thanks, Maggie said.

I'll take one, Turner told Louis, digging around in his back pocket for his wallet. On a whim, he'd had a coffee in Missouri yesterday. He'd nearly forgotten what it tasted like, it had been so long.

Maggie knew about his diet and routine, but she didn't raise an eyebrow. Still, he felt it necessary to explain. I'm fading, he told her as he handed Louis a twenty. The drive.

Don't even talk to me about the drive, she said.

Yours are on me, Turner told Louis. Louis made his eyes comically big, in fake gratitude.

Don't be a jerk, Maggie commanded.

When the kids were out of earshot, he turned to Maggie. So what happened?

She sighed. This guy Eric Hammel came after me.

Who's he?

No one. He's new, young. Christ, he can't be more than twenty-nine. He doesn't even have any gray hair.

There's something else about him, though.

You know how these people are, Turner. Academics. They're just mean in their hearts.

I would be careful about limiting that diagnosis to academics. What are you keeping from me?

He's sort of Charles's protégé.

On the phone Sunday, she had told him about how this all came to be, mainly about an aging woman named Stallings who studied arthropods of all things, whom Maggie had taken a class from all those years ago. When Maggie started poking around, looking for a new advisor, this woman had been eager, even though it didn't make too much sense scientifically, given the differences in the types of work they did. But Stallings was adamant, and she helped Maggie put together a committee and in fact pushed the dissertation through, spending significant political capital along the way, Maggie had guessed. It was personal, between Stallings and

Cinca, she was sure. But as they were fielding a committee, Stallings admitted that there had to be a regeneration person, which obviously couldn't be Cinca. That left Hammel.

And was it serious, his objection?

Oh, it doesn't matter. He was after me about some minutiae to do with the regeneration mechanism. Fibroblasts. I guess maybe I've not kept up quite well enough with some of the literature. I don't know.

Around them, a few grad students and professors drifted past toward the coffee cart or the nearby exits. Turner had forgotten how quiet university buildings were during July and December; only foreigners and those trying to get a step-up ever showed their faces. Everyone else was vacationing with their families or sleeping in and catching up on their TV.

I'm sure it was just a show of force, he told her. It's almost always just a show of force, a way of saying, You've got a long way to go. It doesn't matter if you do or you don't.

Turner's own defense had gone off without a hitch, actually, but bioinformatics was a very different field, new and anxious and without the internal conflicts of evolutionary biology. It also lacked all the gray-suited antecedents. He figured she was thinking about his exam, but he didn't feel it was the time to delineate the differences for her. Again.

I've got to find a bathroom, Turner said. I had about a half gallon of iced tea at the house.

It's just down there, she said, pointing down a corridor.

He could see that she was on pins and needles. Maggie, he said.

Yeah?

This is going to be okay. It's normal to have what feels like a bad defense. It's normal. Hardly anyone has a perfectly uncontentious defense.

You did.

You weren't there.

I know what happened.

Surely you're not competing with me.

I'm thirty-nine years old, she said.

So?

I want my life back. I'm counting on this to give me my life back.

You have your life, Maggie. And if you want to compete, I'll happily show you someone whose life is off the rails.

Goddamnit, Turner. I've been limping around this city for too long. I don't have forever.

None of us do, he said.

—

The bathroom was in the old part of the building and was tiny, the doors of the stalls crowding into one another. He had to turn sideways to get the main door closed behind him before going through a second door, a kind of stall door that was apparently necessary to shield the view to the urinals when the main door was open.

Inside, he saw that there were just two urinals, side by side. One of them was occupied. He thought about turning around before the man saw him, but he really had to piss, so he went ahead and sidled up next to him. It was quiet in the room except for the man's startlingly healthy stream into the small pool at the bottom of the urinal. Turner felt an anxiety rise inside as he unzipped his pants. He would not be able to do this. Perhaps, he hoped, this man was nearly done, and he would flush and leave. But no. He kept pissing, as if he had reserves of the stuff running through his body from some external source. It hit the pool, sometimes the white porcelain, like the stream of a little boy, a two-note cacophony.

Turner cleared his throat, waited, concentrated. But his mind kept circling back to the man standing next to him, his healthy stream. On the heels of this thought lay thoughts of the little walnut-shaped organ that had been such a trouble. Turner had arrived at forty without having been injured, without missing a day of work, without ever really going to the doctor. It was strange how differently you saw the world once you'd been in the hands of medical professionals, once your body had somehow failed you. Of course no one lived forever, but no amount of evidence could convince the human mind of this until the data started rolling in from your own life.

He gave up. He zipped up and flushed because that's what people did in this situation, and then he pivoted and went to the sink. He would have to go deeper into the bowels of the building and find another bathroom. Standing there washing his hands, he could hear the man continue to release his water. He's got the bladder of a giraffe, he thought. Turner's bladder had actually lost its zeal years before he started having prostate problems, and he begrudgingly had to admire an older man with that sort of stream.

He looked in the mirror and could see the back of the man's head, mostly bald but shaved in the few places where hair still grew. He was a big man, thick in the midsection and with broad shoulders, older than Turner by at least ten years, judging by the way the skin of his neck sagged. He wore a suit that was shinier than it was well-cut.

Just as he was about to dry his hands, the man finally finished and, after a few shakes, zipped up his pants and himself swiveled toward Turner at the sink. Turner just wanted to get out of there, didn't want to have to make embarrassing small talk with the guy, but then he saw his face. He recognized it easily from the man's website. Charles Cinca, World-Famous Marine Biologist. These were the first words that floated through Turner's mind because the site proclaimed it in exactly this language at the top of the homepage. *Renowned for his work with limb regeneration in amphibians*, the bio began, *Charles Cinca has reshaped our understanding of stem cell research.*

Did other academic scientists have their own flash-driven websites? Turner had wondered when he'd found the site the first time. He wasn't positive, but a quick survey suggested not. Cinca. He had been hearing the guy's name in his head for coming up on two decades. A part of him had known that his sister was fine, that she had made her peace with the way it had all shaken out. But it had never quite assuaged Turner's deep anger over those events. What an arrogant asshole, Turner thought now. What a megalomaniac.

For many years, he'd wanted to hurt this man, to fuck up his life in some small way. But in the end he'd never met him because he was not in evidence during Turner's visits to Columbus. Apparently, Louis hadn't had much to do with him, finally, in spite of Maggie's sacrifice—her choice, he had to remind himself—to stay in Columbus.

If not for the embarrassing circumstances, he might have gone after him right here in this tiny, fetid room. He would have perhaps accused him of being small about Maggie's defense, sending his attack dog. But he had to swallow all of that now. Also, it was so cramped in here that if Cinca took a swing at him, they'd both end up in one of the urinals.

Back out in the hall, he turned away from the main lobby and followed a corridor that moved into a different section of the building. He dropped down a floor, and after some searching, finally found a restroom tucked between a staircase and a dissection lab. It said *Faculty Toilet*, obviously a remnant of another era. He relieved himself in a much more expansive and clean room. Alone. Charles Cinca, he was still thinking, washing his hands. Why did he care so much? It was like the time a fat little girl whose name he could miraculously still remember—Monica Thayne—was bullying his little sister after school. Nothing raised ire in him in just this way, not his father leaving or his brother's brush-off, not even Jill's cold departure; he and Maggie were a binary star system—it was elemental, their connection.

Climbing the stairs, he was hoping all of this hadn't taken too long. Just as he came even with the main hallway again and could peer down the long corridor into the lobby to where Maggie and the kids were—they were all still standing there—he caught a flicker of Cinca's shiny suit ahead of him, turning the corner, cutting into another long hallway. He casually strode across the passage and continued on toward Cinca, following him at a safe distance. At the end of the corridor, Cinca went into an office, and Turner lay back. He could see a sign that read, *Ecology and Evolutionary Biology*. He waited, pretended to read advertisements on a bulletin board for graduate biology programs at Emory and the University of Montana. After a few minutes, Cinca came back out carrying a stack of papers and continued on around a corner. Turner followed. Another long hallway, again changing buildings, from the old one into a different new one, all connected seamlessly, except that the new buildings were so clean, with sleek windows and floor tiles.

Finally Cinca turned into another office, presumably his own. Turner neared and saw that a plate on the door confirmed this.

He passed the door and peered in. There was an empty anteroom—reams of biological journals lining its walls, one large lab table in the center of the room stacked with more of the same—and beyond that, a larger room with a number of computer stations, occupied, Turner noted, by a handful of female students, one more attractive than the next. Turner could see that beyond these two rooms, there was a small office. Cinca stood inside, surrounded by many plaques and awards on the walls behind him, talking on a phone while simultaneously rearranging his genitals through the pocket of his pleated pants. Could the suit be sharkskin?

Turner backed away from the threshold and leaned against the wall. Was he going to do this? After the many promises he'd made to Maggie, one as recently as two days ago? Her admonition did come to him briefly, but was quickly overwhelmed by a more powerful force in his heart. He didn't know what it was he was going to do.

He straightened himself up and headed through the anteroom toward Cinca. At least one of the grad students had already begun to track him as he was about to cross the second threshold, when he heard the too-loud opening bars of "Like a Virgin." It was playing very close by. Too close. He stopped, uneasily taking in the fact that now all five of the beautiful grad students and Cinca himself were looking at him. He arrived then at the uncomfortable conclusion that the song was coming from him, Turner, somewhere on his person.

His mind finally began to catch up. Brian. Brian had done this. Brian was on the phone. He thought, Fucking Brian. But then: That little card. It's adolescent, but it *is* funny.

Dad, Brian had said during his last visit—it came back to him now, time standing still there halfway into Cinca's lab. Next time I call you, you're going to be really fucking surprised. Turner had been in the sunroom dealing with the ficus that had been threatening death all spring, and only half-registered that Brian was messing with his phone.

Turner looked around the room now and nodded, reaching into his pocket. He held up a finger toward Cinca—who was still on the phone and looking at him with a mix of curiosity and annoyance—and turned and pulled the phone out of his pocket and returned to the hallway.

You're a shitbird, Brian.

Brian was cackling. Isn't that awesome?

I wish you could see where I am.

You're not in church are you? That would be fucking sweet.

It's Tuesday afternoon, Brian.

But Madonna? Everybody likes Madonna, right?

Everybody liked Madonna's *body* when she was nineteen.

You're a pig.

What's going on, Brian?

You're in the middle of the debriefing.

We're still at the university, waiting to hear.

It's so easy to get you frazzled, Turner. I won't keep you. I was just thinking of you. I'm standing on the top of Rendezvous. I think I can see Canada from up here. I had to tell someone.

Sounds nice.

You were supposed to call me and let me know how you were doing. That drive hate on the family jewels?

I'm fine, Brian. I gotta go now.

Alright, hoss. You listen to your sister. She's way smarter than you.

Brian. How do I disable this ring?

You're the one with the doctorate. Even though it's in information technology or whatever.

I'll talk to you later.

He flipped the phone shut and looked up. Standing in the main office doorway was Cinca, apparently curious as to who this man was. This was not exactly how it was supposed to go. None of it had been. But, he thought, Here we are.

But then another interruption. In his periphery, he saw people approaching, Louis and Beth, he knew. They had been sent to track him down. They had no doubt been sent to exactly this spot.

There you are, Louis said in a tone that suggested normalcy.

Here's your latte, Beth added, handing him the paper cup. I'd be surprised if it's still hot. She probably didn't know too much of the context for this little moment, only what Louis had been able to fill her in on during the thirty second walk to Cinca's office.

Louis, Cinca said, an astonished quality in his voice. Now he was even more confused. Who was this man and what does he have to do with my son? his face, now sagging with lips downturned, seemed to ask.

Louis took no notice of Cinca whatsoever, though, made no response to his name. It's happening, he said to Turner. Louis, who gestured then with a quick shake of his head in the direction of the lobby, seemed quite adult all of a sudden.

Before the three of them strode off, Turner stole a glance back at Cinca. His posture, his very essence, seemed to be deteriorating: he appeared to Turner as if he had been shot, the color draining from him, a confusion suffusing his face, his figure crumpling, as if an imaginary bullet had entered on the left side of his body, perhaps his shoulder. He was hurt. Turner felt some pang of compassion for him, in spite of it all, recognizing in him some piece of his own flawed self, some part of his own terrible mistakes come to collect.

The three of them were silent as they walked. When they turned the corner toward the atrium, Turner finally looked toward the kids. She got called back in?

Yep, Beth said.

She send you to retrieve me?

A nod.

So she knew where I was?

Not exactly, Louis said, and then, correcting himself, adding, not for sure.

Back in the lobby, they sat and waited. A lone sparrow flew around the atrium above them. Eventually Louis said, We're not going to tell her anything, Uncle Turner.

Doesn't matter, Louis, he said. He wanted to explain himself to the kid, but there were no words for it. What he might have said would sound stupid because it was stupid.

When the door opened fifteen minutes later, the first person out of the room was Maggie's chair—the only woman on the committee—Dr. Stallings. She was smiling, laughing almost. It was a good sign, but Turner waited to see his sister's face for confirmation. She was next and he saw that she had come out the other side of this.

—

Later at the house, dozens showed up for the impromptu party. Maggie's friends—her community—had been on standby. He met at least forty people, many of them trailing children of various ages. They were from the community college and Louis's school, an entire book group. Church. Even Beth's plumber dad was there with her mom, who it turned out directed an environmental institute at the university. Her dad, it eventually came out, was himself an aerospace engineer with a low tolerance for the corporate world.

None of it was quite what it had seemed, in his mind, or when he was 1,500 miles away.

Maggie finally sat down next to him in the kitchen at midnight; just a few stragglers were left out on the lawn, talking too loudly about politics and listening to a boom box that played some Rolling Stones album Turner didn't know. He was exhausted. She probably was too.

She thanked him for coming. I know it must seem ridiculous now, but if you could've seen me before you got here—

You have a great group of people, he said, then looked at her and smiled. I had no idea that you went to church.

Well, she said. It's never seemed to me an important subject to talk about.

You thought I would judge you.

I'm sure I don't know every little part of your life.

He thought about that for a moment, about what in his life he kept from people—from Maggie in particular. His heart raced a little as something did come to mind. There was this one thing that he could not tell anyone. He wanted to in a way, because he felt so lonely sometimes holding it to himself. During the last year, for the first time in his life, he had thought about killing himself. It was surprising when the idea had first come to him. Because he'd just spent all of this energy trying to stay alive. But this thought crept in almost every day, usually for just a moment. You could just stop, it said. You don't have to do any of this anymore.

He smiled at her.

We are a mystery, aren't we? he said.

You and me?

No. You know. The other 'we.'

———

Late that night, Turner lay in bed, unable to sleep because of the time difference. His mind drifted through a menu of worries. For six months, he had marshaled his forces against the disease. Very little remained of the life that had preceded all of that, and it was easy in a moment like this—away from home, tired—to feel sorry for himself for the way his world had been shaken up; it was perhaps even natural to feel that. Though he knew, too, to still count himself lucky.

He had gone a few months now without really longing for Jill. He remembered this way of forgetting love from high school and college, when a breakup's pain had been so acute that his entire being was encompassed by it. There were two girls like this—Tammy Cline his senior year of high school, who had broken up with him after a track meet for a list of convoluted reasons he never could understand until years later, when it dawned on him that she had just lost interest. The other was Celia Sheldrake, whom he had broken up with when he'd graduated from the University of Missouri and headed to UCSD. She had been moving back to Kansas City, to attend law school. Neither of them had been willing to forego their plans, so he was the brave one—he thought—who said that they should probably just call it quits.

For months, he thought he'd never be able to function in the world again, so accustomed to their company had he been, so tightly had he wound his future with theirs in some late-adolescent way. But eventually, the spell broke. Eventually, a year later or more, he came to regard the situation with a sense of embarrassment because though he had sworn to himself that his life had been ruined, that he had known this loss would bleed from him for all of his future days, he had woken one day and without even noticing the absence, that strong presence, that weight on his chest, was gone.

With Jill it had been different because she was woven so fully into the fabric of his life. He had spent nights with her in far-off places—McMurdo Station in Antarctica, the U.S. Embassy in Dhaka during an uprising; they had gotten lost and subsequently left behind by a small tour group in the jungle of Belize and had sat on the jungle floor all night, taking turns sleeping on each other's lap until dawn, keenly aware of the fer-de-lance, the puma. And these experiences bound you in a way few other things could.

And then all of this is not to mention the worries over their son along the way—the bacterial meningitis he contracted at four, the severe concussion he suffered when a high-and-inside fastball cracked his helmet in two and landed him in the ER for a night.

But now it was, after all, falling away, like the booster of a rocket that has achieved outer space. He could see that the mind was just as set up to deal with such a loss as it was, at first, not to.

His phone emitted a three-note burst, a noise he didn't recognize. New message, he read. He only received calls from two people now, and he was with one of them.

You awake? the message said.

It was the first text he'd ever received, and it took him a few minutes to figure out how to respond.

Just seconds after he'd sent his reply—*Yeah*—it buzzed again.

Go outside, the new message said.

Oh Brian, he thought. The living of life in the moment came so much more naturally to a young man; to someone like Turner, more than halfway down the path, his son's mode sometimes seemed rooted in a quaint and naive sanguinity about what life could offer you. But then, he could not lie to himself about the sheer force of his son's will in keeping him buoyant this past year. He could not discount the power of his son's ethos. Perhaps life would erode it; perhaps not. But for the moment, it was the greatest force he knew. He put on his shirt and carefully made his way through the house to the sun porch and then out the screen door. He had to admit, he was curious where this was heading.

Okay, he typed.

It cloudy? Brian asked.

This is dumb, he thought. He dialed Brian's number.

What's going on? he asked.

North, low on the horizon. It won't be quite the same because of Cowtown's lights.

Turner looked into the sky, after he situated himself to the north. He saw the cluster of stars he now understood he was being pointed toward.

Sagittarius, Brian said.

Yeah? Turner said.

Yeah, Brian said, a little indignant. It's your goddamn sign.

So it is, Turner said.

You don't know the goddamn constellation for your astrological sign? Brian said.

He's a centaur, a hunter.

Yeah. I've seen his picture.

Jesus, Turner. What else don't you know?

Turner just caught the question at the edge of his consciousness. What else don't I know? he wondered, understanding that in the answer to the question lay valuable, crucial information—the sort of thing that might change his life altogether if he could name it, come to terms with it, let light seep into it somehow.

The list is long, Brian, he said.

Don't get sappy on me, Brian said.

Why not? Will there be a better time?

Brian was quiet for a moment, a rare moment of reflection for him.

Probably not, he said.

Thank you, Brian, he said.

It's my job, Brian said.

What's your job?

Keeping it real.

I don't think you say that anymore.

I say it all the time.

Of course you do.

Everything okay?

A hunter, he said.

A badass hunter, he said.

A hunter, Turner said one more time, trying to make out the figure in the sky for the first time in his life.

Acknowledgements

No one writes a book without immeasurable amounts of help. I have many people to thank for their part in the creation of these stories—some whose critical eye helped me to hone the stories, others whose conversation and presence in my life impacted the work. In no particular order, those people are: Chuck Holden, Jon Tompkins, Ann Buechner, Kathleen Hughes, Mona Anderson, Greg Anderson, Michael Glaser, Brice Frasure, Matt Burgess, Patricia Henley, Elizabeth Arnold, Ana Maria Spagna, Matthew Henry Hall, Mark Rader, Ben Warner, Patrick Somerville, Nicole Walker, Ann Cummins, Kevin Moffett, Corinna Vallianatos, Sam White, Gillian Kiley, Caroline Casey, Paul Lisicky, Sasha Todak, Michael Collier, Maud Casey, Charles Baxter, Hannah Tinti, Seth Brady Tucker, Kevin Wehmueller, George McCormick, Lee K. Abbott, Brandi Stanton, Roger Stanton, Jen Michalski, Cathy Chung, Steve Halton, William Tyree, Rob Roensch, Dave Ellsworth, Colby Caldwell, Sam McClelland, Bram Riddlebarger, Amy Spencer, Erik Stump, Amy Swanson, Carl Swanson, Lisa Frasure, Tom White, Alexi Zentner, Michael Downs, Joe Martin, Sally Keith, Petter Nordal, Mark Iwinski, Bruce Cohen,

Leslie Johnson, Katherine Fausset, Lyrae Van Clief-Stefanon, Robert Danberg, Matt Boone, Craig Anderson, and my colleagues in the English Department at St. Mary's College of Maryland, though especially Jennifer Cognard-Black and Jeffrey Hammond. I owe great debts of gratitude to my mother, Norma Gabriel, my sister, Cheryl Arnett, and my brother-in-law, Greg Arnett. I would like to thank the participants at the Chesapeake Writers' Conference over the past several years, and I would especially like to thank the magazine editors who worked with me on these stories: Heather Jacobs at *Big Fiction*, Michael Koch at *Epoch*, Evelyn Rodgers and Speer Morgan at *The Missouri Review*, Ronald Spatz at *The Alaska Quarterly Review*, Libby O'Neill at *Atticus Review*, and David Daley at *Five Chapters*. I would like to thank Dennis Savage, whose photography and discussion was instrumental in helping discover a cover design that was right for the book—and Brian Mihok for his amazing work on that design. And of course Erin McKnight for believing in the book and for her hard work on making it the best version of itself.

Finally, none of this would have been possible without the constant encouragement, support, and love from my wife, Karen Leona Anderson.

Jerry Gabriel's first book, *Drowned Boy* (Sarabande, 2010*)*, won the Mary McCarthy Prize in Short Fiction. It was a Barnes and Noble "Discover Great New Writers" selection and awarded the 2011 Towson Prize for Literature. His stories have appeared in *Five Chapters*, *EPOCH*, *One Story*, *Alaska Quarterly Review*, *Big Fiction*, and *The Missouri Review*, among many other journals. He lives in Maryland, where he teaches at St. Mary's College of Maryland and directs the Chesapeake Writers' Conference.